# Morgue Mama

## The Cross Kisses Back

WITHDRAWN

### C. R. Corwin

Poisoned Pen Press

Copyright © 2003, 2006 by C. R. Corwin

First Trade Paperback Edition 2006

10 9 8 7 6 5 4 3 2 1

Library of Congress Catalog Card Number: 2003104911

ISBN: 1-59058-205-5 Trade paperback

Poisoned Pen Press
6962 E. First Ave., Ste. 103
Scottsdale, AZ 85251
www.poisonedpenpress.com
info@poisonedpenpress.com

Printed in the United States of America

To my sister, Joyce

What an odd-looking pair Aubrey McGinty and I must have made those weeks we investigated the Buddy Wing murder. She was twenty-four. I was sixty-seven. She was a sturdy five-foot-eleven. I was a shriveled five-three. She was all legs. I was all arms. Her red hair was thick and sexy and draped over her shoulders like the fringe on an admiral's epaulets—the faintest twist of her neck sent it flying like a spray of fire. My old gray hair was chopped at the jaw, a Prince Valiant look that back in the fifties made me look peppy and professional, but now only amplified my squirreliness.

Dolly Madison Sprowls
Head Librarian
*The Hannawa Herald-Union*

# 1

The poor lamb. One week on the job and she made the worst mistake a reporter on *The Hannawa Herald-Union* can make.

She called me Morgue Mama—to my face.

It was right after lunch, on a horrible Tuesday in March. I was perched at the counter that separates the library from the rest of the newsroom, going through the metro section of that morning's paper. I saw her coming at me over the top of my 250+ drug store reading glasses. She was tall and willowy and young. And good gravy, she was smiling.

She plopped her arms on the counter, side by side like the runners on a bobsled, and leaned forward, actually casting a shadow over me. "Hi, Morgue Mama," she said. "I need all the files on the Buddy Wing murder."

I kept working, marking which stories should be saved, and where. In the old days I'd cut the stories out of the paper, scribble a date on them, stick them in an envelope and feed them to the file cabinets. Now stories are filed in cyberspace. *Click* and the job's done. No more scissors. No more envelopes. No more of that wonderful inky newsprint on your fingertips. Anyway, I ignored the Morgue Mama thing and kept on working.

"The Buddy Wing files—I'd like to see them," she said, a little louder but no less cheery.

I peeked over the top of my glasses again. "You're the new police reporter."

"Aubrey McGinty," she said.

"Well, Aubrey McGinty, just so you know, Morgue Mama is what you call me behind my back."

"Oops."

"In front of my back you call me Maddy."

"I'm really sorry."

"No crime committed. You called me Morgue Mama because that's what you hear everybody else call me."

"I really am sorry."

I hate contrition, even when it's sincere, which in this instance it seemed to be. "Apologize if it makes you feel better," I said. "In a month you'll be so sick of my crap you'll be calling me Morgue Mama like the rest."

I was expecting her to hop back to her desk like a frightened bunny. Instead she winked at me like we'd been friends for a hundred years. "But only behind your back?"

"If you know what's good for you."

So that's how I met Aubrey McGinty, maybe the best police reporter the *Herald-Union* ever had, maybe even better than my dear Dale Marabout. "You can call up all the Wing murder stories on your computer," I said. "Just type his name in the search box."

She puckered her lips. Apparently she found it funny that an old bag of prunes like me would be telling someone her age how to conduct a computer search. The computer chip has turned the world upside down, I'll tell you. Today the young teach the old. Can't figure out all those teeny weenie buttons on your TV remote? Ask a three-year-old. Can you imagine five hundred years ago some pre-pubescent apprentice showing Michelangelo how to hold his chisels?

"I've already got all the on-line files," Aubrey said. "I'm interested in the older stuff."

I tried to preserve my perfected sour countenance, but I'm sure my delight was smoothing out my wrinkles. The sweet girl actually wanted something from the filing cabinets. She actually wanted something printed on real paper. I wiggled my finger for her to follow.

Let me explain a few things for those of you who don't know diddly about the newspaper business. Newspapers report what's new, what's happening right now, history on the hoof as they say. But news is meaningless unless it's put into some sort of perspective. Let's say you read that the sewer pipes under Cleveland Avenue are exploding, and you think, boy, that's too bad. Then you read that those sewer pipes are only four years old, and you think how can this be? Then you read that the contractor who installed those sewer pipes is the mayor's cousin, who after serving eighteen months in a state correctional facility for stealing cars went on to operate a shady television repair business, and despite having not one day's experience laying sewer pipe, got the Cleveland Avenue contract because he submitted the lowest bid, and that the pipe he installed was made of low-grade iron, illegally imported from the former Soviet republic of Belarus, and you begin to get some perspective.

And how did the newspaper discover all this interesting stuff?

Every paper from the smallest weekly to *The New York Times* has a library. In the newspaper business we call these libraries *the morgue*. And it's a fitting name. Just like they tag and store bodies in the city morgue, stories are tagged and stored in the newspaper's morgue. But unlike the city morgue, the stuff we tag and store is never buried and never forgotten. It's always there, waiting to be resurrected by some ambitious reporter. Waiting to give perspective to some current story. Waiting to send mayors and their shady relatives to prison.

So every newspaper has a morgue and every morgue has a crusty old pain-in-the-ass librarian like me, Dolly Madison Sprowls, whom, as you've already learned, the reporters call Morgue Mama.

But only behind my back.

The *Herald-Union's* computer system was installed in June, 1985. So everything written before then was saved the old-fashioned way, clipped and crammed into a manila envelope, sardined into a file cabinet drawer.

You'd think the younger reporters could *access* information from a file cabinet without too much trouble, wouldn't you? But file cabinets are as strange and mysterious to them as the computer system is to me. Oh, they can pull a drawer open—I'm not saying that—but they seem totally incapable of knowing where to begin. "Good gravy," I hiss at them, "don't you know the alphabet?"

I took Aubrey to the W cabinets first. We had three thick envelopes tagged WING, THE REV. BUDDY. Then I took her to the C cabinets and dug out four envelopes tagged CHURCHES, HISTORY. "There's plenty of stuff on Buddy Wing's ministry in here," I said, "going back to the Fifties, when he first moved here from West Virginia." Next I took her to the T cabinets. Two envelopes were marked TELEVISION, EVANGELISTS. "He started his television show in 1964," I said, "the same Sunday in February that the Beatles appeared on the Ed Sullivan Show."

"My mother wanted to marry George Harrison," Aubrey said.

Good God, I thought, they make these reporters younger all the time. I was already twenty-nine years old in 1964, already divorced, already working here for five years.

"Who was your favorite Beatle?" she asked.

"Mel Torme," I said.

We headed back toward the counter. "You got a videotape of the murder yet?" I asked.

"You've got that?"

"Honey," I said. "Follow me."

Like a lot of TV preachers, Buddy Wing had too much hair and wore expensive white suits. The day after Thanksgiving, he dropped dead, at the ripe age of seventy-six, in front of fifteen hundred people, during his regular Friday night Hour of Everlasting Life services at his opulent Heaven Bound Cathedral on Shellborne Street.

Far more than fifteen hundred witnessed his murder, of course. Wing's Friday night services were broadcast live over some two hundred cable channels nationwide. So I suppose a couple hundred thousand were watching when he grabbed his neck and staggered backward into the fake palm trees. By the time the TV networks got through replaying the tape, everybody in the country had seen Buddy Wing die a dozen times. We ran a four-column photo of it ourselves. Page one. Above the fold.

Wing's theological claim to fame was that he had Jesus's phone number. Sometime during every broadcast he'd say: "Jesus gave me his phone number when I was just a little boy. And I've been calling him every day, ever since. And Jesus is always at home. His line is never busy. Hello Jesus! Hello Buddy!"

People in the audience would shake their arms and shout, "Hello Jesus! Hello Buddy!"

I remember Dale Marabout saying the night of Wing's murder, "At least Buddy will save a bundle on long distance from now on."

So the murder was shown again and again on every newscast in the country, probably in the world, especially after the coroner announced just how Wing had been poisoned.

"I'd sure like to Jack-and-the-beanstalk my way up those legs," Eric Chen said, shaking the last drop of a Mountain Dew into his mouth. He'd returned from lunch just in time to watch Aubrey retreat to her desk with the Buddy Wing files.

"She is a pretty girl," I agreed.

"And I hear a kick-ass reporter."

Eric Chen has worked in the morgue since graduating from college, which makes him about thirty-three or thirty-four. Technically I'm still the head librarian, but Eric is really in charge. That's because he understands how and why the computers do what they do. It's all I can do to double-click my mouse.

The paper had figured I'd retire at sixty-five like everybody else. Then they'd move Eric up to my position, finally completing the modernization program that editor-in-chief Bob Averill initiated about a dozen years ago. But I had no intention of going peacefully. "Maddy-Maddy-Maddy," Bob said to me after receiving the bad news about my intention to keep working, "don't you want to enjoy life a little?"

"That's why I'm staying," I said.

And that's why I'm going to stay just as long as I can. I love this paper. I love the morgue. And so the modernization program remains stalled, one Dolly Madison Sprowls shy of completion.

You'd think Eric would be pissed at me for hanging on, wouldn't you? He stands to make at least $15,000 more a year if I retire. But he never says boo about it.

"I wonder if she likes Chinese?" Eric said when Aubrey sat down and propped her knees against the edge of her desk. He was referring to himself, of course, not won ton soup.

Eric Chen is always nurturing the stereotype that Asian-Americans are smarter than Other-Americans. But the only things Chinese about Eric Chen are his eyes and his last name. He was born in Youngstown, for goodness sake. And while he certainly knows what all the buttons on his keyboard are for, he's a world-class doofus when it comes to things that really matter, like feeding his belt through all the loops in his pants, or making sure there's enough antifreeze in his pickup truck, or having a relationship with a woman that goes beyond watching her carry an armful of files back to her desk. Still, I like Eric Chen. He's funny and polite and honest. He's one of the few people in the newsroom who isn't afraid of me.

To tell you the truth, I've spent years perfecting my act as the newspaper's rottweiler-in-residence. Every morning I come to work determined to be as cranky and uncooperative as I can. It keeps the reporters and editors from asking for information they really don't need—which they'll do every damn day, ten times a day, if you let them.

But Eric Chen saw through me the day he was hired. And Dale Marabout sure saw through me. And now I knew that Aubrey McGinty saw through me, too.

As soon as Eric wandered off, I went to my desk and dialed Dale Marabout's extension. His desk was way over by the elevator but I could see him pick up the receiver and cradle it under his neck. "Hi, Mr. M," I said.

He swiveled in his chair and smiled in my direction. "What's shakin'?" he said.

"Up for lunch tomorrow?"

"Something interesting cooking?"

"Just lunch. Speckley's at noon?"

"Noon it is."

I watched him hang up and swivel back to his computer screen. So many stories to edit and so little time.

◇◇◇

I came to Hannawa, Ohio, in 1953—the most timid eighteen-year-old on the face of the earth—to attend Hemphill College. Hemphill at that time had one of the best library science programs in this part of the country. I was going to get my degree and go back to New York, get a job in one of the big library systems in Albany or Syracuse or Utica, anywhere but my home-town of LaFargeville, a crossroads clutter of two hundred and eighty-five people surrounded by seven thousand dairy cows. Instead I fell in love with Lawrence Sprowls and after graduation stayed right here in Hannawa.

Lawrence was a journalism major and made the dean's list every semester, and so while other J-grads went off to little piss-ant papers around the state, Lawrence went right to the *Herald-Union*. They assigned him to the business section, where he quickly made a name for himself covering a vicious three-month strike at the Ford plant. Like other big cities in the Midwest, the 1950s in Hannawa were boom years. Factories were popping up everywhere, outstripping the local supply of workers. Poor families by the thousand streamed out of the South to work twelve hours a day, six, seven days a week, making things they could not yet afford to buy for themselves. It wasn't long before those workers, their feet now firmly planted in the middle class, got sick of the low wages and long hours. They joined unions and bargained as hard as they worked. Their strikes were long and often violent, and the times being as prosperous as they were, they almost always got what they wanted.

For the first couple of years after Lawrence and I married, I worked part time at the city library. Then Lawrence saw the posting for a job in the morgue. I found myself in the newspaper business, too, clipping stories, stuffing them in envelopes, feeding them to the file cabinets, every night trying to scrub the newsprint off my fingers with Boraxo.

In 1961, Lawrence was lured away from the paper by the local office of the United Auto Workers to handle their public relations. It was irresistible money and we bought the bungalow on Brambriar Court where I still live. In 1963, Lawrence was lured from our marriage by a secretary with irresistible tits.

So Lawrence got the irresistible money and the irresistible tits and I got the bungalow. Over the years Lawrence moved from city to city doing PR for unions and banks and phone companies and race tracks. He would divorce and marry three more times before dying of a heart attack at age fifty-seven. I stayed right here in Hannawa. Stayed divorced. Stayed in the morgue. I was named head librarian in May, 1970, the same week those four students were shot by National Guardsmen at Kent State University, not thirty miles down the road from here. Every time I run across those KENT, MAY 4 SHOOTINGS files I just boil inside.

Hannawa is a lot different today than it was in the Sixties. The good union jobs are pretty much gone. Almost anybody with money has fled to the suburbs. City Council keeps launching various redevelopment schemes, but the downtown remains a canyon of empty storefronts and the neighborhoods continue to crumble. Only on the west side, in the hills surrounding Hemphill College, are there still some safe and tidy middle-class neighborhoods, including mine.

I'd say the city has lost a good seventy thousand people over the last couple of decades, some to jobs in the New South— Atlanta, Houston, Charlottesville, places like that—but mostly to the city's own suburbs—Greenlawn and Brinkley, North Hannawa and Hannawa Falls—once beautiful rural townships now choking with strip malls and big showy houses with adjustable mortgages.

While a lot of the factories have closed, Hannawa has one industry that just keeps growing and growing: Evangelism.

Hannawa has more evangelists per capita than any city north of the Mason-Dixon Line. I'm not kidding. Several years ago we ran a six-part series on the phenomenon. It seems that all those southerners moving up here in the Fifties and Sixties—whites from Appalachia, blacks from the delta states—brought their own brand of Bible-believing Christianity with them. Preachers in need of flocks made the move north, too, setting up shop in vacant breweries and bowling alleys, anywhere they could put up a row or two of folding chairs. Buddy Wing was one of them. He was a high school dropout from Webster Springs, West Virginia, a young man with a knack for healing both spiritual and physical ailments. He also understood early on that God had permitted the invention of the cathode ray tube for one reason and one reason only: to save souls.

Before tumbling into the fake palms, Buddy Wing was the most well-known TV preacher in Hannawa. But he was hardly the only one. Today, I bet there are a dozen preachers here with their own shows on cable.

Anyway, Hannawa is known for its evangelists. So much so that ever since the paper's series brought the phenomenon to light, Hannawa has been known as "The Hallelujah City." I think it's a hoot, but Mayor Kyle Finn sure doesn't like it. Of course he can't say so publicly, but Sylvia Berdache, who covers city hall for us, says hearing that nickname literally turns his orange Irish freckles maroon. She does a wonderful impression of him: "We're workin' our arses off trying to build a progressive city here—attractin' high-tech jobs and foreign investment

dollars—and what are we known for? Faith-healin' hillbillies!"
Sylvia claims she actually overheard him say that to a Catholic
priest once, at the Feast of the Assumption carnival at St. Patrick's
on West Molamar.

Sylvia didn't say what the priest's reaction to the mayor's blas-
phemy was, but I'll tell you mine: People can believe anything
they want and worship any way they want—just as long as they
stay the hell away from me.

At four that afternoon, I saw Aubrey McGinty heading toward
my desk with the envelopes I'd given her. Her youthful bounce
made me nibble on my bottom lip. I'd been much too helpful
earlier. Much too friendly. I needed to re-establish my witchi-
ness. "You sure you're done with those?" I asked sourly. "I don't
like digging out the same stuff twice."

"I'm pretty sure I Xeroxed everything I need."

"Only pretty sure?"

"If it'll make you sleep better tonight I could go Xerox some
more," she said.

I'd wanted to see her wilt. But she'd only bloomed. I motioned
for her to put the envelopes on my desk. They slid in every
direction, one nearly capsizing my end-of-the-day mug of Darjeeling tea.

Before waltzing back to her desk she said something that
was going to upset my applecart for months to come: "Maddy,
I don't think Sissy James did it."

# 2

Speckley's is a wonderful little restaurant about a half-mile west of downtown in the Meriwether Square district. Dale Marabout and I pulled in at the same time.

Meriwether, I suppose, is Hannawa's Greenwich Village. In the Fifties there were a handful of jazz clubs there, and an assortment of all-night diners and serious drinking bars. In the Sixties the city's small contingent of Hippies hung out in "Meri" and in the Seventies it was the Disco set. Nothing happened there in the Eighties. In the Nineties it became a trendy area again with coffee and bagel shops, art galleries and antique stores. Speckley's has been there all along, serving the same famous meat loaf sandwiches, huge gob of au gratin potatoes on the side.

We slid into a window booth. The waitress immediately descended on us and, without asking, turned over our coffee cups and started to pour. I waited for my cup to be full before telling her I wanted tea. The waitress apologized with feigned sweetness and stormed off to find a pot of hot water.

My orneriness made Dale chuckle, as it always did. "So what's up, Maddy?"

"I told you yesterday—nothing."

"That you did. So what's up?"

Dale Marabout knows me too well. He came to the *Herald-Union* in 1975, when he was twenty-four, after two years at the *Elwood Telegraph-Review*. I'd already been divorced for ten years and he was sixteen years younger than me. But somehow we started having an exhausting sexual relationship. I'd never been with any man other than Lawrence, and Dale, pudgy and bland and timid as a mole, had never been with any woman. We were exactly what the other needed.

The sex lasted for five years, until I was forty-five. By then Dale had lost some weight and gained a modicum of self-confidence, and I was in full-blown menopausal decline, every part of my body with sexual application going south.

Our nights together dwindled to once a month and then stopped completely when a young kindergarten school teacher named Sharon moved into his apartment building. I missed the sex but understood Dale's needs. He needed someone he could have a family with, someone to share a mortgage and car payments. He and the teacher married. Twenty-two years later they have a nice house in Greenlawn, a daughter working on her master's in psychology, and a teen-age son who wants to be a professional wrestler.

Maybe the sex between Dale and me stopped, but our friendship didn't. Every once in a while I'll call him, or he'll call me, and we meet at Speckley's.

"What's your take on Aubrey McGinty?" I asked.

It took some real *cojones* for me to ask him that. Aubrey was Dale's replacement on the police beat. Dale had covered the cops since Eddie Nogolo retired in 1974, and he loved it. But our new managing editor, Alec Tinker, decided Dale was too cozy with Police Chief Donald Polceznec. So Dale was shuffled to a deputy copy editor slot on the metro desk.

"I've edited a couple of her stories already," Dale said. "She's good."

I watched him stir a packet of sugar into his coffee. "Well, you were plenty good, too," I said. "It still pisses me off the way—"

Dale reached across the booth and patted my knuckles. There were granules of sugar on his fingertips. "It's okay. Nobody stays on the same beat forever."

I couldn't help but think about those fingers. We never loved each other, not in an ooey-gooey way, but it was still a blow when he broke things off, even though I totally understood it. I blew the sugar off my knuckles and told him about Aubrey calling me Morgue Mama to my face. I told him she wanted everything we had on the Rev. Buddy Wing.

Dale stopped stirring. "Really?"

"So she hasn't been assigned to look into it?"

"Not that I'm aware of. Though I'm not exactly in the loop these days."

"She doesn't think Sissy James did it," I said.

"Sissy James confessed," he said, sipping. Bitterness was spreading across his face. "There was a shitload of evidence."

"You think Sissy did it then?"

"Well—sure. The cops found the poison in her garbage. She confessed, for christsake."

Dale's bitterness had bloomed into anger and I felt terrible for bringing it on. Being replaced by a kid from a podunk newspaper couldn't have been easy for him, even though I'm sure he was sick to death of the beat. It wasn't that Dale was too cozy with the police chief. Dale was too cozy with being cozy. He was forty-nine. He'd written hundreds of murder stories, fatal car-crash stories, kids-fried-to-a-crisp-in-rundown-apartment-building stories. I love Dale Marabout to death, but he was burned out, and he knew it. Still, getting exiled to the copy desk is a real ballbat in the ribs. I've seen it happen too many times over the years. Reporters of a certain age just wilt.

"Maybe there's something new with the story," I said.

"Like I said, I've been de-looped."

When I got back to the morgue I found a Post-it on my computer screen:

Can we have lunch tomorrow?
Aubrey Mc.
ext. 326

◇◇◇

# Thursday, March 9

Twenty-four hours later I was back in Meri, back at Speckley's, two booths down from where Dale and I sat. "Go crazy," Aubrey said, "I'm buying."

"Don't be silly," I said.

"No, I'm buying—I want to thank you for your help with the Buddy Wing files."

"If every reporter I helped bought me lunch, I'd weigh four hundred pounds."

We both ordered the meat loaf sandwiches, au gratin potatoes on the side.

"By the way," I said after the waitress was gone, "you could have e-mailed me about lunch—I'm not the high-tech dodo everybody thinks."

Aubrey's lips contorted into her laugh-preventing pucker. "I did e-mail you," she said, "about an hour after you got the files for me. You never answered."

"Oh."

Now the conversation turned to my name, which conversations with new people always do. "So," she asked, "were you named after Dolly Madison the president's wife, or Dolly Madison the pickle?"

"Both," I told her. "If it hadn't been for the pickle jar in the refrigerator, my parents never would've known there was a president's wife named Dolly."

"Then is Madison your middle name or your maiden name? I don't even know if you're married."

"The beautiful name Sprowls came with my divorce settlement."

She liked that. "So when Ma and Pa Madison had a girl they couldn't resist."

"You have no idea the crap that passes for clever in LaFargeville, New York," I said.

"New York? You sound so Ohio."

"Upstate New York is Ohio," I said.

I learned long ago that it's dangerous going to lunch with reporters. They don't talk to you. They interview you. By the time the check comes, they know what brand of underwear you're wearing. So, the best thing to do is go on offense. "You're from Rush City, right?" I asked.

She rolled her eyes. "Farm foreclosure capital of the Midwest."

"And after college you went back and worked at the hometown paper?"

"Everybody's got to start somewhere," she said.

"It was a good place for you to start. *The Gazette* is a good paper. What's the circulation now? Fifteen thousand?"

"They wish."

"How old are you, anyway, Aubrey? When you get my age everybody looks about twelve."

"Twenty-four."

"You couldn't have been at *The Gazette* for very long."

"Year and a half."

"And you worked like a maniac and got some good clips for your file—good for you."

She smiled. "I was lucky. I got to cover some terrific stories."

I prodded them out of her: an Amtrak derailment, the arrest of a scout master for molesting boys on a canoe trip, and best of all, the murder of the high school football coach by the cuckolded husband of the cheerleading advisor. She was right. She was lucky. Reporters on little papers like *The Gazette* rarely get to cover good stories, just car accidents, county fairs, and an occasional embezzlement by a township clerk. "Dale Marabout says you're a very good writer," I said.

The sandwiches came. Aubrey peeled back the bread and poked the meat loaf with her finger to make sure it was cooked thoroughly. It was and she took a huge bite. For the rest of our lunch our conversation was filtered through mouthfuls of meat loaf and potatoes.

"So, why don't you think Sissy James killed Buddy Wing?" I asked.

Aubrey, chewing away, held up her index finger like a number one. "First, when I saw the police tape of her confession on TV, she just didn't look guilty." She swallowed and held up a second finger. "Two, that murder of the football coach taught me never to trust the police—I don't mean their honesty, most cops are pretty honest—but their work. They're human and humans fuck up."

I've got an absolutely filthy mouth myself, but there are certain words that simply cannot be formed by the lips of a woman of my generation. The one that starts with F is one of them. "So how did they *screw* up the football coach's murder?"

Aubrey put down her sandwich and folded her hands under her chin. "About a month before the coach was killed, he threw this big deal senior off the team for repeatedly peeing in the gym bags of the junior varsity players. The coach warned him a bazillion times to stop. But he kept it up. So the coach tossed him off the team. And the kid's father went berserk at the next school board meeting. Threatened the coach and everybody else. His son wouldn't get a scholarship now, just for kidding around in the locker room, blah-blah-blah. So when the coach was shot three times in the head, they immediately arrested the kid's father."

I remembered the story from our own coverage. Rush City is only forty miles south of Hannawa, right on the edge of our circulation area. Big papers love it when people in those little Norman Rockwell towns go nuts. "Then you're that local reporter who found the real murderer?"

Aubrey stabbed the last au gratin potato on her plate. "No biggie. Everybody in the high school knew the coach was doing the cheerleading advisor. And knew that her husband knew. How much police work does it take to find something like that out? It took me about an hour."

I felt a sudden need to confess. "I think I let the cat out of the bag."

"Which cat is that?"

"The Buddy Wing cat," I said. "I mentioned to Dale Mar-about that you were looking into it. I figured you'd already cleared it with Tinker."

I could see from the way she was chewing that she wasn't pleased. "At this point I'm just trying to see if there's a story there."

"I was a little concerned, that's all," I said. "Big papers are more complicated than small papers. The pace is crazier. In order to make it work, everybody has to know what everybody's doing." I wasn't trying to inflict one of my infamous Morgue Mama lectures on her. I was genuinely concerned.

"I'm not doing this at the expense of my other stories, if that's what you're worried about," she said. "Buddy Wing is totally on the side until I have something solid to go to Tinker with. Okay?"

I knew the *okay* meant that I should mind my own business. "Okay," I said.

The waitress brought the check. Aubrey turned it over and winced.

I pulled it away from her. "How about you just pay the tip?"

On our way to the car she asked me if I'd go with her to the Heaven Bound Cathedral on Saturday. "Just to snoop around a little," she said.

◇◇◇

When I got back to the morgue I first helped Doris Rowe, editor of the paper's Weekend section, search the B cabinets for our old files on the history of the Bowenville Blueberry Festi-val—"How hard can it be, Doris? It's under either Bowenville or Blueberry"—then I got on my computer and called up our stories on the Rush City football coach murder.

For all that baloney about the public right to know, news-papers don't like to mention competing papers. But we had no choice with the football coach story. We not only mentioned *The Gazette* by name, we mentioned Aubrey McGinty by name:

## Reporter uncovers "the real shooter" in football coach murder

RUSH CITY—Police conceded yesterday that they arrested the wrong man for the Oct. 12 shooting death of Rush High School football coach Charles "Chuck" Reddincoat.

Two days after the shooting, police had charged 48-year-old Stephen Stuart. Stuart had publicly threatened Reddincoat after the coach benched his son for harassing junior varsity players.

But based on information provided to police last week by Rush City Gazette reporter Aubrey McGinty, Chief Paul Rafael said his department now believes that "the real shooter" is Darren Yoder, a 38-year-old home improvement contractor.

Yoder was arrested at his Marlboro Ave. home yesterday morning.

According to Chief Rafael, McGinty not only uncovered information about an alleged affair between Reddincoat and Yoder's wife, high school cheerleading advisor Carolle Yoder, but also located a hunting cabin in Coshocton County where detectives

```
Saturday recovered a pair of
blood-splattered overalls and
a .45 caliber pistol.
```
SEE SHOOTER PAGE B5

I read the rest of our stories on the murder: the release of the irate father; Yoder's arraignment and not guilty plea; his trial and conviction. Then later in the afternoon when things eased up, I rummaged through our stacks of *Gazettes*—we keep a year's worth of all the little newspapers around us—and found Aubrey's own stories on the murder.

I could see why Aubrey got the police reporter job here. She was not only a good writer, she was a *digger*. She had that healthy cynicism a reporter needs and can't be taught. I was looking forward to our visit to the cathedral on Saturday.

# 3

## Saturday, March 11

Wouldn't you just know it that one of those damn late-winter snows pushed down across Lake Erie Saturday morning. It had been a pretty stiff winter and the city was out of road salt. So we all had to fend for ourselves, including Aubrey and me. All the way to the Heaven Bound Cathedral she apologized for the heater in her old Ford Escort not working. "Soon as I've got $2,900 in the bank I'm buying an SUV," she said.

"How much you got saved so far?" I asked, knowing reporters are always pipe-dreaming about new cars.

"The saving starts just as soon as my Visa gets under control."

We came up behind a city bus. It covered our windshield with slush. When Aubrey turned on her wipers, the one on my side only smeared the slush worse. The one on her side flew off. "What kind of SUV you thinking about getting?" I asked.

"A bright yellow one," she said.

We turned onto Shellborne Street and started to wind into the city's South Ridge neighborhood. Mercifully, the street already had been plowed and the Escort climbed bravely. For a mile or so the street was lined with abandoned storefronts and rundown apartment buildings. But as soon as we passed McKinley Park the neighborhoods became more prosperous. This part of town was built in the early Sixties when the city was still growing.

There was street after street of tidy ranches with attached garages. We passed a Kmart and a strip of auto dealerships. The Heaven Bound Cathedral was on the right.

The entrance was guarded by two cement angels, frozen outstretched arms welcoming us in. The parking lot was massive, and except for five or six cars, empty. The morning's snow had been pushed into neat mounds around the light poles.

The Heaven Bound Cathedral was one of Hannawa's most recognizable landmarks, a three-sides wedge of glass and serious-looking beige brick. Huge neon crosses rose from all three corners. A pretty ugly building in my opinion.

"It looks bigger on television," Aubrey said.

The sidewalks had been sprinkled with blue de-icing pellets and we made it inside without incident.

For a while we just wandered the halls. There were JESUS DIDN'T SMOKE—WHY DO YOU? signs on every wall. In one hallway we found a long bulletin board thumb-tacked full of Polaroids—new members, Sunday school classes, family outings to various campgrounds and amusement parks. Buddy Wing was in every photo, smiling wide under his huge head of heavily sprayed hair.

We came to a set of wide oak doors. Raised bronze letters told us it was the BROADCAST CHAPEL. We peeked inside. This *chapel* was big enough to hold a Miss America pageant. We heard a pair of hard shoes behind us.

It was a security guard. He was tall and chubby. There was a sadness about him, the kind you see on a lot of middle-aged men as they plow along through a life loaded down with failure. His high cheekbones and protruding ears gave away his Appalachian ancestry. And so did his voice. "Might I be of assistance?" he asked.

Aubrey immediately shook his hand. "We're from the *Herald-Union*. We've got an appointment with Guthrie Gates."

"Thought as much," said the guard. He led us off, at a pace that would make a Galapagos turtle proud.

I was surprised that Aubrey had made an appointment. "I thought we were just snooping?" I whispered.

Aubrey didn't care a whit about the security guard's Appalachian ears. "Guthrie Gates is the associate pastor," she said loudly. "He'll probably be named full-blown pastor pretty soon."

"Already has been," the security guard said.

I knew what Aubrey was doing. She was playing dumb. It's an old reporter's trick. Ask a direct question and people get scared and tell you nothing. Wheedle them into volunteering information and they'll just blab and blab.

"I hear he's very good with kids," Aubrey said to me. "He's got like three or four of his own."

The security guard politely corrected her. "Oh, no, ma'am. Guth's not even married yet. But he is good with the kids. That's for sure."

"And I hear he grew up in the church," Aubrey said to me.

"No ma'am. He came to the cathedral just a year before I did, seven years ago now. He's like family though."

Aubrey filled her voice with apology. "Of course. I was thinking of that other guy, Tim Bandicoot. He's the one whose parents were members of the Clean Collar Club."

"That's right—but Tim's no longer with our church," said the security guard.

I was surprised that Aubrey knew about the Clean Collar Club. They were the five families back in the Fifties that invited Buddy Wing to stay in Hannawa and start a congregation. Until they could scrape up the money to rent their first little storefront church, they met Sunday mornings at six in a Laundromat, over on South Canal Street. Nobody came around to wash their clothes at that hour and it was almost a year before the owner caught them celebrating the Lord's Supper around the folding table.

◇◇◇

We passed yet another JESUS DIDN'T SMOKE—WHY DO YOU? sign and I made some crack about the church not being very brotherly toward the tobacco industry.

"Pastor Wing was firm about cigarettes," the security guard said. "He lost both his daddy and his wife to tobacco. But it ain't just the cancer. It's the weakness. Pastor used to call smoking a manifestation of spiritual sloth. I was hooked a long time myself before he healed me of the habit."

We reached the church offices. The security guard rapped on the door respectfully. I heard the lock unclick. A thirty-some-thing man welcomed us in. He was thin and unathletic and not very tall. He had too much hair and a ridiculous necktie. He couldn't decide if he should smile or not.

Maybe Guthrie Gates had been named pastor but he hadn't moved into Buddy Wing's big office. That room, with its long wall of windows looking down on the parking lot, remained exactly as Wing left it on the night he was poisoned, or so Gates whispered as we padded by. The door was open so people could look inside, but a metal folding chair kept anyone from entering. On the chair rested a huge arrangement of plastic white roses.

Gates' own office was small. So was his desk. Sunday school drawings—animals entering Noah's ark, Jesus taking off like a rocket—were taped to the walls. While Aubrey chit-chatted about the weather I watched Gates try not to look at her legs. Even in a baggy pair of khakis her legs seemed to short circuit male brains.

When the weather was out of the way, and the pastor adequately seduced, Aubrey pulled a notebook from her coat pocket—one of those long, skinny spiral jobs reporters carry so they can take notes while holding it in the palm of their hand. While she flipped through her notes, Gates leaned over his little desk and tried to read upside-down what it said. What a lost cause that was. Reporters develop their own shorthand systems—scrib-bles even they can't decipher half the time. I can't tell you how many times I've overheard reporters cursing their own notes at deadline: "What the blankety-blank does that mean?"

So Aubrey flipped through her notes and told Gates she didn't think Sissy James poisoned the Rev. Buddy Wing. I was expect-ing the pastor to react as Dale Marabout reacted, pointing out that Sissy confessed, that police found the poison in her garbage can. But that wasn't his reaction at all.

"Half the people in this congregation don't think she did it," he said.

Aubrey apparently wasn't as surprised by his confession as I was. "Who do they think did?" she asked.

Gates smiled a little. "People here try to mind their Christian P's and Q's."

Aubrey smiled back. "But—"

"Well, who else. The boyfriend." By *the boyfriend* he meant, of course, Tim Bandicoot, Buddy Wing's one-time heir-apparent. Tim had grown up in the church—the Clean Collar Club and all that—and the childless Wing had carefully groomed him to run the whole show someday. He even paid Tim's Bible college tuition. But when Tim started questioning his penchant for speaking in tongues, Wing very publicly threw him out of the congregation, along with Tim's wife, Annie, and two hundred of Tim's supporters. It happened about six years ago. There was a big debate in the newsroom about how to play the story. Some editors thought it was interesting but inconsequential church stuff that should be held until Saturday and run on the Faith & Family pages, or maybe during the week as a human interest feature in the Living section. Others insisted it was hard news—trouble right here in Hallelujah City and all that.

Hard news won. The story ran below the fold on Page One. What a headline:

```
TONGUE LASHING
Buddy Wing, protégé split over
strange church practice
```

"But Tim Bandicoot is such an obvious suspect, isn't he?" said Aubrey, sliding down in her chair and propping her knees on Gates' desk, the way she did at her own desk.

Gates' eyes locked on Aubrey's knees and pretty much stayed there the rest of the interview. "What's obvious is that Tim really hated Pastor Wing," he said.

Up to now I'd just sat there like a bump on a log, but I remembered that whole story so well. "Enough to kill him and frame his own girlfriend?" I squeaked.

Gates' face started to twitch like a boiling sauce pan of Cream of Wheat. "Tim is an immoral man. Wife, two young sons, and a girlfriend on the side. He stole a big chunk of our congregation."

"He didn't exactly steal them," I pointed out. "They merely agreed that your church could draw a bigger audience if Wing stopped speaking in tongues. And when Bandicoot was given the boot, they followed him. And as far as him having a girlfriend on the side—"

I was way out of line and Aubrey's eyebrows were telling me to shut up. But Gates answered me politely, as if I was a real reporter, and not just a librarian out on a Saturday snoop. "The very fact that Tim thought speaking in tongues was something Pastor Wing could stop, tells you right up front that he didn't belong in this ministry. Tongues isn't some cheap theatrical device to get people excited. It's a gift God gives to the truly saved." Gates grabbed his eyes and squeezed them together. He started reciting scripture: "And they were all filled with the Holy Ghost, and began to speak with other tongues, as the Spirit gave them utterance." He blinked and grinned. "Acts 2: 4. Praise God."

"Do you speak in tongues?" Aubrey asked him.

"Am I truly saved? Yes, I am. How about the two of you?"

Aubrey squirmed. I suppose I squirmed a little myself. "Right now," Aubrey said, "we're only interested in saving Sissy James from spending the rest of her life in prison. Assuming she doesn't belong there."

"We love her whether she does or doesn't," Gates said. "I hope you understand that."

"And I hope you understand that we're not trying to do either God's work or the police department's work," Aubrey answered. "If Sissy James is innocent, that's a great story."

It was the pastor's turn to be uncomfortable. "I hope you're not going to make a lot of good people look silly."

Aubrey closed her notebook and slowly slid it in her coat pocket. It's another old reporter's trick, making people think an interview is over when it isn't. "Any story we write about this is way down the line," she answered. "And only if there's absolute proof that Sissy is innocent. At this point we're just fishing. But her court appearances—her arraignment and the sentencing—she just seemed too calm."

Gates hissed a single word: "Svengali."

Aubrey nodded. "Given her sad personal life—the miserable childhood and prostitution stuff—you're probably right. She could easily come under the control of some manipulative bastard—sorry."

Gates shook both his head and his hands. "No need. Tim Bandicoot is a manipulative bastard. He hoodwinked Pastor Wing for years. All of us."

"What about the confession?" Aubrey asked. "Do you think Sissy could come up with that on her own? It's just a scenario, of course, but say the police suspected Tim Bandicoot from the beginning—which they obviously did—and started looking for evidence. They find out he's got a girlfriend on the side. Check out her house. They find the poison-making stuff in her garbage. Now, she didn't know it was there. But she quickly realizes her wonderful Timmy boy has done one of two things: either he's stupidly tried to get rid of the stuff in her trash can, or he's intentionally set her up. She loves him. Believes his rap that Buddy Wing is embarrassing the Lord with his old-fashioned practices. She also hates herself. Knows she's not worth much in the bigger scheme of things. She figures it's her godly duty to save her man and his important ministry, even if he betrayed her. Not a word would have to be exchanged, would it? She realizes what she has to do and does it. She confesses to the murder of Buddy Wing."

Gates leaned back in his swivel chair, raking back his TV preacher's bangs. "I can believe any or all of that."

Aubrey lowered her knees, stood up and zipped her coat with the fluid grace of a ballerina. She smiled and extended her hand across his desk. "I would like to get a church directory for our files, if that's possible."

From the Heaven Bound Cathedral we drove to the mall in Brinkley. Aubrey had an Old Navy gift certificate that her sister gave her for Christmas. She bought a hooded fleece jacket from the sixty-percent-off rack. Then we had lunch in the food court. I had a slice of pizza and small lemonade. She had a soft pretzel an enormous diet Coke.

For the longest time we made cracks about the crazy things different people were wearing. Then out of the blue Aubrey asked me if I thought Guthrie Gates could be the real murderer.

"Heavens no," I said. "He worships Buddy Wing like he was God."

"Like he was God or like Buddy Wing was God?"

I finished my noisy sip. "I see what you're saying."

And I did see what she was saying: When Tim Bandicoot was tossed out over that speaking in tongues business, Guthrie Gates became heir apparent. When Buddy Wing was killed, Guthrie Gates became the new Buddy Wing. "Maybe he stirred up that speaking in tongues business to get Bandicoot out of the way," I said. "Then, feeling his Wheaties—"

Aubrey squinted at me like I was the one speaking in tongues. "Feeling his Wheaties?"

"You know, feeling strong and confident? Don't tell me Wheaties doesn't use that in their ads anymore?" I could see Aubrey didn't have a clue what I was talking about. I dropped it and continued: "So, after Guthrie successfully secured his position as heir, he figured, why wait for Buddy to die on his own?"

I thought she was going to choke on her pretzel. "You sound like what's-her-name on *Murder She Wrote*—the one who played the teapot. Anyway, Guthrie Gates is a puppy dog. No way in the world he killed Buddy Wing."

"You just said he did."

"No no, Maddy. I only asked if you thought it was possible—assuming that Sissy didn't do it."

Now I was the one without a clue. "You don't think she's innocent?"

Aubrey nibbled and nodded and shrugged at the same time. "I think she's innocent. But even if I can prove it—and get her to admit it—I'm not sure I want to investigate any further than that."

"You wheedled Gates into giving you a church directory. That's not for our files. That's to run background checks on the membership."

"Maybe it's for that." She filled her cheeks with pretzel. "God, Maddy, I've so much to do. I've got to learn the police beat. That's a big department. Rush City had eleven goofy cops. And Chief Polceznec is gearing up for this major internal reorganization. And as soon as spring gets here people will start killing each other left and right. The paper took a big risk on me. I've got to do well. And I've got so much personal shit to do. I don't own anything except a futon and an old Radio Shack computer. I'm an adult now. I need a sofa. Table and chairs. A hutch full of fancy plates I never use. A real bed. Somebody to put in it."

There was something about sitting in that food court full of twitchy kids that made me feel young and wicked myself. "That last part ought to be easy enough."

Aubrey groaned and rested her forehead on the cold Formica tabletop. "Don't even go there," she said.

I suddenly felt hot and silly. I'd gone too far. She was one of the paper's reporters, the enemy, an overly ambitious kid I didn't know and didn't particularly want to know. I quickly got back on safe ground—the murder of Buddy Wing. "So it's down to three then? Sissy James, Tim Bandicoot, or Guthrie Gates?"

Aubrey had finished her pretzel. Now she was harvesting the salt crystals on her paper plate, dabbing them up with her index finger, licking them off. "If only it were three."

"Good gravy—who else?"

"Who benefits from a dead TV evangelist, Maddy?"

"Well—me for one. But I guess you mean specifically."

She giggled deep in her throat, the way Beelzebub might. "From what I've read, some of these TV preachers have no problem living as kingly on earth as they expect to live in heaven."

"You think maybe Buddy Wing was killed for his money? From what I gather, he lived fairly modestly."

We shook off our trays in a trash can shaped like an open-mouthed frog. "My first week at *The Gazette* I did a story on a school custodian who'd lived his entire life in a ramshackle house without running water or electricity," Aubrey said. "He left a half-million dollars to the local ornithological society."

"You're making that up."

"Have you ever been to the new Wyssock County Wild Bird Museum, Maddy? It's really something."

I still didn't know if she was joking or not. But I got her point. "So Buddy Wing might have left somebody a bundle?"

The automatic doors deposited us in the parking lot. "Maybe, maybe not," she said. "We do know from the morgue files that his wife died of cancer, and that they didn't have any kids. But certainly he had other family. Brothers. Sisters. Greedy nephews and nieces. Who knows how much money he had? Who knows who has it now? I'll have to make nice with the gnomes at probate court."

# 4

## Monday, March 13

Nine-o'clock Monday morning Police Chief Polceznec announced his department's reorganization plan. It set off the biggest political row of the winter. The police union filed suit at noon, claiming too many white officers were overlooked for promotions. An hour later the NAACP filed its suit, saying exactly the opposite was true. The local chapter of NOW held a press conference at two and demanded that at least one of the new district commanders be a woman. City Council called a hurry-up hearing at four. Some members of Council chastised Mayor Finn for not exercising enough control over the police department. Some charged that he exercised too much. Aubrey didn't even have time to wave *Hi* across the newsroom. "The poor lamb's working her pants off," I whispered to Eric Chen.

"If only it were true," he answered.

The police reorganization story dominated the news all week. Aubrey covered the police department angle while Sylvia Berdache covered the bickering and back-biting at City Hall. A couple of junior metro reporters were sent into the neighborhoods to gauge public reaction. On Thursday the paper ran a rare front-page editorial chastising all parties concerned for their selfish behavior. "The first thing Council should do," we sarcastically wrote, "is change the city's motto from Building A Beautiful Life to What's In It For Me?"

Friday morning I found a Post-it on my screen:

Super news. Speckley's for breakfast?
A.

◇◇◇

## Saturday, March 18

Aubrey was already in a booth by the door when I got there. She was wearing the hood from Old Navy. Her hair was a mess and her eyes looked like yesterday's bagels. It was ten-thirty and Speckley's Saturday breakfast crowd was already thinning out. French toast was enough for me. Aubrey got the Big Meri: scrambled eggs, bacon, home fries, two buttermilk pancakes. "You're going to explode," I said.

"I'm going to will the calories to my breasts," she said.

"Be thankful they're small. Look where my big beautiful tits ended up."

"They still look pretty perky."

"The wonderful world of wire," I answered.

We laughed and then she told me the great news: She'd talked the police department's PR officer into giving her copies of their Sissy James videotapes—the interrogation, arraignment, even stuff from the crime scene. "It's all public stuff, of course," she said, "but they can be real tight-ass about it if they want. You've got to employ just the right psychological crowbar."

I wanted so much to keep my distance from her. But how can you not like someone that earthy? "And what crowbar did you employ?"

Aubrey's eyes were following our waitress as she much-too-slowly made her way up our aisle with the coffee pot. "The grateful-dumb-girl-way-over-her-head-that-someday-just-might-sleep-with-you crowbar."

"I've heard of that crowbar," I said.

She explained the police-beat facts of life to me: "Once the cops get sick of your reporting they'll shut you out all they can. But I'm new, so they're in their buddy-buddy seduction mode, trying to make me like them, so later when the poop hits the propeller, I'll dutifully report it's milk chocolate. Two months from now it might take a court order to get those tapes. You have a VCR at home?"

"Of course I have a VCR at home—not that I know how it works."

And so we drove to my bungalow on Brambriar Court. She in her old Escort. Me in my old Dodge Shadow.

I call my house a bungalow because it makes living in a shoebox sound cozy. There's hardly enough counter space in the kitchen to make a sandwich and the closet in my bedroom only holds one season at a time. I bang my hip on the bathroom sink every time I get out of the shower. I've got bruises so old you'd think they were birthmarks.

"It's really cute," Aubrey said.

What could I do but give her the grand tour? "This is my bedroom—"

"I love that old iron bed."

"—and this is the guest room. As you can see it's sort of a catch-all—"

"Where'd you get that dresser? It's fantastic."

"It was my grandmother's. There's a gash in the side from the U-haul."

"You can't really see it."

"And this is the bathroom—and we're back in the living room."

Aubrey knelt in front of my VCR and in a few seconds the blinking 12:00 was gone. "I'll know not to listen to Doreen Poole from now on," she said.

I was straightening up the seed catalogs on the coffee table. Once, about fifteen years ago, I ordered some daffodil bulbs from some seed company or the other and now every winter I get a wheelbarrow full of catalogs. I look them over, see if there's anything I want, and then go three miles down the road to Biliczky's Garden Center. "Doreen Poole? What did that lunatic tell you?"

Doreen Poole is the reporter who started the Morgue Mama thing, or so I've always suspected. Even if she didn't start it, she sure perpetuates it. I'm sure that's where Aubrey got it from.

Aubrey was lining up the videotapes on the floor. "She said every room of your house was filled with rusty old filing cabinets. I'm sort of disappointed."

I laughed. I just love the rumors people spread about me. "The filing cabinets are all in the basement."

Aubrey got saucer-eyed, as if I'd just admitted having those little spacemen from Roswell, New Mexico locked away down there. "Can I see them?"

"They're filing cabinets. Gray rectangles of sheet metal."

"And filled with a hundred years of history." She pulled me off the sofa and led me by the arm toward the basement steps.

At the time I must have had fifty filing cabinets in my basement. I've added several since. Every time Eric Chen finishes putting a cabinet of old files on microfilm, the files and the cabinet go directly into the backseat of my car.

"It smells wonderful down here," Aubrey said.

"If you like mold," I said.

She pulled six or seven drawers open, marveling at the manila treasures inside. Then we went back upstairs. I made popcorn, of all things, as if we were going to watch an old Bette Davis movie, and not the police tapes on a murder.

I made the popcorn the way I always do, like I made it back in LaFargeville when I was a girl: I melted a dollop of Crisco in my big iron kettle, plopped in a coffee cup of popcorn, shook it on the electric stove until the lid lifted. I poured it in two aluminum mixing bowls and gave the bigger to Aubrey. I offered her a glass of Pepsi but she wanted milk. That made me smile. That's the way I eat popcorn, too. Glass of milk, a small sip with every mouthful.

Aubrey sat on the floor in front of the TV. I thought about doing that myself. But I was sixty-seven years old. I'd never get back up. So I sat on the couch and Aubrey pushed the PLAY button on the VCR.

The first tape she played was the newspaper's own copy of the murder, the one I gave her that day she called me Morgue Mama to my face.

The Hour of Everlasting Life started with a peppy song by the Canaries of Calvary Choir called So G.L.A.D. I'm Saved. There was a live band heavy on drums and electric guitar, and a stage full of dancers, The Sweet Ascension Dancers, twirling like Sufi Dervishes. Cameras kept searching the audience. Then there he was, the Rev. Buddy Wing, dancing up the center aisle, clapping his hands over his head.

Aubrey clapped her own hands, just once, and pointed at the screen. "There, see that, Maddy? He's not carrying his Bible. That's why he didn't notice that the gold paint was wet. The Bible was already on his pulpit."

I knew what she was getting at. One of the two poisons used to murder Buddy Wing—the heart drug called procaine—had been mixed into the paint that was used to repaint the gold cross on the Bible's old leather cover.

Wing danced up the stage steps and did a couple of fancy Temptations-like steps with the Sweet Ascension Dancers. "Pretty limber for a man in his seventies," I said.

Aubrey answered sarcastically through a mouthful of milk and popcorn. "He was a faith-healer. Every time he got an ache or pain he could ask Jesus to make it better."

It was my turn. "Too bad he couldn't get the Lord's attention before the poison got him."

Oh, we were being cold. It's just the way newspaper people get. They see so much pain and hear so much crap. They're as soft inside as anybody else. Maybe softer. When they were kids they read novels and poetry and let flies and spiders out the window rather than squish them. The sarcasm is just a cover, a way to cope. Nurses and cops are the same way.

Buddy Wing rocked on the balls of his feet for a good fifteen minutes, sharing the good news. He ended every sentence with that rhythmic *uh!* all the TV preachers use:

"God told Eve not to eat the fruit of that tree-*uh!* But Eve disobeyed-*uh!* Oh, that fruit looked so good-*uh!* And the serpent said it was okay-*uh!* Oh, that beguiling serpent-*uh!* And so Eve ate and ate-*uh!* And made Adam eat too-*uh!* And every day since, men and women have been eatin' and eatin' from the tree of sin-*uh!* And God is not happy-*uh!* No, he is not happy at all-*uh!*"

Anyway, Wing ended his sermon with his famous bit about having Jesus's phone number. Then there was a long commercial—I guess you could call it a commercial—where he offered viewers his latest book for free, mentioning several times they also should send in their best financial gift. "Some can send $1,000," he said. "Some $500, some only $100. Even if you can send only $20 or $10, send for this free book today-*uh!*"

The Sweet Ascension Dancers danced and the Canaries of Calvary Choir sang and Guthrie Gates brought out a wheelbarrow full of prayer requests and dumped them on the stage. While Gates sang the sourest hymn I'd ever heard, Wing crawled into the unopened envelopes and prayed his heart out, until his English was transformed into some heavenly tongue. Then there was another commercial, this one for a free videotape of his most-recent soul-saving mission to Africa. "Some can send $1,000. Some $500—"

Aubrey had already watched this tape a dozen times, I'm betting. She kept saying, "Listen to this" and, "You're going to love this." Now she said, "Here it comes."

We both stopped chewing and sipping. The Rev. Buddy Wing was going to die in front of our eyes and there wasn't anything we could do about it. Five months earlier when that church service was for real, and not magnetic impressions on a spool of tape, somebody else knew Buddy Wing was about to die.

It was the part of the broadcast where un-saved people in the audience were called to the edge of the stage. Everybody had their arms lifted over their heads. The Canaries of Calvary were soaring, the Ascension Dancers were opening and closing their arms, imitating blooming roses. Wing walked slowly to his pulpit and raised his Bible over his head. Then, tears seeping from his tightly closed eyes, he drew it to his lips. He kissed the gold cross. "Twenty seven minutes into the service," Aubrey said.

Buddy Wing had been kissing that cross for at least forty years, in every service he'd ever conducted, on television or off. Any other time he would have folded his Bible across his heart and walked to the end of the stage, and saved those who had gathered. This time he just stood there, surprised, worried, frantically licking his lips. The camera had zoomed in for the kiss and Wing's head was ear-to-ear across my television screen. You could see the gold paint on his lips and busy tongue.

Aubrey pushed the PAUSE button. "Procaine is a synthetic version of cocaine. It's a powerful anesthetic given to people having heart attacks—to get their hearts beating normally again. It immediately numbed his lips. That's why he started licking like that. And the licking numbed his tongue. Then the inside of his mouth and then his throat."

She pushed the PLAY button. Wing was trembling now. He dropped his Bible and reached for the glass of water on the shelf under the pulpit. He drank in big fast gulps, water leaking from the corners of his quivering mouth.

Aubrey paused the tape again. "Even a tiny overdose can cause immediate convulsions and a coma. Death in a half hour maybe. But it's iffy whether the amount of procaine the killer was able to mix into the paint would have killed Buddy by itself."

"So the killer poisoned the water, too—a double whammy?"

Aubrey filled her mouth with popcorn. "Lily of the valley is so toxic that even the water in the vase can be lethal. It pretty much causes the same reaction as the procaine. Lungs stop breathing. Heart stops pumping." She pushed PLAY and Buddy Wing continued swallowing the water. "One thing is clear—the killer wanted old Buddy's death to be grotesque and horrible. Right there on the stage. For all the world to see."

When Wing began to stagger back, the director, trained to follow his every move across the stage, went to another camera and a wider angle. Wing stepped backward toward the curtains, like someone retreating from an onrushing tide at the beach. He fell into the fake palms and slid to the floor, convulsing and vomiting.

Some members of the Canaries of Calvary Choir shrieked while others kept singing. Some members of the Ascension Dancers froze while others kept dancing. A low groan of uncertainty spread across the audience. Guthrie Gates ran across the stage and pulled Buddy Wing into his lap. The director switched to a commercial. There was Buddy Wing, alive on tape, promoting his upcoming Jesus-trip to Tallahassee. "So many will be healed," he said.

Aubrey ejected the tape. "Weird combo, isn't it? Procaine and lily of the valley—a sophisticated heart drug found only in hospitals and a weed that grows everywhere."

"Sissy apparently isn't the sharpest cheese in the dairy case," I said, remembering Dale Marabout's stories on the murder. "But she did work as a food service aide at Hannawa General Hospital, taking trays to patients. Theoretically she could have known what procaine was, and what it could do. She could have stolen it from an unlocked drug cabinet, just as she confessed." I poured some of my popcorn into Aubrey's empty bowl. "As for the lily of the valley, you're right. It grows everywhere. I remember picking it in the spring for my mother. She loved those little nodding white bells. Who knew the water in the vase could kill you."

Aubrey filled her fist with popcorn and fed the kernels into her mouth one at a time. "You know what really intrigues me about all this? The tongue thing."

That's the part that had intrigued Dale Marabout, too: Buddy Wing's flap with Tim Bandicoot had been over speaking in tongues. And the killer had chosen a drug that instantly numbed Buddy's lips. Surely the killer knew Wing's first reaction to the poison would be to lick his lips. Surely the killer knew there would be a close-up on Wing's face. Dale had asked the police about it, but their PR guy just shrugged and shook a Tic-Tac into his mouth. They already had Sissy's confession.

"What about the lily of the valley?" I asked Aubrey. "Think there's anything symbolic about that?"

She had the next tape in the VCR ready to go. "I've thought about that."

"And?"

"Bell-shaped flowers? For whom the bell tolls? Sissy's not that deep and neither is anybody else. More than likely, it was just a very handy poison to get down Buddy's throat in big gulps."

The next tape was a short one: the police department's jerky shots of Sissy James' ramshackle garage. The digital time and date on the tape showed that it was made on the Monday morning following the murder, shortly after they showed up at Sissy's door to question her. The camera panned the cluttered workbench inside the garage and then showed several different angles on the garbage cans lined up on the sidewalk behind the garage. Finally it zoomed deep inside one of the cans, focusing tightly on a Ziploc freezer bag. Now we could see Hannawa's top homicide man, Scotty Grant, examining the bag's contents: a small jar of gold paint, a tiny paint brush, a pair of vinyl surgical gloves, a tiny glass bottle with a syringe stuck in the top.

"That's all too convenient, isn't it," Aubrey said. "All that evidence in one bag in one place. The bag wasn't even stuffed down inside a milk carton or anything. Just lying there on top. Puh-leeze."

The next shots were of a spare bedroom in Sissy's house where she kept her crafts supplies: jars of paint and glitter, brushes, a glue gun, shopping bags filled with feathers and plastic beads, Christmas ornaments at various stages of completion. Aubrey paused the tape. "So we know from this shot that Sissy knew her way around slow-drying paint. Too easy, don't you think?"

I was no more impressed than Aubrey. "If Sissy was into crafts," I said, "then everybody who knew her knew she was into crafts. And no doubt ran the other way screaming every time they saw her coming with her shopping bag full of her cutsie-wootsie crap."

Aubrey stretched out on the floor, flat on her young straight back, chewing popcorn. "A lot of planning went into that murder, Maddy. Either the killer knew Sissy very well—all about her hospital job and her stupid hobby and her absolute worship of Tim Bandicoot—or they researched the hell out of her. They designed the murder around her. But the evidence is too perfect. A killer that methodical must have figured the police would find it too perfect, too."

"And go arrest Tim Bandicoot?" I asked.

"Yeah."

"But then Sissy confessed."

"Yeah."

"But wouldn't the killer also know she might confess to save Bandicoot's neck?"

Aubrey sat up in one flowing motion—I hate how young people can do that—and propped her chin on her knees. "Maybe the killer didn't care who got arrested. As long as it wasn't him—or her."

I went to the kitchen for more milk and came back with the most brilliant thought. "Maybe the real killer did care. Maybe the real killer knew Tim Bandicoot had a solid alibi for that night."

"Somebody like Bandicoot's wife, maybe?"

"Maybe."

"And why would she kill Buddy Wing?"

"To get Buddy Wing out of her husband's way," I said. "And Sissy out of hers."

Aubrey covered her head with her arms, as if the ceiling were going to come down. "We are absolutely evil. And absolutely in over our heads."

She resumed the tape. There were shots of Sissy's closets and the shelves of junk in her basement. Nothing interesting or unusual. Then there were various angles on the house's exterior. It was one of those old two-story frame houses built just before the Depression. Hannawa is full of them. They were once the dream homes of big middle-class families. Now they rent cheap to people on the edge.

Next came the interrogation tape. It was slightly out of focus and the voices were barely audible. Aubrey didn't pause it once. She just let it run. It lasted about fifteen minutes.

Sissy was only twenty-six, but on that tape she looked forty-six. She was a tad plump. Her hair was ridiculously blond. Despite her blank face and sunken eyes she was pretty. She was wearing an enormous ill-fitting sweater with a Thanksgiving turkey on the front. I'd guess she knitted it herself.

Detective Scotty Grant asked her if she killed the Rev. Buddy Wing and she said yes. He asked her how and she said with a combination of heart drugs she stole from the hospital and drinking water laced with lily of the valley. Every question was more specific and so were her answers.

"Her confession sounded pretty convincing," I said when the tape ended.

Aubrey agreed. "She did have it down pretty good. The poisons. The paint. How she got in the church. The whole deal."

"Maybe she did do it."

Aubrey slid in the next tape. "I wonder if she would have been so convincing if she'd been interrogated before Dale Marabout's story on the poisons ran?"

"Dale's story ran before her confession?"

"Three days before. You can see why I don't trust the police. Kudos to Marabout, but they should never have given him that evidence so early."

The next tape was from the arraignment. Sissy was wearing an orange jumpsuit now. Her hair was flat and greasy and pulled back into a makeshift ponytail. She told the judge she was guilty. She said she was ready for whatever punishment God and the state of Ohio had in mind. The judge ordered the obligatory psychological testing.

The last tape was from the sentencing. Sissy's childhood had been horrible enough for her to avoid a death sentence but not life without parole. Deputies led Sissy from the courtroom. You could see Guthrie Gates sitting in the gallery.

# 5

Monday evening Aubrey got into a big mess with Dale Marabout and managing editor Alec Tinker. I'd already gone home for the day, but Eric Chen was still in the morgue and overhead most of it.

Chief Polceznec's reorganization plan had reassigned all of the district commanders but one, the 3rd District's Lionel Percy. Aubrey thought that odd, given that most of the city's problems with police corruption came out of the 3rd District. The 3rd is a royal mess, that's for sure. Hardly a month goes by that some cop there doesn't get demoted or indicted for something. Sometimes a whole slew of them get in trouble at once, like the time two years ago when TV 21 reporter Tish Kiddle found eight officers moonlighting at a Morrow Avenue *show bar* where the lap dancers were completely naked and cocaine as easy to get as pretzels.

So Aubrey wanted to investigate why Chief Polceznec didn't reassign Commander Percy. Tinker was all for giving her the green light, but Dale filibustered: It wasn't the paper's job to go on fishing expeditions—that, he said, was the job of the state attorney general, or the U.S. Justice Department, or the department's own internal affairs division.

But Aubrey insisted there'd been enough crap in the 3rd to question why Lionel Percy was left in place when all the other district commanders were either given administrative jobs at headquarters or tempted into retirement.

Eric told me the argument went on for a half hour, ending with Aubrey screeching obscenities, Dale storming off to the men's room, and Tinker wondering out loud why he'd accepted the transfer from our sister paper in Baton Rouge.

I'd have to say both Dale and Aubrey were right. A newspaper shouldn't go on fishing expeditions. But when something already smells to high heaven? Well, that was a judgment call Tinker had to make and he gave Aubrey the green light she wanted.

Let me give you a little background on the *Herald-Union*, and how Alec Tinker landed here as managing editor.

The *Hannawa Herald* was founded in 1855 by Elton Elsworth Newkirk, a Connecticut-born abolitionist who helped bankroll the anti-slavery crusade of John Brown, who, before achieving infamy in Kansas and Harper's Ferry, toiled for many years right here in Hannawa. The *Hannawa Union* did not appear until 1876, late in the corrupt second term of President Ulysses S. Grant. It was an unapologetically Republican paper that championed the region's industrial growth. It reigned as the city's biggest newspaper until the Great Depression, when its anti-New Deal rantings cost it half of its circulation.

In 1937, the *Herald's* then-publisher, Bix Newkirk, bought the near-bankrupt *Union* for a song. By the time I came along in the Fifties, the *Herald-Union* was a vibrant, well-heeled afternoon paper, the fourth largest in the state. Then suburbia raised its ugly head and families by the thousands moved to the cornfields. By 1972, the paper's circulation and advertising revenues had sagged so badly that the heretofore industrious Bix Newkirk suddenly developed an interest in sailboats. In 1974 he sold the *Herald-Union* to the Knudsen-Hartpence chain, headquartered eight hundred miles away in St. Paul, Minnesota. In addition to its flagship paper there in St. Paul, *The Northern Star-Pride*, it owns papers in Duluth, Tampa, Baton Rouge and a dozen or so smaller cities.

Knudsen-Hartpence brought in Bob Averill as editor-in-chief and changed us from an afternoon paper to a morning paper. Home delivery increased by a third and the suburban malls boosted advertising revenues. We've been languishing lately—nobody under forty reads newspapers and everybody in America is unfortunately under forty, or so it seems—but the corporate gurus in St. Paul have plans for changing that. They've sent us Tinker, a thirty-two-year-old wunderkind from our paper in Baton Rouge.

At the time of his appointment the company newsletter said Tinker would make reading the *Herald-Union* "Not only irresistible but imperative." So far he's done that by running shorter stories and larger photographs, though he has promised to initiate what he calls "a synergistic blend of in-your-face and in-your-mind journalism." Talk about bullshit.

Tinker's arrival at the *Herald-Union* was anything but good news to veteran reporters like Dale Marabout. Knudsen-Hartpence sent Tinker here to get the paper's circulation up, which meant shaking the town up, which meant shaking the editorial staff up.

Dale is certain, and I'm sure he's right, that Tinker's marching orders were to fill as many of the paper's major beats as possible with as many indefatigable kids as possible. So the arrival of Tinker was a godsend to Aubrey McGinty. She'd been trying to get the *Herald-Union's* attention since her freshman year at Kent State. She'd repeatedly applied for stringer work—to cover boring suburban school board meetings and the like—but she never got a call. Nor was she ever chosen for a summer internship. During her senior years she lobbied every department editor except sports for a job after graduation. Her stories in the college paper were good enough to get her a couple of interviews, but not good enough to get her a job. And if I know Aubrey, all the time she was trying to get our attention, she was trying just as hard to get the attention of every big-city newspaper in the Midwest. Like most journalism grads, she ended up on a small paper in a small town, covering small stories, trying to survive on a pitifully small paycheck, plotting her escape.

The way young reporters escape small papers is through the stories they write. They clip them out and stick them in manila folders. As soon as they've got six months or a year under their belt, they start sending those *clips* to bigger papers. The better their clips, the bigger the paper they'll land on. So they joyfully work their brains out at those small papers, praying that the good-clip gods let something horrible happen on their beats, like the murder of the local football coach, so they can cover the hell out of it.

Tinker liked Aubrey's clips on the football coach murder. He liked how she didn't accept the Rush City Police Department's verdict. He liked how she pursued the rumors of the coach's affair with the cheerleading advisor. He liked how her relentless pursuit led to the arrest of the cuckolded husband. Aubrey McGinty was just the kind of reporter he wanted covering the cops in Hannawa, Ohio.

From what I gather, Tinker and Aubrey started wooing each other a good year before she was actually hired. Aubrey sent him her clips and he took her to lunch. There were letters and phone calls and then finally a firm commitment that she'd be hired just as soon as there was an opening.

Dale did a wonderful job covering the Buddy Wing murder in November. Everyone in the newsroom praised him to high heaven. But Tinker had already made up his mind and when Wally Kearns announced in January he was taking advantage of the paper's early retirement program to write that novel he'd been putting off, there was suddenly a copy editing slot on the metro desk for someone with an experienced eye. For Dale Marabout.

Aubrey, as you know, showed up the first week of March, full of vinegar.

◇◇◇

# Wednesday, March 22

On Wednesday I took Dale to lunch at Speckley's.

I was expecting him to be pissed off by Tinker's decision. Instead, he was concerned only about Aubrey's safety. "Maddy," he said, "the 3rd District has been corrupt for decades. I don't know if Percy is part of any illegal stuff or not. And I bet Chief Polceznec doesn't know either. But what both the chief and I do know is that Lionel Percy is a five-hundred-pound piranha. You don't swim in his pond. Polceznec probably figures Percy will retire in a couple years and then he can put some Spic-and-Span guy in charge and turn things around."

I tried to get Dale to eat his meat loaf sandwich before it got cold but he just kept playing with his potatoes. "Why didn't you tell Tinker all this?" I asked. "It looks like you're trying to protect your pals on the force again."

Dale wasn't happy with that. "Again?"

"You know what I mean."

He stuck his fork in the top of his potatoes and folded his arms. "If I tell Tinker I'm afraid for Aubrey's safety, that will only prove her point, won't it? If only Aubrey wasn't so damned gonzo about everything."

Well, Dale was right about that. Aubrey was one very determined young woman. Most reporters are emotionally detached from the stories they cover. It doesn't matter much if they're covering a murder trial or a Red Cross blood drive. They go where they're assigned, gather up the who-what-when-where-and-why, come back and write the damn story, go home and feed their cats. They get whooped up about a story from time to time, sure. But when they do, it's the *story* that gets them excited, not the reality.

From what I'd seen, Aubrey McGinty was different. With her it was the reality. Yes, she'd told Guthrie Gates she was only interested in Buddy Wing's murder because it was a good story. But I had the feeling she really wanted to help Sissy James. And if she wanted to investigate why Chief Polceznec left Lionel

Percy commander of the 3rd District, it was because the people living there deserved better.

"Now Mr. M," I said, "It might turn out to be a good story."

He decided to eat. "It's not sour grapes. She really could get hurt."

## Friday, March 24

Aubrey not only sat on my desk, she pulled her legs up under her chin. It was one of those late March days in Ohio when the weather should have been a lot better than it was, when wet snow covers the sprouting daffodils and tulips, when people are torpid and testy, bundled up in sweaters they'd already put away for the summer. "Look around the newsroom," I hissed at her. "Do you see anybody else sitting on the top of their desks?"

She didn't get off, but she did lower her legs and dangle them over the side. I accepted the partial victory. "So, what brings you to the morgue on this wonderful afternoon?"

She yawned. "I finally got that stuff from probate on the good reverend's estate."

Suddenly it wouldn't have bothered me if she were standing on her head. "And?"

"It seems the money trail leads straight to God."

"You don't think He poisoned Buddy Wing, do you?"

She was no more in the mood for my smart-assed remarks than I was for hers. "It's really quite remarkable. Wing only had $6,400 in the bank. A $10,000 life insurance policy. A tiny paid-for colonial in South Ridge. A 1987 Pontiac Sunbird valued at nothing. All left to the Heaven Bound Cathedral."

"What about all the white suits and loud ties?"

"God got those, too."

"Then he wasn't killed for his money."

Aubrey handed me my tea mug and we headed for the cafeteria. "Do you know Wing only made $34,000 a year. You'd think he was a member of the newspaper guild."

"And how do you know he only made $34,000 a year?"

"I goo-goo eyed one of the young studlies in homicide into showing me the church's financial report from their files."

"You think Guthrie Gates will settle for $34,000?" I asked.

"He was already making $60,000 when Wing was killed."

"And now?"

"Well, that's this year's financial report, isn't it? Which the police don't have. And I'm guessing Gates wouldn't be too crazy about sharing with us. But it doesn't matter anyway."

We'd just walked through sports. I took a look over my shoulder. A half-dozen sets of male eyes quickly shifted from Aubrey's jeans, some to the ceiling, some to computer screens, some to the floor, none to me. "It doesn't matter?"

Aubrey was looking over her shoulder, too. Making sure she was being appreciated. "Even if Gates killed poor old Buddy for the tithes and offerings, he'd have to take it easy with the church elders for a while."

This late in the day the cafeteria was empty. I headed for the hot water. Aubrey headed for the candy machine. "So where does this leave your investigation?" I asked.

"Nowhere and everywhere," she answered. "Just like before."

# 6

It was a toss-up whose car we'd take that morning. Neither my Dodge Shadow nor Aubrey's Ford Escort was in any shape for a long drive. But if we were going to Marysville somebody had to drive. My car got the nod when we compared tire tread.

I picked her up at her apartment building, a crumbling old Art Deco palace at West Tuckman and Sterling. It had been a wonderful neighborhood once. I've seen the old pictures: muscular oaks lining brick streets, trolley cars, big old Tudors surrounded with wrought-iron fences. Now the oaks are gone, the bricks paved over with asphalt, the trolleys replaced by boxy buses, the wrought-iron by chain-link, and the wonderful old homes chopped up into efficiency apartments for poor souls who don't have two nickels to rub together.

Aubrey was waiting outside for me, in the rain. She got in the car with soaked hair, a mug of black coffee, and cheeks as pink as bunny slippers.

"Good gravy," I scolded, "you'll catch pneumonia."

"Pneumonia is caused by micro-organisms, not raindrops," she said.

It was only six-thirty and I made an illegal U-turn to get back to the I-491 interchange. "I don't think so, Aubrey." I told her how President William Henry Harrison gave a four-hour inaugural speech in the rain, contracted pneumonia, and died four weeks later.

She was pressing the coffee mug against her forehead. "Don't mother me, Maddy."

I took I-491 to I-76 to I-71. We hit one pocket of rain after another. Aubrey was driving me nuts changing stations on the radio.

My lunch with Dale Marabout the previous week had poured more fuel on my already combustible curiosity and sent me looking for answers about what made Aubrey tick. Whenever I'd gotten a spare minute, I'd snooped through the files looking for anything to do with Rush City or a McGinty. And now I was chomping at the bit to ask her about something I'd found. However, what I'd found wasn't good, and that kept me chomping instead of asking. It kept me disappointed in her, and disappointed in me, all the way to Marysville.

Marysville is a little city of eleven thousand or so in Union County, a half hour northwest of Columbus. Back in the Eighties the governor persuaded the Japanese carmaker Honda to build a big auto plant there, providing thousands of good jobs and ruining thousands of acres of good farmland. Until then the county's biggest employer was the Marysville Reformatory for Women. It's where they sent Sissy James after she confessed to poisoning Buddy Wing.

Saturday morning is not a good time to visit someone in prison. It's when everyone wants to visit. So there were quite a number of cars lined up at the gate and the guards were taking their time checking people in.

Except for the chain-link fences and Slinky-like rings of razor wire, the prison looked like a small college. Some of the buildings were old and strangely quaint—the first were built in the early nineteen hundreds—while others were cold and modern. There were a few bunches of trees here and there, though the prison clearly could have budgeted a little more for landscaping. On the drive from Hannawa, Aubrey told me that Marysville housed eighteen hundred women, most for non-violent crimes like drugs or forgery or prostitution, most for getting mixed up with the wrong kind of man.

I was surprised that Sissy James had agreed to talk with Aubrey. I also was glad Aubrey invited me along. I'd sat in the morgue for forty years watching reporters rushing in and out, watching the stories they banged out turn into neat columns of print. Now I was getting a chance to see a reporter in action. I knew that Aubrey cared how this whole Sissy James thing panned out, but frankly I just liked the snooping and the lunches afterward.

The guards directed us to the maximum security building. It was big and new. Except for the bars in the windows it didn't look much different from the middle school they built up the street from my bungalow a few years ago. Inside we were politely interrogated, checked for drugs and weapons, and led into a tiny windowless room. It was furnished with an uncomfortable-looking blue sofa, a single wood chair without armrests, and a small coffee table made of molded plastic. The walls were bare except for a closed-circuit TV camera and a framed photo of Republican Governor Dick Van Sickle.

Aubrey motioned for me to sit in the chair. She sat in the middle of the sofa, so Sissy would have to sit close to her no matter which end of the sofa she chose. We only had to wait a couple of minutes before Sissy was ushered in. Her baggy cotton slacks and blouse were the same gray as the floor tiles. The guard positioned herself in the doorway, arms folded across her mixing-bowl breasts.

Sissy was surprisingly friendly. She smiled and shook our hands and sat on Aubrey's left side. She'd only been in Marysville for four months, but she looked thinner than she did on the interrogation and arraignment tapes. Aubrey took a notebook and pen from her purse, but she didn't open the notebook or click the pen, her old off-the-record trick. "What job do they have you doing here, Sissy?" she asked.

"Flag shop."

"Making flags you mean?"

"American flags. Ohio flags. I like it."

"Keeps your mind off things?"

"It makes the day go by."

"You've got a long row to hoe, don't you? Life without parole."

"Life goes by in a minute. Then you've got eternity with the Lord."

"Confident you're going to heaven then?"

Sissy's smile turned hard and uneasy, like the seat of that damn wooden chair I was sitting on. "I've already been forgiven," she said.

Aubrey put her notebook on the coffee table and twisted until her arms and chin were resting on the back of the sofa. She was close enough to stroke Sissy's cheek if she wanted. "And what has God forgiven you for? Murdering Buddy Wing or covering up for somebody else?"

Sissy's eyes floated up to the governor's picture, her popularly elected lord here on earth. "I know there's still lots of talk about me taking the blame for somebody else."

Aubrey nodded. "For Tim Bandicoot, your lover." ·

Sissy just stared at the governor. "Everybody knows me and Tim did wrong. That's no secret. God's forgiven me for that, too."

"And apparently Tim's wife has forgiven him," Aubrey said. "I hear they're a happy family again."

Said Sissy, "As it should be." ·

"You don't think Tim was just using you for sex? The way other men had used you for sex?"

I watched Sissy's eyes cloud over, her nostrils glow pink. "You just know everything, don't you?"

Aubrey's voice shriveled into a whisper. "I read the transcripts of your sentencing hearing. If it hadn't been for all that stuff that happened to you when you were a kid, you might be on death row right now."

I'd remembered Dale's story on the sentencing: Sissy's lawyer had talked for an hour about her illegitimate birth, her mother's early death, the shoplifting, the running away, the drugs, the stripping in rathole bars, the escort service stuff, how she'd been rescued by the Rev. Buddy Wing, pressing his open hands against the inside of her television screen. Her lawyer was followed by a dozen members of the Heaven Bound Cathedral, forgiving her the way they knew Pastor Wing surely would have forgiven her, praying that Sissy be allowed to live and be a witness for God's love inside the secure walls of the Ohio Reformatory for Women.

"What happened to me ain't important," Sissy told Aubrey. Her head was bent over her knees now, and her arms wrapped around her waist, as if she had a bad case of menstrual cramps. "All that matters is that Satan got the best of me and I killed Pastor Wing."

If I'd been the one asking the questions, I would have been rocking Sissy in my arms. But Aubrey pulled back, making sure there wasn't a whit of compassion in her voice. "I don't think you killed Buddy Wing," she said. "And I don't think Tim Bandicoot killed him either, though I'm sure that's what you think."

Sissy almost screamed it: "I killed Pastor Wing. Why don't anybody believe that?"

Aubrey put her notebook back in her purse. She hadn't written a word. "Well, the police believe it. The judge believes it. So you've got them on your side. But me, I'm not on your side. I'm going back to Hannawa and I'm going to prove beyond a shadow of a doubt that Tim Bandicoot didn't do it, even if he's the world's biggest asshole in every other way. And then I'll come back and we'll have another talk."

Sissy James walked out of the room before another word could be said. Her arms were still wrapped around her waist. She was crying.

Aubrey and I drove into Marysville and had an early lunch in a restaurant that looked a lot like Speckley's. The specialty of this place was fried bologna sandwiches. We were both intrigued. The bologna was a half-inch thick, smothered in cheddar cheese. The bun was soaked with grease. They were absolutely wonderful. After lunch we checked out the antique shops. I bought an old Lassie novel for Joyce, my niece back in LaFargeville. Like every collie owner I ever met, Joyce collects anything Lassie. Then we started for home.

In the hilly part of Richland County traffic stopped. Both lanes north, both lanes south, thousands of idling cars and trucks spewing blue exhaust. It was raining so hard you'd of thought we were in a car wash. We couldn't see a thing. Aubrey punched the radio buttons for the right song to soothe her growing anxiety. Finally she squealed "Shit!" and jumped out of the car. She disappeared up the berm.

I was antsy, too. Not so much about the traffic jam—sooner or later we'd start moving again—but about the lie Aubrey told me that day we went to see Guthrie Gates at the cathedral. One of the first lessons new reporters at the *Herald-Union* learn is that you don't bullshit Morgue Mama. Heap all the bullshit you want on your sources or on the editors. On Morgue Mama, not even a teaspoonful. But now there I was, being bullshitted by Aubrey McGinty and afraid to confront her about it. I was simply furious with myself.

Aubrey was gone for a half hour. She jumped into the car soaking wet. "Remember Maddy," she said even before the door was closed, "pneumonia—virus."

She took her cellphone from her purse and punched in a flurry of numbers with her little finger. Somebody picked up right away. "Metro," she said. And so I learned about the accident up ahead at the same time the desk did. A skidding semi full of Florida grapefruit had been broadsided by another semi hauling steel I-beams. Bouncing, flying, rolling grapefruit had caused six separate accidents. Nobody was dead, but several had been seriously injured, among them 25th District congresswoman Betty Zuduski-Lowell. "Her nose is broken and she's screaming at the top of her lungs that she's a member of the U.S. Congress," Aubrey told the desk. "There must be fifty or sixty people standing in the rain eating grapefruit—God, I wish I had a camera."

It was exciting to see Aubrey in action like that. She was thorough, detached. For some reason it gave me the courage to confront her about the lie. As soon as she was off the phone I dove in. "Forgive me," I said, "but I have to ask you about that fleece jacket you bought at Old Navy."

She reached for the radio knob, unconcerned and probably not listening to what I was saying. I softly pushed her fingers away. "You told me the gift certificate was from your sister. Your sister is dead."

Her eyes froze on me. "You been snooping, Maddy?"

"I don't snoop," I said. "I get intrigued."

She slid down and rested the back of her head on the seat. "It's all there, isn't it. In print forever and ever. Everybody's dark secrets. I'm sorry I lied to you."

"It's not that you lied to me," I said. "I'm concerned why you lied to yourself like that."

She started to cry, the way Sissy James had cried when Aubrey pressed her. "I just miss her, Maddy."

We didn't discuss it any further. There was no need to. I knew all that I needed to know from the stories in the files. She knew all she needed to know from having lived it. The poor lamb. It was a horrible thing:

Aubrey's older sister had committed suicide fifteen years before, when she was thirteen and Aubrey just nine. She'd sprinkled an entire bottle of her mother's antidepressants inside a peanut butter and banana sandwich. She made that sandwich three months after their stepfather was tried and acquitted for repeatedly having sex with her. Was Aubrey abused like that, too? Probably. I did find her mother's divorce listed in the courthouse news, eight months after the suicide. If Aubrey was molested, it ended when she was ten.

So, of course Aubrey gave herself a Christmas gift from her sister every year. She missed her sister. She needed to keep her alive any way she could. And of course she lied to me, if you really want to consider it a lie. Why would you explain something like that to a stranger? I was angry at myself for bringing it up

Angry for snooping. Yet it seemed to explain why she wanted to help Sissy James. Why she went looking for the truth back in Rush City when the football coach was murdered. Cops screw up. Courts send innocent people to jail. Courts set guilty people free. Somebody has to care.

# 7

## Sunday, April 2

The next day I worked on my tomato and pepper plants. It's an annual ritual that always leaves me hating myself. The process actually starts in September when I take four or five of my best-looking green peppers and a couple of my fatter tomatoes and rip them open for the seeds. I spread the seeds out on pieces of newspaper and let them dry. Then I roll the papers up and put a rubber bands around them and write TOMATOES on one and PEPPERS on the other.

Then the first week of April I plant the seeds in a tray and put them on a card table by the window in my bedroom that faces south, so they get a full day of sun. I keep the trays watered and watch the tiny sprouts pop through the potting soil. They come in thick as grass. When they get so big, I pluck out the scrawny ones, so the healthier ones have plenty of elbow room. I water them and talk to them and when they're three or four inches high they shrivel up and die. Then Memorial Day weekend, I drive to Biliczky's Garden Center and buy a half-flat of tomato plants and a half-flat of pepper plants, and plant the damn things in my garden. The rabbits whittle the leaves off three-quarters of them, but the rest survive. I get enough peppers to cut into my summer salads and enough tomatoes to get my fill of BLTs. Right after Labor Day I pick a few of each and rip them open for the seeds. Spread them out on newspaper to dry.

◇◇◇

# Monday, April 3

Monday morning I got on the elevator with Nanette Beane, the religion editor. She was cradling another cactus for her desk. She already had a dozen of them, some of them two feet tall. The newsroom joke is that they thrive on Nanette's dry prose. Instead of making my usual beeline to the morgue, I meandered through metro to Aubrey's desk.

Aubrey was busy putting a human face on the half-naked female corpse found over the weekend in the parking lot of an abandoned factory on Morrow Street. Morrow runs parallel with the interstate, in the southern end of the 3rd District. There are lots of abandoned factory buildings there. They find lots of bodies there.

"Prostitute?" I asked. The female bodies were almost always prostitutes, the male bodies almost always drug dealers.

She gave me an of-course-she-was shrug while looking for her coffee mug among the clutter. "Mother with three little kids, too. She had their pictures in her purse. Among the needles and condoms, and the wad of lottery tickets."

"You want me to pull any files for you?" I asked.

"Eric's already on it," she said. She took a gulp from her mug—I could tell from her expression that the coffee was cold. "Just stay on him, Maddy. He's got the attention span of a snowflake in Honolulu."

I squinted toward the morgue. Eric was at his computer, eyes six inches from the screen, arched hands attacking his keyboard like tap-dancing tarantulas. "He looks sufficiently motivated," I said.

She knew what I meant. "Don't even go there—he's the world's biggest geek."

"A geek in heat," I said.

She dismissed me with a long "Puh-leeze" and another gulp of cold coffee.

I circled through the morgue to hang up my coat and get my mug, and then went to the cafeteria to fix my first dose of Darjeeling tea. When I returned Doreen Poole was waiting for me at my desk. "I need some stuff on the mayors' wives," she said.

"The mayor has more than one wife? Now that's a story."

Doreen started nibbling at her lower lip. I love to piss her off. And it's not just because she's the one who started the Morgue Mama thing. It's the way she floats through her day like a soggy cloud, oblivious to all the parades she's raining on. "The wives of past mayors," she said. "I'm thinking of doing a story about how their role has changed over the years."

"Thinking of doing a story?" I asked. This is the part of my job I've always hated. Reporters are always *thinking* of doing a story on something. What it means is that they don't have anything important to write about at the moment, so they try to pull some flimsy feature story out of thin air. They'll have Eric or me work for hours finding *stuff* about the story they're *thinking* of writing. Then something important does happen on their beat and they're off on that and all our work was for nothing. "Let me guess, Doreen," I said. "You saw that documentary on A&E last night about the presidents' wives and you thought it might be interesting to localize it."

"I think it would be interesting."

I fished the tea bag out of my mug. At home I always add a couple squirts of skimmed milk and honey to my Darjeeling tea. At work I drink it straight. Darjeeling is one of the famous black teas from northern India, grown in the shadows of Mt. Everest, which has always been my favorite mountain. When reporters come to the morgue begging for my files on this or that, I want them to go away feeling they've just climbed Everest. "My guess is that the lives of mayors' wives haven't changed much over the years," I said. "They slowly turn into alcoholics waiting for their husbands to come home at night."

I told Doreen to make me a list of some specific mayors' wives and I'd see what I could find. After she threw back her head and stormed off, I threw my teabag in the trash and went to work finding everything we had on Tim Bandicoot, his wife Annie, and his rival, Guthrie Gates.

# Friday, April 7

Aubrey's story on the dead prostitute was terrific. It turned out she'd been an outstanding basketball player in high school. The sports department had even run a feature on her. "For all her physical gifts it's her heart that puts her head and shoulders above the rest," her coach said at the time. Aubrey re-ran that old quote from the coach and added this new one: "If she hadn't gotten pregnant and dropped out, she could have gotten a full-ride from any number of colleges. Now she's just another dead girl from the inner city."

The rest of the week Aubrey concentrated on her investigation of the 3rd District. She got several officers, some retired and some still on the job, to talk off the record about Commander Lionel Percy. She compiled all kinds of crime figures, contrasting the 3rd to other districts in the city. Eric and I pulled together all the old stories on past corruption we could find. By Thursday she'd interviewed Chief Polceznec and Mayor Flynn—neither of whom had much of anything to say—as well as several members of City Council and a number of self-appointed community leaders—all of whom had plenty to say.

By Friday afternoon, Aubrey's story was pretty much finished except for an interview with Lionel Percy himself. He called her back at six-thirty and told her she had exactly one minute to ask her "worthless questions." So she started rattling off various facts and accusations. He answered, "Same old tired shit" to every one of them. Before hanging up he said this: "If those dumbfucks on City Council think they can do a better job cleaning up the 3rd, let them gather up their shit shovels and come on down."

Aubrey put the quotes in her story and sent it to the desk, knowing they'd never get past Dale Marabout.

Which they didn't. Quotes like that wouldn't get by any copy editor on any newspaper. So Dale told her to kill the quotes and *paraphrase*, the tried-and-true trick for circumventing profanity. When Aubrey refused to paraphrase, Dale rewrote the story himself, which sent Aubrey straight to Tinker. People in the newsroom still debate whether Aubrey intentionally set up a confrontation between Tinker and Dale. I can go either way. One thing was sure, Aubrey knew Tinker's mind better than the rest of us. Tinker told Dale to put the quotes back in and dash the bad words, *s--t, dumbf---s.*

Dale shouted, "You've got to be kidding!"

Tinker shouted back that he wasn't: "Lionel Percy had the opportunity to answer our questions any way he chose. Readers have a right to know how he chose."

Dale filibustered about the *Herald-Union* being a family paper, about our never using language like that before, not even with the appropriate dashes.

Tinker threw back his head and shared his disbelief with the fluorescent lights. "This is the twenty-first century, Marabout. Nobody gives a rat's ass about those words anymore."

"Then why not print them without the dashes?" Dale wondered. Even the sports guys were gathering around the metro desk now.

Tinker continued to commiserate with the lights. You just knew he was wondering why on earth he'd accepted the transfer from our paper in Baton Rouge. In his three years as managing editor down there, he'd not only stopped the paper's horrible slide in circulation, he'd helped the paper win a Pulitzer Prize. He'd done all the usual things papers do when panic sets in—he redesigned the paper to look like *USA Today*, created trendy new sections to appeal to people's active lifestyles, and put pictures of the paper's columnists on the sides of buses. But the biggest thing he did was spice up the reporting. The *Business Week* feature on him recounted a pep talk he gave reporters one afternoon: He stood on his desk and told them to start writing like the novelists they all really wanted to be. "Treat the truth just like it's fiction," he was quoted as saying.

Tinker wasn't up on his desk now, but he was joyously giving the same sort of speech. "From now on," he said, "when profanity is pertinent to a story, we dash it and run it."

Dale, to his credit, didn't back off. "And how is it pertinent here, Tinker? Everybody knows cops have garbage mouths. All you're trying to do is sell papers."

Tinker's head lowered as slowly as my automatic garage door. "And you're not trying to sell papers, Marabout? I'm not so happy to hear that."

Well, that's how it went. Dale lost the argument and on Saturday the story ran with the dashes. Dale called me at home on Sunday. He tried to sound carefree and chatty, but I knew he was worried. "People do need to know what kind of bastard Lionel Percy is," he admitted, "and maybe Aubrey's story will do some good. But she's going to pay for it. She's made one of their own look bad. They'll close ranks, freeze her out for a couple of months until it looks like she's sloughing off, then feed her bad information on some big story to make her look incompetent."

"She's hard as nails," I said.

That made him laugh. "You used to tell me I was hard as nails. Now I'm just another worn-out lump on the copy desk."

It was the first sexual innuendo between us in years—if you want to call anything that blatant an innuendo. I let it go by. "You're a good copy editor," I said.

I spent the rest of the day kicking myself for that *good copy editor* remark. What a horrible thing to say. It was like praising some old geezer architect for the log cabin he was building out of Popsicle sticks at the rest home. At least I knew he was probably kicking himself for his hard as nails crack. We'd been lovers once. But Father Time and that damned kindergarten teacher had put an end to that. Now we were friends. That was enough.

◇◇◇

# Saturday, April 15

Letters to the editor started pouring in on Monday. By fifty to one they lambasted us for sinking to such a new low. The girls in circulation were busy all day with people calling to cancel their subscriptions. At Tuesday night's City Council meeting, several of the backbenchers used language they wouldn't have dared using in public before, presumably in the hope of finally being quoted in the paper. On Wednesday, Charlie Chimera, afternoon drive-time host on WFLO, ranted all four of his hours about what he repeatedly called the *Herald-Union's*, "disgusting descent into the murky mire of irresponsibility." Every caller agreed with him.

Our circulation started climbing back up on Thursday.

Finally it was Saturday again and Aubrey and I were on our way to see Tim Bandicoot.

At first we discussed the weather—the first thing all Ohioans discuss when they crawl into a car—and then why Tim Bandicoot would agree to talk to us about Sissy James. "It sure can't be for the free publicity," I said. "Sissy's name all over the front page could destroy him."

"I'm the enemy," Aubrey said. "He wants to take my measure."

"Take your measure? Somebody's been watching too many old movies."

She knew I was joking. She also knew I was taking her down a few pegs. "Then how about this?" she asked. "He knows Sissy will be all over the front page with or without his cooperation. So he might as well appear helpful."

"*Appear* being the key word?"

She repeated my question as a declarative sentence. "Appear being the key word."

"Which raises all sorts of possibilities?"

"Which raises all sorts of possibilities."

Tim Bandicoot's New Day Epiphany Temple was located east of downtown, on Lutheran Hill, at the corner of Cleveland

and Cather, an old commercial district that once served the city's German enclave. By the Fifties those Germans had been absorbed by other ethnic groups and other neighborhoods. Today Lutheran Hill is populated by South Koreans, Pakistanis, poor blacks and even poorer Appalachian whites. Three-quarters of the storefronts are empty.

The temple was housed in an old dime store, a single-story orange brick building sandwiched between two used car lots. The fat red letters that once spelled W O O L W O R T H ' S across the front of the building were long gone, but you could still see their dirty silhouettes.

Aubrey found a parking spot in front just big enough for her Escort. We checked twice to make sure the doors were locked and went inside. What a difference from the Heaven Bound Cathedral. The New Day Epiphany Temple was a single room. The floor was covered with peel-and-stick tile. The walls were covered with cheap maple paneling. The lights were on but nobody was home.

We stood by the door for a few minutes, wondering what to do, then walked down the rows of metal folding chairs to the stage at the back of the room. The stage was carpeted with red shag. There was a modest pulpit up front and a row of ugly, throne-like chairs across the back. The monstrous cross on the wall was wrapped with hundreds of miniature Christmas lights. "You suppose they're the twinkly kind?" Aubrey asked.

"Of course they're the twinkly kind," I said. We each chose a throne and sat.

Tim Bandicoot arrived maybe five minutes later. He came through the front door, three tall Styrofoam cups of coffee balanced on a box of Krispy Kreme Doughnuts. "Comfortable, aren't they?" he called out when he spotted us in those ugly chairs.

I felt like a royal fool and started to get up. But Bandicoot motioned for me to stay put. He came up the center aisle with the coffee and doughnuts, snaring a pair of folding chairs as he went. He set the coffee and doughnuts on one and himself on the other. And so our visit began, Aubrey and I on our thrones, Tim Bandicoot on a folding chair, debating between creme sticks, glazed crullers, and cinnamon twists.

I don't know what Aubrey expected, but I expected Tim Bandicoot to be some kind of icky egomaniac. I figured that, more than likely, he was the real murderer. I figured that after he'd gotten all the sex and mindless adoration he wanted from Sissy James, he set her up to save his own neck. And now here we were having doughnuts and coffee with this nice, down-to-earth young man. Maybe under that pleasant façade he really was icky and egomaniacal, and maybe even the real murderer, but I felt surprisingly comfortable that morning, sipping coffee, nibbling on a cruller, looking into those chocolate-brown cow eyes of his.

When we'd gone to see Guthrie Gates, Aubrey got right to the skinny: Did he think Sissy did it? This morning was different. She let Tim Bandicoot go on and on about his growing congregation and his plans to build a new temple right there in that rundown neighborhood, with a day care center, soup kitchen, and food bank for the city's poor. He also talked about building his electronic church. Currently his services were only broadcast on the local community-access channel, but he was determined to be on a regular local cable channel within a year and on cable nationally within five years. He had plans for saving millions of souls in Africa and China and the former Soviet Republics.

By the time Aubrey asked him about Sissy James, we'd eaten half the doughnuts in the box. "Did you really love Sissy?" she asked. "Do you still love her?"

He was clearly embarrassed. And clearly nervous. "I did not love her the way I love my wife," he said. "I let my flesh take over." He searched the box for the plainest doughnut he could find. "I've already admitted all this to my wife."

"Has she forgiven you?" asked Aubrey.

"I did not ask her for forgiveness. I want her to be disappointed in me for the rest of my life. I'm weak. I'm a sinner."

Aubrey took a doughnut oozing raspberry. "And your congregation? Do they know how weak and sinful you are?"

"A few. I suppose they all will after you're done with me."

Tim Bandicoot clearly was trying to manipulate Aubrey—make her feel guilty if he could manage it, at least a little sympathetic if he couldn't—but Aubrey wasn't falling into that trap. "We went to see Sissy at Marysville," she said.

"I heard."

Aubrey had her doughnut clenched in her teeth while she dug in her purse for her notebook. "I get the impression Sissy loves both you and the Lord about the same."

When she couldn't find a pen, Bandicoot gave her the Bic from his shirt pocket. "I hope that isn't the case," he said.

What a nifty little Kabuki dance that was. By pulling out her notebook at that very touchy moment, Aubrey was openly challenging his rectitude. She was telling him that the questions were going to get really tough now, and that from now on everything would be on the record, that anything he said would be judged in the court of public opinion, and maybe even a court of law. And Bandicoot, by handing her his Bic the way he did? Well, you didn't have to be a theologian to interpret a Jesus-like act like that.

"There are those who don't think Sissy did it," Aubrey said.

Bandicoot answered slowly, watching her scribble his quotes as he talked. "There are those who think she didn't, those who think she did. There are those who think I put her up to it. There are those who think I did it myself, and framed her. There are those who think somebody else did it."

Aubrey tapped the Bic on her nose. "Who do you think did it? There was a lot of physical evidence supporting Sissy's confession."

"I don't want to believe she did it. But I don't know."

"How about somebody like Guthrie Gates?"

"I absolutely do not think Guthrie did it. He loved Buddy too much."

"Interesting. You're absolutely sure your rival didn't kill Buddy, but not so sure about the woman you were screwing?"

If Tim Bandicoot was going to pop his cork and beat us to death with a folding chair, that was the question that would do it. He just smiled sadly. "Sissy has a lot of problems. I'm sure you know all about that stuff."

Aubrey nodded as sadly as Bandicoot smiled. "How about you? Did you love Buddy too much to kill him?"

"I did love him. I just didn't agree with some of his—"

He couldn't find the right word. Aubrey could: "Theatrics?"

"I wouldn't call them theatrics. He truly believed in those things. I didn't."

"You're putting a pretty mild spin on it, aren't you? Your break with the Heaven Bound Cathedral was pretty nasty. And very public."

Bandicoot took several slow sips of coffee. His chocolate eyes, for the first time, focused squarely on Aubrey's blue eyes. "It was your paper that made it very public. But I could have handled it better. I caused a lot of pain."

Aubrey now turned to the murder itself, wondering how someone could have moved through the Heaven Bound Cathedral unnoticed, filling Buddy Wing's water pitcher with poisoned water, painting a poisonous cross on his old family Bible. "Sissy told police she pulled her coat collar up around her ears and walked right in. Did her dirty business and walked right out. Given what you know about the Heaven Bound Cathedral, do you think that's possible?"

Bandicoot shrugged. "I suppose anything's possible."

"The police talked to a lot of people who were there that night. Nobody saw her."

"I've read that."

"But that doesn't prove she wasn't there."

"I guess not."

"Nor does her saying she was there prove that she was."

"I guess that's right."

"Now let me ask you this," Aubrey said. "Could anybody else from your flock—including yourself—have walked around the cathedral without wearing a disguise?"

"No more than Satan could have."

"How about with a disguise?"

"Satan maybe. I doubt anyone else."

The Krispy Kreme box was empty when we left Bandicoot's storefront church. Aubrey's car was still out front. "You know," she said as we pulled away, "we never should've pigged out on those doughnuts."

"Don't I know it," I said. "We'll have to fast for a week."

Aubrey U-turned through an abandoned Sinclair station. "Screw the calories. Think about who gave us those doughnuts. A man who, maybe, poisoned Buddy Wing twice. Maddy—we have got to be more careful."

Even after all those Krispy Kremes Aubrey wanted to go to Speckley's for lunch. The place is as busy Saturday mornings as it is weekdays, so we had to wait in line. Aubrey bought a *Herald-Union* from the box outside and read it standing up. I got a menu from the counter and looked for something light that might counteract any slow-acting poison. When we finally got a table—in the smoking section—I ritually ordered the meat loaf sandwich and au gratin potatoes as usual. Aubrey got a house salad and tomato soup.

I started our debriefing session: "Tim Bandicoot was nice enough, wasn't he?"

"Too nice."

"Think so? Other than the doughnuts I don't think he spread it on too thick."

My appraisal angered her. "These TV preachers manipulate people for a living. They get perfectly sane people to jump up and down and roll around on the floor and then hand over the grocery money. And when they get caught with some bimbo in a motel room? They simply trot out their *God's already forgiven me—won't you?* shtick and everything's hunky-dory until the next time they get caught. Remember Jimmy Swaggert? 'I have sinned! I have sinned!' I think we just got Swaggert-ed, Maddy."

I wasn't so sure. Tim Bandicoot had seemed sincere to me. "He told us he didn't want forgiveness," I said.

"Shtick. He gave me his Bic for christsake. What was that all about?"

"You needed a pen?"

"That was my shtick. I've got a purse full of pens."

The waitress brought our food. Aubrey used her little finger and thumb to fish out the curls of raw onion from her salad. She deposited them in the ash tray. "Did you hear what he said when I told him we'd been to visit Sissy at Marysville? 'I heard.' How did he hear? Who told him?"

"Sissy?"

"Of course, Sissy."

"So they're still communicating."

Aubrey filled her mouth with Romaine lettuce. "So he's still manipulating."

Maybe she was right. Maybe Tim Bandicoot was the icky egomaniacal murderer I thought going in, before the Krispy Kremes, the chocolate-brown cow eyes and that big dose of contrition. "So where do we go from here?"

"Shopping."

# 8

I planned to spend Easter cleaning out my raspberry bed. But it was raining when I got up, and it continued to rain all morning. At noon I gave up and drove to the paper, to catch up on my work. Not that I had any work to catch up on. As empty as the newsroom was on holidays, it was a lot less empty than my bungalow.

There were just eight cars in the parking deck, including Aubrey's Escort and Eric Chen's little pickup truck. They were parked side by side in the Handicapped Only slots by the elevator. When I got to the morgue I tossed my raincoat on the counter and went to my desk for my tea mug. Everywhere in Hannawa families were setting down to baked beans, Jell-O salad, and spiral-cut ham. I'd be having a mug of Darjeeling tea and a package of stale oatmeal cookies from the vending machine. I cut through sports to the cafeteria. That damn sign was still taped to the back of Chip McCoy's computer:

HER NAME IS
DOLLY MADISON SPROWLS,
BUT HER FRIENDS
JUST CALL HER MADDY.
TO THE OTHER 99.8% OF US
SHE'S JUST PLAIN MAD

Those signs used to be stuck everywhere. Now there are just two, that one on Chip's computer, and the one I framed and put on my kitchen wall at home.

I found Aubrey and Eric sitting together in the back. Aubrey was eating yogurt out of a plastic cup. Eric was eating potato chips and sucking on a can of Mountain Dew. Good gravy, how odd finding those two together. I just stood there in the doorway with my empty mug.

Which made Aubrey laugh. "You caught us together in the cafeteria, not in bed," she said. "You can come in."

I looked at Eric. He was as stunned by what she said as I was. "Are there any cookies in the machine?" I asked.

Eric leaned back and checked. "Nada. But there's some of those indigestible cheese cracker things."

I bought the crackers, filled my mug with hot water, and started for the door.

Aubrey called out, "For christsakes, Maddy, sit down."

I sat.

Eric didn't say a thing—I'm sure his brain was full of dirty pictures of Aubrey and him in bed—but Aubrey launched into a nervous explanation of their togetherness. "Eric's going to help me with the computer searches for other possible suspects. Just some quick checks for strange behavior, criminal or otherwise. I knew you wouldn't have time."

What she meant, of course, is that I wouldn't have a clue on how to do it.

It was about then that Eric regained the use of his brain and remembered that he had to be in Youngstown for Easter dinner in a half hour, about eighty miles away. He got three cans of Mountain Dew from the vending machine—fuel for the road—and left. Aubrey took a cleansing breath and rolled her eyes. "What a *boy* that boy is."

"You're not going to your mother's?" I asked.

"She's having dinner at five and I'm going to point my car in that direction about three. But am I actually going to go to my mother's? God only knows."

While Aubrey cleaned up Eric's mess, I gathered up her folders. Her SISSY folder was already an inch thick, and her T. BANDICOOT folder not much thinner. The folder marked HEAVEN BOUND CATH had two copies of the church directory rubber-banded together. "Two copies?" I asked. "Didn't Guthrie give us just one?"

"I went back later for another one," she said. "An older one. I got thinking about Tim Bandicoot breaking with Buddy Wing and realized that former church members were more likely to be suspects than present members. You know? Somebody mad enough at Buddy Wing to quit his church might also be mad enough to kill him."

I handed her the folders. "Smart. How old is the other directory?"

Her faced scrunched with disappointment. "Just three years. But we might find somebody interesting. You don't mind Eric doing this for me, do you? I should have asked."

"What's there to mind? Just be gentle with him."

"Puh-leeze."

I stayed at the paper until four, organizing my desk drawers, playing solitaire, calling my relatives in LaFargeville on the paper's dime. Then I went home and opened a can of vegetable soup. I ate it right out of the saucepan, on the porch my Lawrence built on the back of the house the same summer he started screwing his secretary. It's a wonderful porch, running the full length of the house, screened in to keep out the bugs, wide enough for my picnic table and a propane grill. The door opens right into my vegetable garden.

By eight I was in bed reading Jane Smiley's new novel. Trying to read it, anyway. It was Easter Sunday and I was alone. I should have gone to church that morning. I should have stopped off at the drug store and bought myself a chocolate rabbit and some marshmallow peeps. I should have taken a week's vacation and driven to LaFargeville to visit my brother and my niece. After Lawrence flew the coop I should have remarried somebody and had some children. I took the notebook and a pen from my nightstand and used Jane Smiley's book as a desk. Lawrence was gone and Dale Marabout was gone and the only people I had to sponge the loneliness out of my life were Aubrey McGinty and Sissy James.

I started making my own notes on the Buddy Wing murder: Was Sissy James really innocent? Or had we just talked ourselves into believing she was? And what about all that evidence right there in Sissy's garbage can? Yes, somebody who knew Sissy inside and out could have framed her. But Sissy was also troubled enough to frame herself, either intentionally or through her own stupidity.

I scribbled all sorts of crazy things in that notebook that night. I was lonely and frightened and just plain unsure.

## Monday, April 24

"Well, did you make it home yesterday?" I asked Aubrey. I was so glad it was Monday and that horrible Easter weekend behind me.

She leaned across the counter and answered "Yeah," as if she was angry with herself.

"Everybody has to go home once in awhile," I said.

She asked, "And why is that?"

## Friday, April 28

I hardly saw Aubrey that week. She was busy doing interviews for her series on the ghastly lives of the city's street prostitutes. The idea for the series, of course, had grown out of her story on the body they found on Morrow Street. Aubrey wanted to explore the lives of these women while they were still alive. She had no trouble finding women still working the streets, and no trouble getting them to talk. What she wanted, and couldn't find, was someone who'd escaped and built a new life for herself, on a better street.

Friday morning she asked if I wanted to go back to the Heaven Bound Cathedral with her, that evening, to see how easy it would be for a stranger to sneak in and kill someone. I wasn't crazy about the idea. But I went along.

The televised Friday night services continued after Buddy Wing's murder without missing a week. For a while, in fact, more people attended, and more people watched, than had before Buddy gave his Bible that fateful kiss. In the story we ran on that ironic fact, Guthrie Gates said it was a tribute to just how much people loved their martyred pastor. If you ask me, it was the same morbid fascination that sends hundreds of thousands of teary-eyed tourists to Graceland year after year, even though they didn't give a rip about Elvis when he was alive. Anyway, attendance and viewership dropped off after a couple of months.

We left the paper at six and drove in my Shadow to Aubrey's apartment. It was my first visit and I was appalled. Her living room furniture consisted of an old kitchen chair with a ripped vinyl cushion, a big yellow ceramic lamp sitting on a folding TV table, and a pyramid of cardboard boxes.

Some of the boxes were marked SHIT FROM COLLEGE and some were marked SHIT FROM HOME. Coats and sweaters and newspapers and magazines and God only knows how many shoes were strewn everywhere. "How can someone own nothing and still live in a hovel?" I asked.

Aubrey was in her bedroom changing into a dress so she could fit in with the Christians. "I'm a young and carefree writer with a brilliant mind," she called out. "So leave me the hell alone."

When she came out in a dress I couldn't stop laughing. It was not a bad looking dress—a loose-fitting, below-the-knee A-line with a sailor collar and pleats—but I'd never seen her in anything but jeans or chinos and she looked about as comfortable as my brother the dairy farmer looks in his polyester wedding-and-funeral suit from Sears. "All you need is a white purse and pearls," I managed to get out.

Aubrey was laughing harder than me. "I just don't want to look out of place in church."

I opened my arms and turned in a circle. "What about me looking out of place?"

She studied me. I was wearing my usual work uniform: loose-fitting slacks, even looser sweater, penny loafers, and a cheap necklace. "You look fine," she said.

I knew what she meant by *fine*: women my age never look out of place because we never look in place. We are as unintrusive as beige walls.

Aubrey's plan was to sneak into the Heaven Bound Cathedral without sneaking. "I think it's safe to assume that the killer knew his way around the church," she said as we drove toward South Ridge. "So we're going to act like we belong there. We're going to chat and smile and be friendly. You think you can pull that off?"

The service didn't start until eight, but Aubrey wanted to arrive at seven, to be there during the final hectic hour before the cameras clicked on and the Canaries of Calvary started singing and the Sweet Ascension Dancers started dancing. When we arrived, there were already lines of cars waiting to pull into the parking lot. The big-eared security guard we encountered on our first visit was standing beneath the cement angels, directing cars toward empty slots. We smiled and waved as we drove past him. "You suppose he was out here directing traffic the night Buddy Wing was killed?" Aubrey wondered.

We parked and joined the funnel of people heading for the cathedral doors. Aubrey greeted everyone who looked at us with a happy "Good evening."

Inside we followed the flow toward the chapel. Everywhere in the hallway choir members and dancers were mingling with their friends and families. Everyone was so happy. I felt just lousy, like a terrorist with sticks of dynamite taped to her ribs. I wanted to spin around and get the hell out of there. But Aubrey had me by the arm, squeezing a smile out me every time somebody smiled at us.

When we got to the chapel we kept going, up the hallway toward the offices. As we clicked along we looked at each other and started giggling guiltily, like schoolgirls sneaking out of gym class. The hallway was filled with people, all serenely buzzing about, arms full of hymnals or collection baskets or electric guitars.

On our earlier visit the outer door to the offices had been locked. I remembered how the security guard had knocked for us and I remembered that Guthrie Gates had unlocked the door before letting us in. Now this door was wide open and people were freely flowing in and out. We went in.

It was noisy and busy inside. Someone was whistling a hymn. Someone was laughing like Santa Claus. Just a few yards from Buddy Wing's office Aubrey stopped at a water fountain and bent low to drink.

"No security and no suspicion," I whispered. "Anybody could have walked right in."

Aubrey whispered back, "Any stranger at least. But what if it weren't a stranger? What if it were Sissy or Tim Bandicoot? Could they have just walked in like this? I don't think so."

I took a drink myself. The water was warm. "Sissy told the police she just walked in and went about her business."

Said Aubrey, "More proof she's lying."

We walked on to Buddy Wing's office. The open door was still blocked with the folding chair and arrangement of plastic roses. Dale Marabout's story on the murder said that Wing used to keep his old family Bible on his desk, always within his reach. Now there was a framed, eight-by-ten photograph of the martyred pastor in the center of the desk, facing toward the door, smiling eyes fixed right on us.

"Let's think about what we already know," Aubrey whispered as we stood in the doorway like a pair of humble pilgrims visiting a holy shrine. "We know Buddy Wing followed the same routine every week. We know that thirty minutes before every service he left his office and went to the make-up room, and after being painted up to look twenty years younger, went to another room to pray with the church elders. Then, when it was showtime, he went to the back of the chapel and danced his way down the aisle."

"We know all that?" I asked.

"Yes. And we can surmise that the killer knew all that, too."

Just down the hall from Wing's office we found a roomful of middle-aged men in suits drinking coffee and eating pastries. "I'd say those are the elders," Aubrey whispered. We kept walking. In the next room we saw Guthrie Gates half reclined in a beauty shop chair. He was getting his hair sprayed stiff by a woman with painted-on eyebrows. We hurried by. The hallway turned right, then left, then right again. We were near the stage. We could hear the orchestra warming up. We found the main control room and peeked inside. People with headsets and clipboards were buzzing about like honey bees. "What a fancy operation," I whispered. "You'd think they were putting on the Academy Awards."

Aubrey gave me a nudge and we started our retreat. She reconstructed Buddy Wing's last service as we walked: "Sometime while he was in the make-up chair or praying with the elders, the killer slipped into his office to paint that poison cross on his Bible. We know from the police reports, and from your Mr. Marabout's stories—"

I protested. "My Mr. Marabout?"

"You know what I mean. I know you haven't slept with him for years."

"And who said I ever slept with him?"

Aubrey scowled at me. "Will you get your mind back on the murder? Everybody knows you and Marabout used to do the nasty—"

She called it the *nasty*. I knew that was just a word people her age used. But it stung. It had not been nasty. It had been good, clean, wonderful fun between two people who genuinely cared for each other. "Who told you?" I demanded. "Doreen Poole?"

She ignored my question. "So we know—from more than one source—that it was the director's job to take the Bible to the pulpit, along with Wing's notes for his sermon, and make sure he had a pitcher of water for when the sweat started pouring. But the director—her name's Elaine Albert, she's been directing the broadcasts since they started in the early Seventies—told the police that when she went to get the Bible and sermon notes from his office, approximately fifteen minutes before the service was to start, they were both gone. She hurried to the stage and found them already on the pulpit. And the pitcher of water under it."

"And she wasn't a little curious?" I asked.

"She told police she didn't have time to be curious. The service was starting in a few minutes."

"It certainly piques my curiosity. Why wasn't this Elaine Albert considered a suspect?"

"She was the first person they talked to. They gave her a lie detector test the next morning."

"I gather she passed."

Aubrey gave me one of those "Duhs" people her age employ to tell someone they're making a fool out of themselves by stating the obvious.

"But wouldn't a television director have to be a real cool cucumber—always in control?" I asked. "I'd think somebody like that could easily fake a lie detector."

"I'd think so, too."

"But the police wouldn't think so?"

"The police stopped thinking when Sissy confessed."

A slow, melancholy voice put an end to our snoopfest: "I thought it might be the two of you."

It was the big-eared security guard and a minute later we were standing in the make-up room watching the woman with the painted-on eyebrows rub a natural tan into Guthrie Gates' chalky face. He was struggling with every vein in his neck to remain Christian. "I'm guessing you didn't come to worship with us."

Aubrey was doing a much better job at staying calm than I was. "We wanted to see the crime scene—as it would have been the night Pastor Wing was poisoned."

Gates lifted his chin so the eyebrow woman could squirt make-up on his neck. "Let me guess why you didn't call for permission first—you were afraid I'd change things around?"

"I was afraid somebody might," Aubrey admitted. "But not for malicious reasons. When people know the press is coming they tend to put their best foot forward, often subconsciously."

Gates swatted away the make-up woman's sticky fingers. "Like subconsciously bringing you doughnuts?"

I was flabbergasted. "You know about the doughnuts?"

Gates closed his eyes and motioned for the eyebrow woman to resume her rubbing. "Since Tim Bandicoot started that *temple* of his, it's been like the U.S. and Red China between our congregations. Everything they do gets back to us. Everything we do gets back to them." He sat silently until the eyebrow woman was finished, then checked himself in the mirror. He smiled with satisfaction. I watched his eyes shift in the mirror, to the knees peeking from the hem of Aubrey's churchy dress. "Wasn't I open and honest with you, Miss McGinty? Wasn't I respectful and friendly?" He checked his watch and clicked on a small speaker box on the make-up table. The choir was already singing. "Time to go," he said. He stood and pulled a plastic bottle of mineral water from the side pocket of his suit coat. He unscrewed the cap and took a small, quick sip. Then he smiled at us, calmly, neck veins back in place, and said, "You're welcome to stay for the service, if you think it might do you some good. But you are not welcome to come back. Or call me. Or talk to any member of this congregation." He gave us a quick "God be with you" and left. The security guard pointed to the door with his chin. As we left, I poked Aubrey in the arm and pointed back into the room. The eyebrow woman was sitting in the chair, nervously lighting a cigarette.

The security guard followed us to our car. Aubrey and I hardly said a word to each other until we reached Swann's, Hannawa's legendary drive-in restaurant where all the car hops are muscular college boys. The minute you pull into a slot and click your headlights they run to your car—not walk, but run like they were on a football field—and take your order. We both ordered double-cheeseburgers and fries. They have forty-seven different flavors of milkshakes. Aubrey got a large butterscotch-banana. I got a small strawberry.

I watched Aubrey watch the carhop trot inside with our orders. "So," I asked her, "what did we learn today?"

"Well," she said, "we learned that sad-sack security guard isn't the rube we thought. He recognized us when we pulled in and followed us. What we don't know is whether it was on his own initiative or whether he was under orders from Guthrie Gates."

"What difference does that make?" I asked.

"Remember what he said, Maddy: 'I thought it might be the two of you.' He didn't follow us because we were strangers trying to sneak in and poison somebody. He followed us because it was us."

"That doesn't mean Gates has something to hide," I said. "There are lots of innocent people who hate the press."

Aubrey liked that. She laughed. "The first time we went to the church, Gates was as nice as pie. This time he couldn't control himself. He was really p-o'd. And what was that U.S. and Red China stuff?"

"It's no secret those two churches don't like each other," I said.

"Aren't you being a wee bit charitable? They're at war. They *spy* on each other. Gates knew about the doughnuts."

"Yes he did," I said. "It gave me the willies when he said that."

"He wants us to be afraid. He wants us to believe that both churches are full of crazies. He's warning us to back off. What's done is done. Let Buddy Wing rest in peace."

The carhop was running toward us with our food. I rolled down my window for the tray. "And let the real killer rest in peace?"

Aubrey impatiently reached across me for her bag of fries. "But we're not going to let the real killer rest in peace. At least I'm not."

I handed her a cheeseburger. I had the willies again. She was telling me things were going to get dangerous. I could stop tagging along if I wanted.

Aubrey peeled back the bun and delicately removed the onions. She looked for a place to put them. "Did you notice he was carrying his own bottle of water? I don't think he's merely being trendy, Maddy."

I let her put the onions in my hand and then dumped them on the window tray. "You think he's afraid somebody will poison him next?"

Aubrey nodded while she took a bite. "Or maybe he just wants people to think he's afraid somebody will poison him next."

"So Guthrie Gates is still a suspect?"

"Everybody is still a suspect."

"Including Sissy James?"

This bite she shook her head. "I don't see any way she could walk around there without being spotted. Even in disguise. Tim Bandicoot either. I think they're out."

I watched her eat and she watched me eat and we giggled at how messy the cheeseburgers were. "So, did we learn anything else?" I asked.

Aubrey squinted at me. She knew I had seen something she hadn't.

"The eyebrow woman," I explained. "She lit a cigarette. I poked you, remember?"

"And?"

"Jesus Didn't Smoke—Why Do You?"

"Ah—the signs. They're fanatical against smoking."

"Yet she lit a cigarette," I repeated. "I'd say either she's the killer or she's one of Tim Bandicoot's spies."

"Because she lit a cigarette?"

"Because she forgot the rules, Aubrey. Because she was so frightened or nervous, or something, that she just had to have a cigarette." I reminded her of something the big-eared security guard had said during our first visit: "Smoking was a manifestation of spiritual sloth."

I watched Aubrey draw the thick butterscotch-banana shake up her plastic straw. It seemed like she was having trouble fitting a new suspect onto whatever list she had in her mind. Finally she said, "So you think we should talk to this woman with the eyebrows?"

"Yes, I do."

# 9

When I got to work Monday, Eric Chen was wearing a necktie. By all appearances a new one. By all appearances one hundred percent silk. I grilled him about it as soon as I got back to my desk with my tea.

He did not like being grilled. "I just felt like buying a tie," he said. "And if you're going to buy a tie you might as well wear it."

I knew what the tie was all about. It was about Aubrey. "I think maybe you're trying to get my job," I teased. "Next week it will be a sports jacket and the week after that a three-piece suit. Week after that I'll be out on my keister."

Eric loosened the ill-shaped knot under his chin. "You're crazy, Maddy." He knew I knew why he'd bought the tie.

I enjoyed my tea while Eric continued his computer background checks for Aubrey. He was trying to find someone in that church directory with a reason, no matter how far-fetched, to poison the Rev. Buddy Wing.

Our investigation of Buddy Wing's murder was puttering along on three parallel tracks. I say *our* investigation because by now Eric and I were completely seduced by Aubrey's obsession to free Sissy James. Let me take some of that back. I was seduced by her obsession. Eric was seduced by something else. Anyway, the investigation was puttering along on these three tracks:

The first was to prove that Sissy didn't kill Buddy Wing. The second was to prove that Tim Bandicoot was a creep, so Sissy would come to her senses and confess, on the record, that she didn't do it. The third thing was to identify other suspects.

I was searching the map cabinet with Sylvia Berdache—looking for some pre-1950 city zoning maps for some story or the other—when Eric suddenly yelled, "Hello!"

I was bent over the bottom drawer and it took me a few seconds to straighten up. Eric was smiling like a birthday party clown and motioning for me with both hands. I was happy to let Sylvia search by herself. Before going to Eric's desk I circled by my desk to pick up my mug. He kept smiling and motioning until I got there. "Find something, honeybun?" I asked.

He pointed to a name on the screen. "Wayne F. Dillow, 1144 Summerhill Lane, Hannawa. Complaints. Restraining order. Conviction for breaking and entering."

"Does not a murderer make," I said.

"Yeah. But all these charges. Pretty pathological guy, wouldn't you say? And a member of the flock."

"Which church directory you working from?" I asked.

He grunted, "Huh?" and I explained that Aubrey had gotten two church directories from Guthrie Gates, a current one and one that was three years old. He used his thumb to mark his place and looked at the cover. It was the one for the current year. "So he's still a member," I said.

I watched over Eric's shoulder as he e-mailed Aubrey. GOT A NIBBLE, his message said. I wrote Dillow's name and address on the back of an envelope from Eric's wastebasket and went to the old filing cabinets to check the D drawers. There was nothing on Wayne F. or any other Dillow. Eric had better luck. Scanning the on-line obituary files, he found a Dorothea Louise (nee Pauley) Dillow. She died in 1997 at age fifty-seven. She was a member of the Heaven Bound Cathedral. She was survived by her sons James of Hannawa and Howard of Duluth, Minnesota; her husband, Wayne; a sister, Edna Lynn Scarberry of Knoxville, Tennessee.

Five minutes to four, Aubrey hopped out of the elevator and sped to her desk like an angry ostrich. She typed furiously for about an hour then strolled to Eric's desk like a happy swan. "What's the nibble?" she asked. She was absolutely delighted that Eric found a church member with a criminal record. She kissed his cheek. They went out to supper. I turned down their half-hearted invitation to join them and went home.

## Tuesday, May 2

The next day Aubrey got the police records on the charges against Dillow. She also called his wife's sister in Knoxville.

Wayne and Dorothea Dillow had been members of the Heaven Bound Cathedral since 1974. According to the sister, Dorothea was more religious than Wayne—not unusual—but he was faithful enough to go along with her tithing to the church. In 1996, Dorothea started passing blood. Her doctor told her she had a cancerous kidney. Wayne begged her to have the surgery. But Dorothea had watched God cure thousands of people of their terrible afflictions through his gifted servant Buddy Wing. So she joined the healing line at the next Friday night service and walked across the stage and told the Rev. Wing of the evil growing inside her. He put his hand on her belly and told the cancer to leave. "Out, foul flesh," he commanded. "Out! Out! Out in the name of Jesus-*uh*."

After Dorothea's funeral, Wayne stopped going to church. Stopped tithing. Then he started calling Buddy Wing at home, late at night. That Buddy felt almost as bad about her death as he did was of no consolation to Wayne F. Dillow. That God worked in mysterious ways was of no consolation either. When Buddy one night suggested that perhaps Dorothea's faith wasn't strong enough, that perhaps that's why the cancer came sneaking back, Wayne called him a murderer. Call after call he called him a murderer. When the pastor no longer answered his phone, Wayne showed up at his door. Pounding on it. Screaming, "Why Buddy? Why?"

Buddy Wing repeatedly complained to the police and the police repeatedly warned Dillow to stop his harassment. Dillow didn't stop. Wing got a restraining order. Dillow ignored it. Wing had Dillow arrested. Dillow bailed himself out and went right back to Wing's house. He broke out a window and crawled inside. He screamed, "Why, Buddy? Why?" up the dark stairs.

Dillow was charged with breaking and entering but Wing begged police to reduce the charges to trespassing. Dillow was fined $250 and served a month in jail.

The strange thing, the sister in Knoxville told Aubrey, was that after six or seven months Wayne started going back to the church, started tithing again. He had regained his faith.

"Why am I suspicious?" Aubrey asked as we leaned against my car in the parking deck after work.

"I know I couldn't go back to that church," I said.

"Unless you wanted to get even," she said. "Then you might. Then you might sit there week after week swallowing your anger, biding your time, waiting for that right opportunity to see if Buddy Wing could heal himself."

"So Wayne F. Dillow goes on the list of suspects?" I asked.

"You bet he does."

She talked me into going to Speckley's for supper. That's where she told me she was on the cusp of having sex with Eric. "If he plays his cards right, maybe tonight," she said while I winced. She also told me of her plans to ambush the eyebrow woman. "You'll come along, won't you?" she asked.

# 10

Aubrey and I called her the eyebrow woman, but her name actually was Sandra Leigh Swain. She was forty-one, a divorcee with two adolescent daughters. She worked full-time cutting men's hair. On Fridays, she did make-up for the Heaven Bound Cathedral's televised services. She was listed in the directory as a member.

I wasn't at all surprised that Aubrey had learned these things about her. A few minutes on a computer and you can learn all kinds of things about people these days. I was surprised, however, that Aubrey knew that the eyebrow woman would be grocery shopping at Artie's on Saturday morning.

"It was a no-brainer," she explained as we drove to the supermarket for the ambush. "She works full-time days. She has two daughters in middle school who have to be driven like sled dogs on school nights to stay off the phone and do their homework. She spends Friday nights working at the church and Sundays attending. So she simply has to do her grocery shopping Saturday morning."

She was probably right. Saturday is the worst time in the world to go for groceries, yet two-thirds of the women I know do exactly that. They have no other time. "But how do you know she goes mornings? Maybe she goes—"

"Afternoons? No way. She's a single mother with an ex-husband who doesn't pay his child support. She goes mornings for the hamburger and the chicken and whatever other specials she can get to keep down her bill. By afternoon, everything good's picked over."

Aubrey could see the skepticism on my old face, apparently. "I know these things because—as you remember from your own snooping—my mother was often without a man's paycheck."

"And with two daughters just like the eyebrow woman," I added without thinking.

The pain of her childhood worked across her face. Then she smiled wickedly. "I also know these things because I followed her last Saturday."

"Why didn't you ambush her then?" I asked.

"Because I wanted to know more about her first."

"Why are we ambushing her at all? Why don't you just call her on the phone?"

"I tried all week. She kept hanging up."

"You found out where she did her shopping first and then you tried to call her?"

Aubrey's impatience was bubbling into anger. "Why the third degree here? After that scene with Gates in the make-up chair, and what you told me about her lighting up, I was curious right away. And I wasn't only interested in seeing where she did her grocery shopping. I also wanted to see if she'd sneak over to Bandicoot's church, if she really was a spy."

"But she didn't?" I asked.

"She just went to Artie's and Wal-mart and home. And she didn't go out Saturday night. At least by nine o'clock she hadn't."

"Did you?" I asked.

"You're asking if I went out with Eric?"

"It's none of my business."

"You're right. It's not. But so you don't have to ask the next question that isn't any of your business, as of last night, Eric and I have entered the post-cusp phase of our relationship."

We pulled into Artie's. Aubrey spotted the eyebrow woman's car and parked in the next row. We went inside and found her in the dairy aisle, lifting gallon jugs of two percent milk into her cart.

Aubrey descended immediately. "Do you buy your cigarettes here, too?"

The eyebrow woman's eyebrows shot up like the mushroom clouds of two atom bombs. Her pupils froze on Aubrey then drifted toward me. I was several feet behind Aubrey, by the I-Can't-Believe-It's-Not-Butter display. I gave her one of those stupid finger-wiggle waves.

"I'm not talking to you two," she said. She put a fourth jug in her cart and started for the meat department. Aubrey followed her. I followed Aubrey.

"You know we don't think Sissy James killed Buddy Wing," Aubrey said while the eyebrow woman waited for her turn at the hamburger. "And we don't think it was you, either. So don't be afraid of that."

"I'm not afraid of that," the eyebrow woman answered.

Aubrey was almost touching shoulders with her now, getting inside her private space. "You are afraid Guthrie will find out you're one of Tim Bandicoot's spies though."

"I am not one of Tim Bandicoot's spies."

"Of course you are. That cigarette you just had to have gave you away."

The eyebrow woman put the biggest package of hamburger she could find in her cart. We were off to the chicken.

Aubrey assured her that we didn't care if she was a spy or not, that we weren't interested in exposing anybody, or destroying anybody, or doing anything but proving that Sissy James didn't poison Buddy Wing.

The eyebrow woman put a huge family pack of legs and thighs in her cart.

"Do you bread and fry that for your girls?" Aubrey asked her. "At Marysville, they just boil it."

The eyebrow woman pushed her cart up the beverage aisle, past the Coke and Pepsi sections to the cheap supermarket brands. The two-liter bottles of diet cola were only sixty-nine cents. She put eight of them in her cart. The image of bland boiled chicken was apparently still on her mind, though I'm sure Aubrey didn't have a clue whether the prison served boiled chicken or cordon bleu. But the mental image had done the trick. "I don't know if Sissy did it or not," the eyebrow woman said, "but I do know she more than likely had an alibi for that night if she needed one."

Aubrey wasn't expecting to hear that. "More than likely?"

The eyebrow woman slipped through a bottleneck of shopping carts and turned down the snack and cookie aisle. "How much do you know about Sissy's past?" she asked.

Aubrey told her we knew about her mother's death and the years she worked as a stripper and a prostitute, how she found God and gave that awful life up.

The eyebrow woman seemed happy to find the potato chips on sale. She took four bags, the maximum number allowed. "She didn't find God until she found out she was pregnant."

Aubrey wasn't expecting to hear that either. "There's a baby somewhere?"

"There's a seven-year-old girl somewhere," said the eyebrow woman.

"Tim Bandicoot's baby?" I asked.

The eyebrow woman looked at me if I were a deaf mute suddenly healed. "Her thing with Tim came much later," she said. "The girl belongs to some john, I suppose."

Aubrey began thinking out loud: "So somewhere there's a little girl she spends holidays with—and Buddy Wing was poisoned the day after Thanksgiving."

"Like I said," the eyebrow woman said, "I don't know she was there for sure."

"Where for sure?"

We were rushing through the bakery department now. The air was sweet with the smell of fresh-baked bread and doughnuts but there was no room in the eyebrow woman's budget for any of that. "I suppose you know Sissy wasn't born here in Hannawa," she said.

When we reached the produce aisle Aubrey asked her if she'd seen Wayne F. Dillow lingering in the hallways the night Buddy Wing was killed.

"Wayne Dillow? Goodness no."

"Anybody else in the office or stage area that didn't belong there?" Aubrey asked. "Anybody that looked suspicious?"

The eyebrow woman stopped her cart in front of the cabbage and cauliflower. "Nobody suspicious—if that's what you mean. But there are always new people back there before a broadcast."

"New people?" I asked.

"Kids from the college, TV and radio majors."

The thought of someone from my alma mater evil enough to kill someone made me defensive. "Not Hemphill College?"

"Goodness no," she answered. "Kent State." She had a head of cauliflower in each hand, weighing them with her motherly instinct.

"So why are they there?" Aubrey asked. "To see a real-live television show being taped?"

"We put them to work and pay them. Some are there week after week, for the whole year. Some can't take our brand of religion and quit after one night. You never know." She chose the head in her left hand and pushed on.

Next she got a big bag of Idaho potatoes and a bag of those tiny salad carrots. She thought hard about the fresh California strawberries but passed them up. We went to the canned goods aisle. Aubrey continued to press her about the college students. "Were any of these kids ever assigned the job of taking Buddy Wing's Bible to the pulpit?"

"Not that I'm aware of," she answered. "That Bible was sort of an important holy relic, you know? It had belonged to pastor Wing's father, back in his coal mining days. The Bible was always Elaine's job."

Elaine, of course, was Elaine Albert, the director who'd passed a lie detector test the day after the murder.

"Elaine wouldn't have gotten busy and sent one of the college kids to do it, would she?" Aubrey wondered. "And then lied about it so nobody knew she wasn't doing her job?"

"Goodness no."

"What about filling his water pitcher?" I asked. "Was that also part of Elaine's sacred duty?"

"Elaine did that, too. Though I suppose she might've given a little job like that to somebody else. Water's water."

"Except when it's tainted with lily of the valley," I said.

We headed for the front of the store. Every register had a long line. The eyebrow woman groaned and slid behind a woman with a cartful of baby food and disposable diapers. "I want you to know I don't spy," she said. "I love the church. I can't imagine where'd I be without those people. But I also think Tim Bandicoot got a raw deal, the way Guthrie forced him out."

Aubrey caught that immediately. "Guthrie forced him out? It wasn't Buddy Wing?"

"Guthrie put the bee in Pastor's bonnet, little doubt about that."

"Manipulated him into getting rid of his rival?"

"Not that Tim was without sin," the eyebrow woman said.

That afternoon we watched paint dry.

At Pizza Hut.

Eric Chen was already there when we pulled in. He had a window booth, facing the Red Lobster across the street. Aubrey slid in next to him. Their bodies snapped together like a couple of magnets. I slid in the other side. "You two have enough room over there?" I asked. They smiled with embarrassment and moved apart—about a half inch.

Eric had already ordered for us, a pitcher of Pepsi and a large pizza with sausage and green pepper.

We were there not only to assess our ambush of the eyebrow woman—which Aubrey and I agreed had gone better than expected—but also to conduct our paint-drying experiment. Given Sissy's confession, the police hadn't bothered to test how long it took the gold paint the killer used on Buddy Wing's Bible to dry.

Eric was not only responsible for ordering the pizza. It also was his job to bring a leather-covered Bible, a tiny paint brush, and a bottle of Testor's Gloss Enamel, the same kind of gold paint used by the killer, available in any craft store.

According to Aubrey, how long it took the paint to dry was no small matter: "In order for Buddy Wing to get the procaine on his lips when he kissed the cross, the gold paint would have to be tacky. Sissy confessed that she slipped into his office as soon as he left for the make-up chair. She said she quickly painted the cross and then took it to the chapel stage, along with the notes for Buddy's sermon and the pitcher of tainted water, which she claims she'd already filled in the kitchenette in the nursery. Then she rushed home to watch him die on her TV. Which is doable. Her house is only a five-minute drive."

"I gather you've driven it yourself?" I asked.

Eric answered for her. "We drove it six times last night. Every possible route."

Aubrey seemed embarrassed that he told me that, as if he was describing their love-making rather than their driving experiment. She continued: "Buddy didn't kiss the Bible until he was twenty-seven minutes into the service. Add that to the ten minutes he was in the make-up chair, and the four or five minutes he was praying with the elders. The paint would have to stay tacky for thirty-five or forty minutes—so let's see."

She opened the little bottle and started painting over the cross on the cover of the Bible. "The killer had to paint the cross very quickly, but also very neatly. The wet cross had to look just like the old one underneath." Aubrey finished the job in only a minute.

The waitress brought our pitcher of Pepsi and three plastic glasses filled with ice. We sipped sparingly, knowing it was going to be a long wait, for both the paint and the pizza. "So exactly what are we trying to prove here?" I asked Aubrey. "We already know the cross on the Bible was painted during that little window of time after Wing left his office and the service started."

Aubrey was nibbling on her ice. "Do we really know that? What if the paint doesn't dry for an hour? Or two hours? Or ten hours? Then the cross could have been painted long before the service, maybe in the middle of the night, and the Bible put on the pulpit at any time. All we really know—if Elaine Albert's statement is to be believed—is that when she went to get the Bible from Buddy's desk, it wasn't there, it was already on the pulpit."

Eric gently touched the cross Aubrey had painted. He looked at the little circle of gold on the end of his finger and frowned. "If the cross was painted hours earlier, then the killer swiped the Bible from Buddy's desk hours earlier. But if that Bible was as important to him as everybody says, wouldn't he go nuts looking for it? Have everybody looking for it? There's nothing like that in the police reports."

Aubrey wadded her napkin and wiped the paint off his finger. "There's nothing much about anything in the police reports," she said. "As soon as they found the stuff in Sissy's garbage, and she confessed, the investigation pretty much ended. But you're right, Eric. Buddy would've gone nuts if he couldn't find his daddy's Bible. He would've said something to somebody."

It simply popped out of my mouth. "Unless he poisoned himself."

Eric looked at me like I was crazy. Aubrey, however, smiled slyly. "What if he wanted to kill himself but didn't want Tim Bandicoot to replace him as the prince of Hallelujah City?" she said.

"And why would he want to kill himself?" Eric asked.

Aubrey took another mouthful of ice. "The autopsy didn't show any terminal diseases or anything. But maybe he was suffering from depression. Maybe he'd lost his faith. Or never really had any."

The cross on the Bible was seducing me just like it had seduced Eric. I touched it with my pinky. "If that's the case, why would he frame Sissy and not Tim Bandicoot?"

Aubrey dutifully wiped the gold circle off my pinky. "Maybe framing Tim Bandicoot would be too obvious."

This suicide thing seemed utterly bizarre to me. "Wouldn't setting up Sissy to set up Bandicoot be too obvious, too?"

She laughed. And started singing: "I was looking back to see if you were looking back to see if I was looking back to see if you were looking back at me— Maddy, we're talking about real cops here."

I was having a hard time keeping all of the possible scenarios straight. "So if Buddy or somebody else was trying to make Sissy too obvious a suspect, to set up Tim Bandicoot, then I guess that all fell apart when Sissy confessed."

Eric tried to check the paint again but Aubrey slapped his hand away. "That's right," she said.

We waited a long fifteen minutes for the pizza to come and then ate it like it was our last meal. Every few minutes Eric or I poked the cross and held up a shiny gold fingertip. Aubrey never once touched the cross, leading me to gather she already had a pretty good hunch how long it would take. Only after the pizza was gone, a full forty-five minutes, did Eric's finger come up dry.

"So," I said, sucking the gooey tomato sauce out of my teeth, "the poison had to be painted on the cross during that little window of time after all."

Aubrey was pleased with herself. "And that means the killer had to be there right before the service started."

"Which leaves us where?" I asked.

"Which leaves us with a bazillion suspects. Sissy. Guthrie Gates. Tim Bandicoot, assuming he was dumb enough to set up Sissy so clumsily. Maybe Bandicoot's wife. Maybe the eyebrow woman. Maybe Elaine Albert or that Dillow guy, or Buddy Wing himself, or somebody else on the TV production staff, or any member of the church past or present, or somebody we're not even aware of."

"Good gravy," I said.

"Still we've made big-time progress today," Aubrey said.

Knowing the shaky financial condition of those two, I dug into my purse to pay the bill. Neither objected. "We have?"

"Absolutely. The paint proves the killer was there right before the service. All we've got to do now is prove that Sissy wasn't. Which shouldn't be too hard at all."

"That's right," I said as we slid from the booth, "the mysterious baby girl."

Having been assigned to scrounge up the Bible and gold paint, Eric was totally in the dark. "Mysterious baby girl?"

Aubrey wrapped her arm around his. She was almost giddy. "I almost peed my pants when the eyebrow woman told us that."

In the parking lot Aubrey and Eric behaved like a couple of deer in rut, poking and pushing and giggling, squeezing each other's backsides. I wanted to knock them in the head with my purse. I liked them both. But I did not like them together. Oh, I'm sure the sex was more than Eric could ever have hoped for. And I couldn't blame him for taking advantage of his good fortune. I'd once done that myself with Dale Marabout. But Aubrey McGinty was way out of Eric's league. She was worldly and ambitious, and more than a little self-centered. I couldn't picture her staying in any relationship very long. Certainly never long enough to get married and have kids. Once the sex wore off, Eric's penchant for losing things and forgetting things would start driving her crazy. She'd start finding fault with his Mountain Dew drinking and the careless way he dressed. Little by little he'd go from love monkey to lapdog to road kill.

And I'd be the one with the shovel scraping him up.

# 11

## Monday, May 8

Monday afternoon, at exactly four, Dale Marabout pushed himself away from his desk, stood up, swung his chair once around his body like a giant discus and slammed it into his computer. He yelled out the three words I'd been dreading for some weeks now: "I. FUCKING. QUIT."

Before the elevator door closed he shouted a single word at Aubrey, who had her knees on her desk and the Hannawa white pages in her lap: "HAPPY?"

I hurried down the stairwell as fast as I could and intercepted Dale on the parking deck. He was crying like a baby. While we hugged I reached into his pants pocket for the handkerchief I knew he carried there. I dabbed his eyes and whispered "It'll be okay" I don't know how many times.

Dale was ripe for a mid-life crisis no matter what was going on at the paper. He was in his late forties and his kids were grown. Whatever secret dreams he carried inside him were simply dreams now, defeated by the limits of his talent and his metabolism. So in my mind Tinker's transferring in from Baton Rouge, or Aubrey McGinty waltzing in from Rush City, had very little do with Dale's anger. He was angry with himself.

"Wait an hour," I told him, "then go back to your desk with a mug of coffee and a cookie and nobody will say a thing."

He tried to unlock his car but I strategically squashed my backside against the door. "There's no way in hell I'm going back in there," he said.

"Yelling 'I quit' is not the same as writing 'I quit.' Until you give Tinker a written resignation, you haven't officially resigned. You've just gone a little crazy. You're allowed. All will be forgiven."

"Move your ass," he said.

I moved and he drove off. He didn't show up for work the next day and Sylvia Berdache told me Tinker had an e-mail waiting for him when he got to work. It said: "In case you haven't heard by now, I. FUCKING. QUIT."

So Dale's resignation was official and I felt just awful about it. I stewed about it all week and on Friday afternoon sneaked upstairs to see Bob Averill. He smiled and shook my hand with both his hands. "Maddy, why is it we don't get a chance to talk anymore?" I'm sure he figured his horrible week was going to end on a high note, the long-prayed-for retirement of Dolly Madison Sprowls. Instead I dumped Dale Marabout's resignation in his lap.

His smile sagged. "I heard about that."

"Not my version, you haven't," I said.

He listened to what I had to say. Then he called Tinker upstairs and had me repeat the whole thing to him.

## Saturday, May 13

Saturday morning, Aubrey, Eric and I were supposed to drive down to Mingo Junction to check out Sissy's mystery baby. But at eight Aubrey called me. She was absolutely furious. "They smashed out my windows. Went right around my car with a goddamn sledgehammer or something. Right in the goddamn garage."

"Who's they?" I asked.

"Take your pick. Those Nazis cops in the 3rd District who don't want me writing about their asshole commander. Those crazy Christians who don't want me to free Sissy. Those pimps who don't want me talking to their meal tickets. That wacko pal of yours."

"I think we can rule out Dale Marabout," I said.

"Do you? I think we can put him at the top of the list."

"Stop talking crazy."

"He blames me for his lousy life, Maddy."

Now I was the furious one. Dale did not have a lousy life. He had a good life. I came very close to telling her that she was the one with the lousy life. I twisted my bangs until I was under control. "I gather this means we're not going to Mingo Junction today."

"It means that Eric's driving. Unless you want to drive."

I did not want to drive. I did not even want to go.

But I did go.

And I did drive, Aubrey next to me with her knees propped on the dash, Eric sprawled in the back seat with a big bottle of Mountain Dew.

One reason Eric Chen was coming along on this week's snoopfest was that he and Aubrey had copulated into a couple. They were still in the inseparable stage. The more utilitarian reason was that he was from Youngstown, which is just north of Mingo Junction, in that impoverished southeastern slab of Ohio where nobody in their right mind ever visits.

I would have taken the Ohio Turnpike all the way to Youngstown and then followed State Route 11 down the Ohio River. Eric made me zig-zag along a series of narrow county roads. We went through one worthless town after another. We had lunch at a Dairy Queen in East Liverpool and then picked up Route 7 for our final descent into trepidation.

Mingo Junction is a suburb of Steubenville, if that tells you anything. It's a very long town, stretched out in the floody flats along the banks of the Ohio River. Small mountains hold the town in like the walls of a prison. The steel mills where people used to work have rusted away. The chemical plants that sour the air haven't. It's a poor and depressing place. You understand immediately why people like Sissy James move north to Hannawa.

Aubrey had done her homework. She had a street map of the town and the addresses of the James families living there. Her plan was to go from house to house and simply ask if Sissy was there and then interpret the terror she found in her relatives' eyes.

The first house we went to was painted the most awful blue. The window casings were painted pink. The lawn hadn't been mowed in weeks. Aubrey made Eric wait in the car. The narrow porch was lined with plastic Adirondack chairs. A man about my age came to the door. He was wearing a yellowed T-shirt. He had a floppy slice of Swiss cheese in one hand and the piece to a jigsaw puzzle in the other. He glowered at us impatiently.

Aubrey smiled at him like a Girl Scout selling cookies. "Hi—you Sissy's father?"

"Uncle."

"I'm sorry—we were looking for her parents."

"All she ever had was a mama and her mama's dead."

"Her mother was your sister then?"

His impatience was replaced by anger. "Go see Jeanie if you got questions. She's the one Sissy's thick with."

"Jeanie?"

He pointed with his Swiss cheese hand. "My daughter Jeanie. Lives two miles down Georges Run Road there. Brown house with a swing set in front."

"Did you see Sissy at Thanksgiving?" Aubrey asked, as if it were a friendly afterthought.

"Like I told the police when they came—I ain't seen her in ten years." He shut the door in our face.

We found Jeanie's house. It was a skinny two-story, covered with raggedy asphalt shingles and surrounded with overgrown shrubs. There were actually two swing sets in the front yard, an old rusty one and a brand new one with a spiral slide. The porch was covered with green indoor-outdoor carpeting. Eric stayed in the car without being told.

A frazzled woman in her thirties opened the screen door. Aubrey asked her if she were Jeanie.

The woman was suspicious immediately. "I am."

"Has Sissy been here since last Thanksgiving?"

Jeanie's eyes worked back and forth like a Kit Kat clock as she tried to figure out the answer. Inside the house a television was on and children were screaming at each other. Finally she said, "Who says she was here even then?"

"She always visits at Thanksgiving, doesn't she?"

Three girls suddenly appeared around Jeanie's legs. One was maybe seven. The other two in the three or four range. All had red circles around their mouths and big plastic glasses of Kool-aid in their hands. Jeanie slid onto the porch and closed the door behind her. "Who are you two?"

Aubrey introduced us. She told her we were from the newspaper in Hannawa. She also introduced Eric, who had escaped from the car and was now sitting on the lawn with a malnourished cat in his lap.

"We just met your father," I said.

Jeanie looked at me with empty eyes. "Did you?"

Aubrey got back to business. "I guess you know Sissy is in prison for murder?"

"I do."

"Had to be a shock, huh? Your cousin arrested for murder?"

"It was."

"And how did you first hear about it? Read about it? See it on TV?"

The children were banging on the door, wanting out. Jeanie ignored them. "I saw it on TV. I don't get the paper."

From the wry curl on Aubrey's lips I gathered she was not surprised that Jeanie did not subscribe to a newspaper. "But you must have known about it before you saw it on television," Aubrey said. "News like that would spread through a family pretty fast."

Jeanie's face wrinkled with bewilderment, or guilt, or fear, or some other agonizing emotion. Apparently she did not want to tell the truth any more than she wanted to lie. "Sissy told me herself."

Aubrey was delighted to hear that. "Before her arrest or after?"

"I think before."

That delighted Aubrey even more. "And she said what?"

"That she'd just killed a man. That it was likely she'd have to spend the rest of her life in prison, if not be put to death. I didn't know it was that famous preacher until I saw the TV."

"And she told you to watch after her child?" Aubrey asked.

Jeanie's once-empty eyes were now cloudy with tears. I gave her the pack of Kleenex from my purse.

"That's right," Aubrey continued, "we know about the daughter."

"Ain't nobody supposed to know."

Aubrey pointed with her chin at the children playing inside. "Which one is hers?"

"The oldest girl. Rosy."

"She doesn't know Sissy is her mother, does she?"

Jeanie shook her head.

"And when Sissy called you that day—she told you not to say anything about Rosy to the police, right?"

"Ain't nobody supposed to know," Jeanie said again.

"So Rosy thinks you're her mother. And thinks Sissy is Aunt Sissy."

Jeanie nodded as if she had a hundred girls to raise.

"It's really wonderful of you," I said.

She seemed to appreciate that. "What's one more?" When she tried to give the Kleenex back I told her to keep it.

Aubrey kept pressing. "So, did Sissy visit all Thanksgiving weekend?"

"Just Thanksgiving Day."

"Is that what you told the police when they talked to you?"

"It is."

"But that's not true, is it?"

"Just Thanksgiving Day."

Aubrey pulled out her notebook and slipped it under her arm. A threat to start recording Jeanie's untruths for all the world to read. "Let me get a clear picture of this," she said. "Sissy has a daughter one hundred and fifty miles away. A daughter she aches to see, even if it's just as Aunt Sissy. And when the four-day Thanksgiving weekend comes, she drives down for one lousy afternoon? Eats some turkey and says bye-bye? Goes home and kills a man?" She pulled out her pen and tapped it on her nose. "She stayed the whole weekend, didn't she?"

Jeanie watched the pen bounce. "I told the police it was just the one day."

Aubrey pulled the cap off the pen with her teeth. She held it there like a tiny cigar. "And the police accepted your lie because they didn't have any reason not to. Because they didn't know about Rosy. Because they wanted to corroborate Sissy's confession as fast as they could. Because they're boneheads."

Jeanie was crying into her hands now. "Why can't you believe me?"

Aubrey slipped her pen back into the cap. "Because we're not boneheads, Jeanie. Because we know Sissy had an alibi for that Friday night. Just like you know it. Because we fucking care."

Aubrey's crudeness made Jeanie cry all the more. Because she was not a crude woman. Because she was a good woman caught between the truth she wanted to tell and the lie she had promised to tell. "I care, too."

Aubrey handed me her notebook and took Jeanie in her arms. She guided her down to the first step and sat next to her. "Who was at your house for Thanksgiving dinner then? Sissy? Your parents? Your kids and your husband?"

"Just me and Sissy and the girls. I don't have a husband no more and I don't see my parents any more than I have to."

"And now you don't have Sissy anymore," Aubrey said.

My but Aubrey was good. I was beginning to feel my own eyes water up. I kneeled in front of Jeanie and patted her hands. "Why did you lie for her, dear?"

"Because she was in trouble and I knew she didn't want that trouble spreading to Rosy. And I guess I figured if Sissy confessed to killing that preacher it was for a reason. I figured she must have been mixed up in it some way."

None of us said anything for a long time. We just rubbed our eyes and watched Eric play with the cat. The warm May sun was sprinkling across the steps. "Just to get it all straight," Aubrey finally whispered, "Sissy was here that Friday night?"

"She was."

"And when the police came to see you, you told them she wasn't?"

"That's right."

"They didn't press you? The way we did?"

"They was here about five minutes."

"We know they talked to your father. Do you know if they talked to anybody else? Other relatives? Your neighbors?"

"They just got in their car and drove off."

"Fucking boneheads," Aubrey hissed.

This time Jeanie laughed. The weight of the world was off her shoulders. At least some of it was.

We talked with Jeanie for another half hour or so. We told her what we knew of Sissy's new life at Marysville. She told us about Sissy's childhood in Mingo Junction. It was not a childhood anyone would want. Sissy was eleven when her mother died. Her mother was with her latest boyfriend, driving home fast and drunk from a bar in East Liverpool, on a black November night, when a bend in a road that had always been there sent them into the Ohio River. Sissy went to live with her aunt and uncle, Jeanie's parents. It was not long before her uncle started cornering Sissy in dark corners of the house when no one else was around. It went on for years. "He used to bother me like that, too, until Sissy came to live with us," Jeanie said. At fourteen Sissy started drinking. Got into drugs. Got into beds and back seats with any boy who wanted to. When she was seventeen she escaped to Hannawa, to its strip bars and its by-the-hour motels, finally finding her way to the Heaven Bound Cathedral.

"I think having Rosy is what finally turned her around," Jeanie said. "Even if she couldn't raise her baby herself, she could behave better for her."

"Being the girlfriend of a married preacher isn't exactly behaving," I pointed out.

"It was an improvement over what she was," Jeanie said.

We headed for home, taking the same zig-zag route we came on. In the town of Wellsville, Eric made us stop at a convenience store for Mountain Dew and Doritos. I bought a little bag of cashews and Aubrey bought some M&Ms. The chewing got us talking.

"I can't believe how easy that was," Aubrey said, putting one little circle of candy in her mouth at a time.

"Buying snacks is not a difficult thing," Eric answered. He was putting one handful of Doritos in his mouth at a time.

"I mean how easily Jeanie opened up to us," Aubrey said, playfully throwing an M&M at him. "It makes you wonder who'd be in prison if the detectives who drove down here hadn't been so eager to get back to Hannawa."

Eric found the M&M in the folds of his shirt and ate it. "What blows me away," he said, "is that Jeanie lied for Sissy in the first place. Usually relatives lie to keep somebody out of jail."

"That is odd," I agreed.

Aubrey threw another M&M at Eric. "What's odd? She owed Sissy that lie."

Eric retaliated for that second M&M by smashing a Dorito on Aubrey's head. There is nothing worse in the world than young people in heat. "Owed her?" I asked.

Aubrey picked the orange bits from her hair. "You heard what she said—her father stopped molesting her when Sissy moved in. She didn't suffer because Sissy did. How'd you like to carry guilt like that around?"

Eric wasn't buying Aubrey's analysis. "She's already raising the kid for her. How much guilt could she have?"

Aubrey threw an entire handful of M&Ms at him. "Quit having opinions about things you don't understand!"

Aubrey hadn't just thrown those M&M's. She'd thrown them hard. Her rebuke hadn't been playful. It had been loud and angry. In the mirror I watched Eric slide back into the seat and stuff his cheeks with Doritos, already accustomed to her mood swings after only a few days of love. "If Jeanie lied to the police because she owed Sissy that lie," I asked, "why did she tell *us* the truth?"

Aubrey pressed her face against the side window. She stared at the passing sky. "She owed her the truth, too."

We drove along in silence, the playfulness wrenched right out of us from the sadness we found in Mingo Junction. "At least now we know Sissy didn't kill Buddy Wing," Aubrey said after several miles. "I can go to Tinker and start working on the story above ground."

My fingers tightened around the steering wheel. "Tinker already knows about your investigation."

Aubrey wasn't at all pleased to hear that. "Who told him? Marabout?"

I could feel my head shrinking down my sweater like a turtle. "I told him."

She said, "Shit, Maddy!" But it sounded like "*Et tu Brute?*"

I confessed in full: "Yesterday I went to see Bob Averill about Dale's quitting—"

"Averill knows too?"

"He knows, too. I was explaining why Dale went off his rocker."

"That he's jealous of me? Good God."

"That is not why he quit."

Aubrey was an inch from screaming. "That's exactly why he quit."

"No it's not, Aubrey. He's simply afraid you're biting off more than you can chew."

Aubrey put an M&M on her outstretched tongue and flicked it in like a lizard devouring a fly. "That sounds like jealousy to me."

Eric laughed at her. "You are so full of yourself."

"I am not full of myself."

"Of course you're full of yourself," I said. "If you weren't you couldn't be doing what you're doing. There's nothing wrong with being—confident."

Aubrey surrendered. "So if Dale wasn't driven mad by my brilliant reporting, then what was it?"

I wasn't about to share my mid-life crisis theory with her. No one her age could possible understand an excuse like that. So I put it in journalistic terms. "You work all those years as a reporter convinced that the editors on the copy desk are a bunch of drooling old doofuses. Then suddenly *you're* on the desk. *You're* the drooling old doofus. You panic. You embarrass yourself. Anyway, that's sort of what I was telling Tinker and Bob when I let the cat out of the bag about the Buddy Wing thing."

I thought I was getting through to her but I was wrong. "This is the most important story of my life," she said. "I can't afford this relentless busybody crap of yours."

She glared at me and I glared back. The car drifted and I almost clipped a mailbox. "You should have told them yourself," I said.

Aubrey swung her head around and waited for Eric to defend her. But Eric didn't defend her. He offered her his last Dorito. "Okay," she said, "maybe I should have said something. But I wanted to be sure about Sissy first. I didn't want them to think I was some chicky-poo air-head off on some wild goose chase."

"Believe me," I said, "nobody thinks that."

# 12

Aubrey was summoned to Bob Averill's office as soon as she got to work Monday. She was up there for two hours. When she got off the elevator, she gave me a thumbs up. The paper was going to let her proceed with the story.

I wasn't a bit surprised. Proving that Sissy James didn't kill Buddy Wing would be a great story. It would be a nasty, tantalizing drama that would keep the city spellbound for months. Murder. Sex. Police ineptitude. Religious hypocrisy. It would be Hannawa's O.J. story.

Aubrey and I sneaked out of the newsroom at four and walked down the hill to Ike's Coffee Shop. Ike's was the only remaining tenant in the eight-story Longacre Building, a beautiful old art nouveau palace that once housed many of the city's most prestigious doctors and lawyers. The faded sign in the window of the empty storefront next to Ike's had been announcing a major renovation of the building for at least a decade.

But Ike hangs on, selling lattes to-go to harried white office workers and mugs of regular coffee to the retired and under-employed blacks who like to linger at the little round tables. I buy my tea bags there, in bulk, not because I get a better price, but because Ike needs the money, and, well, I just like his company.

Ike was at the sink washing mugs when we came in. He sang out: "Morgue Mama!"

I wriggled my fingers at him. "Tea and a regular coffee, Ike." We sat at the empty table by the cigarette machine.

Aubrey was surprised. "You let him call you that?"

"Ike has earned the right," I said.

"I'm jealous—how has he done that?"

"Driving me home a hundred winter nights when my car wouldn't start. Always making sure I'm having a good day."

Ike brought our mugs. "Morgue Mama ever tell you why everybody calls me Ike?" he asked Aubrey. "Even though my real name is Leonard?"

Aubrey gave me a playful glower. "I'm afraid Mrs. Sprowls keeps lots of secrets from me."

"Well—It's because I was the only black man in Hannawa anybody knew who voted for Dwight D. Eisenhower."

Aubrey looked at me for help.

"You'll have to forgive Miss McGinty," I said to Ike. "She is very, very young." I leaned toward Aubrey and whispered. "Ike was Eisenhower's nickname."

Ike laughed and went back to his dirty mugs. Aubrey and I started making plans for her now-official investigation of the Buddy Wing murder.

"You don't look too happy about Bob and Tinker giving you the go-ahead," I said.

"Every word I write they'll be perched on my shoulders like a couple of big-nosed parrots. *Can't say that! Awrrrak! Can't say that!*"

"That's the way big papers work," I said. "It's your reporting but their reputations."

She sarcastically toasted me with her mug. "Well, just so you can sleep nights, I'm going to play by the rules."

"Which are?"

"That I simply try to prove Sissy couldn't have done it—which we've pretty much done already—and, if I can manage, get her to admit it on the record."

"But not try to find the real killer?"

She imitated Bob Averill's slow, dry Midwestern voice: "That is the police department's responsibility."

"And it is," I said.

She returned to her own voice: "But they do want a series—five or six parts—so we can still do lots of snooping. Background on the atmosphere that led up to the murder. History of the church. Bandicoot's split with Wing. The anger and the rivalry. How easy it would be for someone else to paint that cross. How the police rushed to judgment. Whatever we can put together to paint the big picture."

I sipped my tea and waited for one of Ike's regulars to rattle a pack of Kools out of the cigarette machine. "You still want this to be *we*? Even after I let the cat out of the bag?"

"It's still we, Maddy. You, me and my wild, Asian-American sex toy."

We laughed and sipped and ducked the cigarette smoke wiggling toward the ceiling.

The paper—rightfully—did not want Aubrey looking for the real murderer. But I knew Aubrey would keep looking. She not only wanted to free Sissy James, she wanted an arrest and a trial. She wanted a story that would go on for months. She was as interested in advancing her career as Bob Averill and Alec Tinker were about advancing theirs. The *Herald-Union* was not going to be her last stop. She had her eyes on the *Washington Post* or *The New York Times*. And why shouldn't she?

"What happens," I asked, "if we do stumble onto the real killer? Would you go to the police, like you did with the football coach at *The Gazette*?"

"I suppose."

We passed on the free refills Ike offered us and started back. Central Avenue, pretty much empty all day, was filling up with rush hour traffic. "Did you tell Bob about your car windows?"

"Am I out of my mind?" she asked.

## Sunday, May 21

Before Aubrey could pursue the Buddy Wing story full-time, she had to finish her series on the city's street prostitutes. She worked day and night all week. I dug out all the old files I had on the subject, some going back to the twenties. Prostitution is not only the world's oldest profession, it's one of the world's oldest newspaper stories.

On Sunday the first story of her series ran. "WALKING THE WALK," the headline across the top of Page One read, "THERE'S NOTHING SEXY ABOUT THE SEX TRADE."

Accompanying the story was a shadowy photo of a girl with chubby, naked legs leaning into a car window. Aubrey's story was chilling:

> HANNAWA—Keesha will party with a dozen people tonight, but she will have a lousy time.
>
> That's because Keesha is one of an estimated 50 to 60 women selling sex on Hannawa's bleakest streets. Like Keesha, most of these women are not women at all, but teenage girls, some still attending high school. Most, like Keesha, are black.
>
> "I ain't doing this forever," Keesha said minutes after exiting a dark green Ford Explorer, where she'd performed oral sex on a big-bellied white man.
>
> SEE WALK PAGE A6

◇◇◇

# Tuesday, May 23

Aubrey leaned on the counter where I was sorting out a month's worth of obituaries. She was smirking. "Maddy—you'll never guess who's descended into the dark, slimy world of corporate PR."

I made sure my expression was as flat as an Ohio corn field. "Dale Marabout?"

Her smirk got even uglier. "I figured you already knew about it."

"I course I know about it."

She leaned on the counter. Rested her chin on her knuckles. "I ran into him at the library last night. Working away at a little table in the corner like a Franciscan monk."

"And he told you about the job, did he?"

"Only that he was doing a freelance project for a local company. He was pretty tight-lipped about it."

"And you figured I'd fill in all the horrible details?"

"Well—yeah."

I did not like Aubrey taking pleasure in what she considered Dale's misfortune. Nor did I like her drilling me for information. "Dale and I have been friends for a long time," I said. "You and I have been acquainted for five minutes. If Dale doesn't want you to know more, then neither do I."

The word *acquainted* stung her and I was glad it did. "Come on, Maddy—I'm happy for him," she said.

I batted the air. "Poop! You're just happy it isn't you."

"True enough," she admitted. "I think I'd slit my wrists before I sank to writing PR."

Good gravy, Aubrey made me angry that day. Angry at her and angry at myself. I was helplessly attracted to her sassiness and her tenacity, like a mosquito to a bug zapper, as they say. But I was also helplessly loyal to Dale. "Not if you had a family to support," I growled. I gathered up the obits and headed for my desk. She knew enough not to follow.

I wasn't about to tell Aubrey, but Dale never would have taken that freelance assignment if it hadn't been for me. I'd learned about the job though the grapevine and knew it would be perfect for him. It was with a prominent corporation in town. It would pay big bucks and maybe lead to a full-time job. So I'd invited him to Speckley's and told him about it.

Freelancing always gives reporters the heebie-jeebies—even unemployed ones—so I wasn't surprised that his first reaction was to shake his head like an oscillating fan. "No-no-no-no, Maddy," he said. "There'll be no have-keyboard-will-travel stuff for this boy."

I patted his nervous hands. "I admire your standards. I really do. And I admire the courage it took to walk away from the paper. You've got moxie out the wazoo. But if you're anything like other reporters I know, you've also got bills out the wazoo."

Dale hemmed and hawed through several cups of coffee. But in the end he agreed to put on a suit and tie and meet with the corporate honchos dangling that big, fat freelance job. They offered and he accepted.

I was happy for Dale. And pretty damned pleased with myself. So when Aubrey started smirking at me that morning in the morgue, I guess I got a little crusty. Later in the day I made amends by sharing a pack of stale Fig Newtons from the vending machine with her. Thank God she had the good sense not to bring up Dale's freelance job again.

## Wednesday, May 24

During a little mid-week pillow talk Aubrey learned that Eric was having a birthday on Sunday. Instead of taking him to the Olive Garden and a movie, she got the bug to throw a surprise birthday dinner for him. She not only wanted to bake a cake, she also wanted to make him a lasagna. I was astonished. "This is suddenly very domestic of you," I said. We were on our phones grinning at each other across the newsroom. "You must be either pregnant or in love."

She cradled the receiver under her chin and playfully gave me the finger with both hands. "Those are two things I will never be. I just thought a nice dinner with the three of us would be fun."

"The three of us?"

"You can't possibly think I could tackle cake and a lasagna by myself."

"And here I thought it was because we'd become something of a family."

Again she gave me the fingers. This time I gave them back.

So the secret birthday dinner for Eric was set: I'd go to her apartment early Sunday afternoon and help her make the lasagna and the cake and then when Eric showed up that evening, expecting Dominos pizza and sex, he'd get crepe paper, balloons, and Dolly Madison Sprowls in a pointy paper party hat.

## Thursday, May 25

All week Aubrey worked the phones. All week people hung up on her.

The one person who did talk to her—and talk and talk—was the eyebrow woman. Having spilled the beans about Sissy's child in Mingo Junction, she now freely rummaged through her brain for anything Aubrey might find useful. "And of course you know about Family Night," she said matter-of-factly during one of their conversations.

"Family Night?" Aubrey asked.

Five minutes later Aubrey was standing in front of my desk, telling me everything that the eyebrow woman had told her. "It appears we have a few loose ends to tie around the Reverend Bandicoot's neck," she said.

## Friday, May 26

Aubrey drove. The insurance company had replaced the windows in her old Escort two days after they were smashed, but there were still tiny shards of glass everywhere in the car. So all the way to Hannawa Falls, I sat in the back fishing out the glass between the seats, and Eric sat in front fishing them off the dashboard. It became a game, like seeing how many out-of-state license plates you can spot.

Hannawa Falls is a tidy blue-collar suburb just east of the city. It's where many of the area's autoworkers settled in the Fifties and Sixties. The endless acres of Cape Cods and ranches had been paid for with years of sacrifice. The owners of those tiny palaces were not about to allow the teeniest bit of sloth, by themselves or their neighbors, to eat into their hard-won equity. Every lawn was mowed. Every shrub was trimmed. We wound our way through a series of concrete streets named after deciduous trees until we arrived on the cul-de-sac where Tim Bandicoot lived. We parked and waited.

At six-fifteen, the garage door went up and a dark green minivan backed out. Four heads were visible through the windows: Tim Bandicoot, his wife, Annie, and their two sons. Aubrey waited until they reached the end of the street and then followed. We wound back through the deciduous tree streets pretty much as we'd come in, until we reached East Tuckman, the wide, four-lane street that runs through the suburb like a barbecue spit. The Bandicoots turned left and drove to Eastfield Centre, the gargantuan shopping strip that has sucked most of the retail out of downtown Hannawa.

They pulled into Arby's. We parked across the street at a Burger King. They went inside to eat. Aubrey sent Eric inside for carryout. It took the Bandicoots forty minutes to eat. Then they drove to the book store next to the mall. "How boring is this," Aubrey moaned as we parked five rows behind them. "Friday night at Borders."

I told her I thought a family outing to Borders was actually a pretty nifty thing.

"Putt-Putt golf for the mind," she said.

"To each his own," I said. Aubrey was already heading for the door and Eric and I were walking like quick little penguins to catch up.

We lingered by the magazine racks while the Bandicoots browsed the tables of just-published non-fiction. After a few minutes they split up. Annie headed for the children's section with the boys. Tim wandered into the history section.

We followed Tim, hiding by the books on World War II while he worked his way down the long aisle of Civil War books. When he opened a large gray-covered volume on Robert E. Lee, Aubrey slid beside him and turned sideways, resting her elbow on the top of the shelving. "Civil War buff," she said. "How ironic." She was referring, of course, to his famous split with Buddy Wing over speaking in tongues.

Tim raised his head only slightly. His eyes drifted from Aubrey to Eric to me—by now we were awkwardly hovering behind her—then back to the book. "I thought you hung out in the dairy aisle," he said. He, of course, was referring to our ambush of the eyebrow woman at Artie's supermarket.

"Wherever I can learn something," Aubrey said.

Tim closed the big book on Robert E. Lee and cradled it across his chest. Psychological armor, I suppose. "I knew Sissy had a daughter, if that's what you want to know."

Aubrey curled her index finger under her thumb and flicked the portrait of Lee on the cover. "Do you consider the great Robert E. a hero or a traitor?"

He put the book back on the shelf. He was struggling to remain calm. And failing. "You're insinuating that I knew Sissy was in Mingo Junction the night Buddy was poisoned."

"Did you know?"

"I knew she always went there for holidays. And I suppose she told me she was going there that weekend. But then Buddy was killed and three days later she confessed."

"And it didn't occur to you that she was confessing—just perhaps—to protect you?"

"Why would that occur to me?"

Aubrey tried again. "Did it occur to you that maybe somebody else was setting Sissy up?"

Tim started pawing the books nervously. I figured any second now he was going to pull out the biggest coffee table volume he could find and beat Aubrey over the head with it. "The police were crawling all over my house and my church, trying to prove that I did it," he hissed. "Then they found all that stuff at Sissy's place, and she confessed. What was I supposed to think?"

Aubrey began nodding, sarcastically. "So—just so I'm clear on this—never once did you say to yourself, 'You know, maybe I should tell the police she just might have been in Mingo Junction that Friday night.'"

Bandicoot bent over the bookshelves and pressed his forehead against his folded hands, as if praying on the back of a church pew. "You know for sure Sissy was in Mingo Junction?"

"I know for sure."

He started to cry.

Aubrey only got tougher with him. "It's funny you didn't tell the police about Sissy's possible alibi. A woman you'd been sleeping with, for what, four years? But maybe it was just sex with you. Sex that was getting stale. Maybe you just figured, she confessed, good riddance, that's the end of that."

"I did not think that."

"Maybe you were just afraid that if Sissy was cleared, the police would focus on you again."

Tim Bandicoot peeked at Aubrey through his folded hands. "I did not kill him."

Aubrey leaned on the shelves just like him, their shoulders touching, best friends having a heart-to-heart. "Of course you didn't. It was a Friday night. Family Night. You were having fast food with Annie and your boys. Seeing a Disney movie or something."

This, of course, is why we'd followed the Bandicoots to Borders—to confront him about Family Night. The eyebrow woman had told Aubrey that, unlike the Heaven Bound Cathedral, Bandicoot's new church did not hold services on Friday nights. Friday night at the New Epiphany Temple was Family Night. "A time," he regularly told his flock, "for mommies and daddies and their children to heal the week-day wounds of secular strife, and take the Living Lord out for supper and some G-rated fun."

"I gather you told the police about Family Night," Aubrey said.

"They asked me what I was doing that night and I told them."

"Did they ask you about Sissy?"

"They asked me about a number of people in my congregation."

"Were they aware of your affair?"

"They were aware."

"Did they ask if you knew where Sissy was that night?"

He fed a bent knuckle into his quivering mouth and bit down. "I know I should have told them about Sissy's girl in Mingo."

"Should have but couldn't," Aubrey said without sympathy. "Because that Family Night was different than most—"

His blanched face jerked sideways, the bent knuckle ripping into the side of his mouth like a fishhook.

"—Because that was Father & Son Night at the Gund Arena in Cleveland, where a bus load of men and boys from the New Epiphany Temple saw the Cavaliers squeak by the New York Knicks, 107 to 104. Wives stayed home that Friday night, didn't they? And home alone is not much of an alibi, is it?"

"My Annie did not kill Buddy." It was the loudest, most tortured whisper I'd ever heard.

Aubrey repeated herself: "Home alone is not much of an alibi."

Tim spun around, his back digging into the spines of the books. "You are so full of shit," he growled. He sounded just like that possessed little girl in *The Exorcist*.

Aubrey smiled. "And you are so full of guilt. You had to choose between betraying your lover and protecting your wife. Assuming she needs protecting, something I'm sure you still don't know. No wonder you were drawn to that book about Robert E. Lee."

Wasn't Aubrey something—on the spur of the moment using that book on Robert E. Lee to drill deep into his tortured soul. Lee, if you remember your Civil War history, was forced to choose between the country he loved and the state he loved. When Buddy Wing was murdered, Tim Bandicoot had to choose between his wife and his mistress. Lee chose Virginia. Bandicoot chose Annie. Or so it seemed.

"What do you want me to do now?" Bandicoot asked. His eyes were red. His cheeks were shiny. He was shaking.

Aubrey shrugged her shoulders like some old Italian bocce ball player. "I'm going to see to it that Sissy goes free. What you do is up to you. Thanks for the interview, reverend."

Aubrey walked away and Eric and I followed. I figured we'd be going to a restaurant somewhere, to assess what we'd learned, like we always did. Instead she led Eric and me to the coffee shop right there in the bookstore. While we were standing in line to order, we saw Tim Bandicoot herding his family across the parking lot. "A Family Night to remember," Aubrey said.

We spent a good two hours there, sipping our cappuccinos and munching on biscotti. Eric kept going for computer magazines to read while Aubrey and I listened to the folk singer. He was so loud we could only discuss the story between songs.

"So, what do we make of Tim Bandicoot now?" I asked.

Aubrey was propping up her chin with her knuckles. Her eyes were half closed. I couldn't tell if she was bored by the music, or enjoying it. "He wasn't exactly the same cool and cocky cucumber who filled us full of Krispy Kremes, was he?"

The singer launched into a Beatles' medley: *Eleanor Rigby* followed by *Blackbird* followed by *Fool on the Hill* and *Hey Jude*. It went on forever. I was one of the three or four who applauded. "I gather you weren't moved by his tears."

"When people cry for the right reasons I'm moved."

I knew what Aubrey meant. It wasn't remorse that made Tim Bandicoot cry and shake like that. It was fear. "You really think he's protecting his wife?"

She answered right through *On a Jet Plane*: "A lot of these women-behind-the-throne types are real ballbusters. Let's say Annie Bandicoot didn't give a damn that her Timmy boy was screwing Sissy The Bimbo—as long as he wasn't screwing her—but she *was* worried about his congregation finding out. Worried about Buddy Wing and their enemies back at the Heaven Bound Cathedral finding out. Maybe she was afraid Buddy already knew."

My head was swimming. Not from Aubrey's analysis. From the cappuccino. I'd been sipping my Darjeeling tea all day and the last thing I needed at nine o'clock at night was another strong dose of caffeine. "So she poisoned Buddy Wing and framed Sissy to protect her husband's ministry? You think that's possible?"

Aubrey lifted her cup with both hands and took a slow, thoughtful sip. "We've got to learn more about this Annie Bandicoot, don't you think?"

"Well—I do know a little bit already."

Aubrey squinted at me over her cup. "Been busy with your old files, Maddy?"

I made a joke of it but I could see she was not happy with my snooping on my own. "Sometimes they call out to me at night."

"And what did they have to say about our little Annie?"

I told her what I'd found: that she'd grown up in the Heaven Bound Cathedral; that she'd won the citywide spelling bee when she was in the eighth grade and had been in the National Honor Society in high school; that she'd attended Hemphill College, dropping out in her second year to marry the church's youth pastor, Tim Bandicoot. "Her name and picture have been in the paper a hundred times over the years," I said, "serving on committees, hosting ecumenical lunches, taking food and second-hand clothes to poor churches in Appalachia, that sort of thing."

Aubrey was not impressed. "Nothing important then?"

"Deciding what's important is your job, dear."

◇◇◇

When we left Borders it was already dark. Eric hadn't bought any of the magazines he'd read. I couldn't stop humming *Eleanor*

*Rigby*. About a mile from downtown Hannawa Aubrey started twisting her rear-view mirror. "There's that damned red station wagon," she said.

"Red station wagon?" I asked.

"Don't freak," she said, "but some dickwad's been following me."

Eric and I twisted and looked out the back window. There was indeed a red car of some description behind us, but it was too far back and the night traffic was too heavy for us to tell if it was a station wagon, let alone following us. "How do you know it's the same one all the time?" I asked.

Aubrey squinted at me in disbelief. "Nobody drives station wagons anymore. So when you keep seeing a red one slithering up behind you—"

"You don't think maybe you're a little paranoid?"

She did not appreciate my skepticism. "In case you've forgotten, these are brand-new windows we're looking out."

Eric apparently got a good look at the car. "Ford Taurus. Late Nineties."

Aubrey was encouraged. At least he believed her. "Bubbly shaped, right?"

"Yeah," he said, "Tauruses are kind of bubbly shaped I guess."

"So you think the same people who smashed your windows are now following you?" I asked. "Either the pimps or the cops or the Christians?"

If Aubrey was frightened, it wasn't affecting her ready sarcasm. "A Taurus station wagon rules out the pimps, I think—even if it is a red one."

"So it's down to cops or Christians?"

She looked at me. Her cheeks were suddenly pale and her eyes rabbit-like. "Let's hope it's cops. Cops I can handle."

We drove downtown, turning left onto North Bidwell. A block from the *Herald-Union* parking deck the red Taurus disappeared.

# 13

**Sunday, May 28**

Sunday afternoon I drove to Aubrey's apartment to help her with Eric's surprise birthday dinner. I was the one who was surprised. She had made some improvements. The once empty living room now had a huge white love seat with green and yellow-striped pillows. A small black television sat alone on one of those assemble-it-yourself entertainment centers. There was a poster of Van Gogh's Starry Night on the wall. Her many pairs of shoes, once scattered like bones in the desert, were now piled in a wicker laundry basket by the door. One thing hadn't changed. Her cardboard boxes marked SHIT FROM COLLEGE and SHIT FROM HOME were still stacked in a pyramid against the wall.

She took my shoulders and pushed me into the kitchen, proudly showing me her new table and chairs. Balloons and loops of crepe paper were Scotch-taped on the ceiling. "Can you believe it," she said. "We are actually going to sit down and have a home-cooked dinner like official adults."

"I've been an official adult for a long time," I said. "Where's your cake mix?"

It was a basic yellow box cake which Aubrey intended to cover with Dream Whip and jelly beans. She also had a box of those candles you can't blow out. She poured the cake mix into the bowl and I put in the correct measures of water and oil. She cracked the three eggs and I picked out the bits of shell. She read the baking instructions on the box while I beat the batter with a tablespoon. She opened the oven door and I put in the pans. I don't know which of us was having the better time.

We started on the lasagna. I'd given her a shopping list during the week and she'd dutifully bought everything I said we needed. We worked side by side on the stovetop, me browning the Italian sausage while she boiled the water for the noodles. When I asked for the canned tomatoes, she handed me the canned tomatoes. When I asked for the basil and garlic, she handed me the basil and garlic. When I asked for the ricotta cheese, she asked, "What ricotta cheese?"

"You didn't get the ricotta cheese?" I cackled like some nasty old grandmother. "How can you make lasagna without ricotta cheese?"

She showed me the shopping list I'd given her: No ricotta cheese.

"Looks like you're going to the supermarket," I said.

She was hesitant, almost hostile, as if I was asking her to swim to Sicily for the ricotta cheese. "You're the one who fucked up," she said.

"If you think you're capable of juggling a cake and a half-made lasagna, I'll go," I said.

So Aubrey went to the supermarket for the ricotta cheese. Even if she drove like an ambulance driver and immediately found the right aisle at the market, I figured it would take her a half hour. That would give me time to boil the noodles and maybe tidy up the apartment a bit.

She returned with enough ricotta cheese to make six lasagnas.

## Tuesday, May 30

Monday was Memorial Day. Aubrey and Eric went to the Rock and Roll Hall of Fame in Cleveland. I stayed home and replaced the tomato plants the rabbits nibbled. Hannawa not only has more evangelists per capita than any city of its size, it also has more rabbits. The fear of humans was bred out of them generations ago. Unfortunately, they've never lost their genetic urge to devour anything a human plants.

Tuesday evening I went with Aubrey to see Wayne F. Dillow, the man whose wife had died of cancer after being faith-healed by Buddy Wing. Dillow lived on Summerhill Lane in Elden, a hilly section of town sandwiched between the old Chevrolet plant to the north and the airport to the south. His house was not unlike my own: a boxy ranch with an attached one-car garage. Mine is painted white with dark green shutters. His was painted avocado and had, if you can believe it, pink shutters.

Dillow invited us in the front door and led us straight through the house to the back yard, where a circle of aluminum lawn chairs and a pitcher of lemonade were waiting. It was clear from the get-go that Wayne F. Dillow was a proud and gentle man. He was dressed in a well-starched white shirt and a pair of tan polyester dress pants. His shoes were shined and his thick head of white hair was Brylcreemed and combed. His backyard was mowed short and all the flower beds were neatly mulched. "Everybody want lemonade?" he asked us.

While he poured we engaged in small-talk about his bird houses. There must have been a couple dozen of them, all made of gourds and painted white, hanging from the branches of his lilac bushes like Christmas tree ornaments.

Aubrey got down to business. "I'm sorry I can't tell you everything at this point," she began, trying to sip and open her notebook at the same time, "but there seem to be some unresolved issues concerning Buddy Wing's murder."

Dillow took a long drink of his lemonade and then wedged the glass between his knees. "Everybody at church is talking about the investigation your paper's doing. Apparently you have some evidence that Sissy didn't do it."

"There's some evidence that points in that direction," Aubrey conceded. "But what we're trying to do now is set the scene."

"Set the scene?"

"You know—the atmosphere inside the church since Tim Bandicoot was booted out? Are people still riled up? Are there lingering suspicions? Things like that."

Dillow sprouted a mellow smile. "Guthrie spread the word we weren't to talk to you. But if you ask me, that just looks like we're hiding something."

Aubrey tapped her nose with her pen. "You think anybody is?"

His smile hardened. "I know I'm not."

Aubrey smiled back, just as resolutely. "You gave the Reverend Wing quite a rough time after your wife died."

"I was angry and confused. He forgave me."

"And you forgave him?"

"Nothing to forgive. It was the cancer that killed Dorothea."

"After she was allegedly healed."

The word *allegedly* weakened Dillow's smile. "Dorothea believed in that sort of thing. And of course the pastor did."

"But you didn't?" Aubrey asked.

"Not particularly. But I've come to understand that God accepts a lot of leeway as long as you essentially believe the right things."

Every time I went on an interview with Aubrey that spring and summer I promised myself that I'd keep my mouth shut and let her ask the questions. And every time I broke that promise. "So you don't believe your wife was hoodwinked by the faith healing?" I asked.

*Allegedly* weakened his smile. *Hoodwinked* flattened it. "Hell is filled with people hoodwinked by the miracles of modern medicine. Dorothea, on the other hand, is waiting for me in heaven."

Aubrey scribbled down his quote—it was a fantastic quote— then jumped in to rescue both me and the interview. "After your wife's death you harassed Reverend Wing for quite a long time. So much so that he finally had you arrested."

Dillow's smile returned. "Believe me, I was mad enough to murder him. But God jumped in and wrestled me away from the devil."

Another good quote. "And you went back to church?" Aubrey asked as she scribbled.

A woeful laugh wiggled through Dillow's puckered lips as he sucked on his lemonade. "It struck me one night that I missed my church almost as much as I missed my Dorothea. I cried and prayed for hours and the very next night went to services. Everybody knew what I'd done—breaking into his house and all that—and when I walked in people just divided like the Red Sea. The reverend spotted me during his sermon. He jumped off the stage and came right up the aisle and hugged me and kissed me on the forehead. 'Will you look who's here tonight?' he shouted, just as happy as he could be. 'Will you look who's here?'" Dillow pressed his perspiring lemonade glass against his forehead. "So that, Miss McGinty, was how it was at the church before the reverend was poisoned. And that's how it is now. Some people are suspicious and some are afraid. But everybody loves the Lord."

This Wayne F. Dillow was a regular quote machine. Aubrey wrote it down and closed her notebook. "And you were there the night Wing was poisoned?"

"Oh, yes."

Dillow walked us around his backyard, showing us his day lilies and his rhubarb and the pachysandra he'd just planted around his evergreens. He also showed us the brick barbecue he built in the Sixties. "We used to cook out every chance we got," he said. "Even on rainy days."

On the drive back to the paper Aubrey kept checking the mirror to see if the red Taurus station wagon was following. It wasn't.

"So after your stories run and Sissy is cleared," I asked, "do you think the police will put Dillow on their list of suspects?"

"No matter how Dillow sweetens it up—all that wrestled-from-the-devil crap—he had a motive and he had the opportunity. He'll be on the list. And he knows it. That's why the preemptive strike. Talking openly and honestly about his past sins. Nothing To Hide 101."

"He seemed pretty sincere to me," I said.

"He did to me, too. Cool, calm and tidy. Maybe the kind of guy who could crawl back to the preacher who killed his wife, and then pretend to be lovey dovey for several years while plotting the perfect revenge. Plying us with lemonade for a half-hour would be a piece of cake for an old fox like that."

I rubbed my throat. "First Tim Bandicoot's doughnuts, now Wayne Dillow's lemonade. We've got to stop accepting refreshments from potential murderers."

By the time Aubrey dropped me off at the paper and I drove home, stopping at the new Walgreen's for toothpaste, it was after nine. I wanted to crawl into bed and turn on the TV. But my brain was still buzzing. So I went to the basement and rummaged through the old morgue files until midnight.

I think I've told you how, little by little, I've been pirating the old files out of the morgue. I simply love those old files: The mushroomy smell of the old newsprint. The quiet way the old clippings unfold. The bylines of reporters long retired if not dead. Stories that seem so small and innocent now, but once caused quite a to-do. I love the old file cabinets, too. Some are painted dark green but most are gray. Every one of them is exactly five feet high and 18 inches wide. Every one has four deep drawers that open begrudgingly. Every drawer contains something marvelous.

I know it makes me sound like the most boring woman on the face of the earth, but it's not uncommon for me to spend two or three evenings a week going through the files in my basement. I'll pull out an armful of folders and then sit down at the old chrome-legged kitchen table I keep by the clothes dryer and just lose myself in the magic of the past.

That night I was looking through files from the S drawers. The Heaven Bound Cathedral is located in the city's South Ridge neighborhood. We don't anymore, but we used to keep detailed files on all the neighborhoods, the crimes committed, church and school events, sewer and water projects, the fires and horrible traffic accidents.

The Heaven Bound Cathedral was built in 1978. That section of South Ridge was still pretty leafy and quiet then. The land Buddy Wing bought for his church was the old estate of Ralph Haisley, founder of Haisley's department store. Before the interstate highways and the flight to the suburbs, Haisley's was *the place* to shop downtown. The grand, six-story building closed and sat empty for seven years. Now it's the county welfare offices. Anyway, Ralph Haisley built this incredible Tudor mansion up on South Ridge in the Twenties. After World War II, the woods and fields around the mansion were sold off for housing developments. The Haisley heirs sold the remaining grounds to Buddy Wing just after the department store closed.

My South Ridge files contained a number of stories about the cathedral's construction. People in the surrounding developments did not like the church being built there at all. They complained about the garish design and they complained about the impending traffic problems. They complained that the zoning code change granted to Wing would encourage other unwanted development. Which it did. Today there are fast-food restaurants and car dealerships and a huge strip mall with a Target and a Home Depot.

Soon after the cathedral opened, residents discovered another problem. The parking lot lights. Eighteen steel poles rising over the asphalt like those Martian machines in the War of the Worlds. Each pole was topped with six balls of blinding white light. Neighborhood dogs wouldn't stop barking and people couldn't sleep. One man whose property abutted the parking lot started shooting out the lights with a .22 rifle. The man's name was Edward Tolchak. Between 1979 and 1985, he was arrested and charged six times.

◇◇◇

# Wednesday, May 31

First thing in the morning I gave the files to Aubrey, who already had her knees propped on her desk and her keyboard in her lap, typing furiously. She tossed the file on her desk, where it immediately became lost among the rubble. "A guy dumb enough to stand in his own backyard and shoot out parking lot lights plotting a perfect murder? I don't think so."

"He's been arrested six times, and altogether served over ninety days in jail," I pointed out. "I'd say there has to be some real anger there."

She nodded impatiently and typed even faster.

I persisted. "My files at home only go to 1987. So who knows what Edward Tolchak may have done in recent years. Things may have escalated."

She could see I was irritated by her indifference. "I'll give the files to Eric. Maybe he can find something worth pursuing."

I went from mild-mannered Maddy to bitch-on-wheels Morgue Mama in a hundredth of a second. "What are you saying to me? That if I wasn't such an incompetent old fool I could check the computer files myself? Well, from now on—"

She apologetically grabbed my elbow and slowly pulled me toward her. "You want to go with Eric and me to Meri after work?"

And so that night we met for dinner. I assumed we'd go to Speckley's, but they both wanted to go to Okar's, a trendy new Lebanese restaurant. Instead of the meat loaf sandwich and au gratin potatoes I was craving, I had a fruit salad covered with yogurt and honey and pistachio nuts. Eric and Aubrey had grilled chicken pitas and shared a plate of lawn clippings called tabooli. For dessert we ordered one baklava and three forks.

It was just about dark when we left the restaurant. The sidewalk was filled with old gays wearing pastel baseball caps and noisy college kids covered in tattoos and earrings. I remembered the days when be-bop jazz used to roll out of the bars and give the entire neighborhood a happy epileptic fit. Now the street throbbed like a toothache from that awful rap music. Eric was begging me to join them for cappuccinos at Starbucks when Aubrey spotted the red Taurus station wagon parked along the street just a block from our own cars. I don't know if she was frightened, angry, or simply annoyed, but she began leaking four-letter words. Quite to my surprise, Eric began leaking them, too. Then he started running, right toward the Taurus, fists tucked under his chin like a boxer.

Aubrey and I both yelled for him to stop. But Eric was in protective boyfriend mode. When he got within fifty feet of the station wagon, the man inside jumped out and ran. Eric stayed with him. They crossed the street and ran another block before disappearing around the back of an apartment building.

Aubrey wanted to follow, but I locked my arms around her elbow to hold her back. "Eric couldn't catch a cold," I assured her.

After a minute or two, the man reappeared, trotting, arms wrapped around his face like a babushka. He jumped into his station wagon, backed into a lime-green Volkswagen Beetle, made a clumsy U-turn and sped away. Then we saw Eric, weaving slowly across the street, oblivious to the traffic.

Aubrey and I hurried to him. There was blood on his lip and the bridge of his nose. He was staring straight ahead, acting dopey. I fished in my purse for a Kleenex while Aubrey berated him for not getting the license plate number on the Taurus. "That's all you needed to do," she kept repeating. "That's all you needed to do."

I licked the Kleenex and started cleaning the blood off his face. "Good gravy, Aubrey. He's just been beaten to a pulp."

Actually he hadn't been beaten to a pulp. He told us he'd tried to tackle the mysterious station-wagon man and missed, tumbling over the hood of a Yugo.

"Could you make the guy out?" Aubrey demanded. "White, black, young, old?"

Eric fought off my dabbing Kleenex. "Middle-aged white guy." He swung his eyes across my worried face and stared into the black sky. "I think I'm going home now," he said.

Aubrey followed him to his truck, begging for a better description of the man. He drove away without telling her anything.

I felt so sorry for Eric. He had tried to defend the woman he loved—at least loved to sleep with—only to make a fool of himself. I knew what that kind of embarrassment was like. I once went to Dale Marabout's apartment with a chocolate cake, to rekindle our faltering affair. Instead of knocking, I used the key he'd given me. I found him naked on his living room floor with that kindergarten teacher.

A few days after that incident in Meri, Aubrey confided in me that Eric had stopped sleeping with her. "I guess flying over the hood of that Yugo he came to the conclusion I'm not worth dying for," she said. She said it as if she didn't care. But I could see she did care. For years, Dale Marabout and I assured each other we were just in it for the sex. We laughed and copulated like a couple of those chimpanzees in equatorial Africa, bonobos I think they're called, who just mindlessly screw and screw and screw. After I found Dale on the floor with the kindergarten teacher, I pretended not to care. I went to their wedding and, of all things, gave them a set of fitted flannel sheets. But I cared. And Aubrey cared. She'd been using Eric, no doubt about that, but it was for more than sex.

# 14

Thursday morning I went with Aubrey to Kent State University to see Dr. Howard Cooksey, a professor of television and radio news in the communications department. It would be a forty-minute drive across some of the most forgettable landscape in the state of Ohio.

"Were you still there when the black squirrels were poisoned?" I asked as Aubrey's Ford Escort struggled up the long grade that divides the tiny towns of Richfield and Peninsula.

Her eyes widened. "How do you know about the squirrels?"

"Morgue Mama does not know all or see all," I joked, "but Morgue Mama does remember all." The fact was that after the eyebrow woman told us about students from the university working at the cathedral, I searched through the morgue's Kent State files.

"That happened my senior year," Aubrey said. "I covered it for the college paper."

"So that was just three years ago."

She played with the calendar in her mind. "Yeah."

Kent is famous for its black squirrels and the poisonings shook the town and the campus to its roots, not as badly as the May 4, 1970 shootings, of course not, but it was amazing how worked up people became over the deaths of thirty-seven squirrels.

The black squirrel story actually began decades earlier, in the early Sixties, when the university's grounds supervisor, a guy named Larry Woodell, went to Canada and brought back sixteen black squirrels. In Ohio you only see gray squirrels and red squirrels, so black squirrels popping across the lawns were quite a novelty, and the herd, whatever you call a group of squirrels, multiplied faster than rabbits. In 1982, the university held its first Black Squirrel Festival, complete with rock bands and a barbecue. The annual May 4 memorial commemoration and the Black Squirrel Festival in September are the yin and yang of campus life at Kent State, the sad and the silly if you will.

So, anyway, it caused quite a stir when people started finding the carcasses of black squirrels all over the place. The campus police called in the Kent city police, and the Kent city police called in the State Highway Patrol. "They never caught who did it?" I asked Aubrey.

"Nope. After thirty-seven squirrels it stopped. By Christmas break it was all over. But it was a cool story for awhile—you know what I mean by cool—it was actually pretty sickening."

I did know what she meant by cool. Covering those squirrel poisonings when she was a senior journalism student at Kent was cool the same way covering the murder of that football coach was cool when she was a new reporter at *The Gazette* in Rush City, the same way that digging into the Buddy Wing murder now was cool. Big stories, no matter how tragic, are cool to cover. I'm sure that Aubrey's stories on the squirrel poisonings for the college newspaper helped her get her first job in Rush City, and I know her football coach stories got her into the *Herald-Union*. Soldiers advance through the ranks by going to war. Reporters advance by covering cool stories. "How exactly were the squirrels poisoned?" I asked. "It wasn't walnuts shot full of procaine, was it?"

She winced at my joke. "Ears of corn sprinkled with insecticide—as you well know."

"Well, it's still possible that's it's the same person, isn't it? Psychopathic killers aren't under any obligation to use the same poisons all the time, are they?"

Aubrey agreed that it was possible with an exaggerated, Oliver Hardy nod. "But think about the odds. In order for one of the television students to have poisoned both Buddy Wing and the squirrels, that student would've been at Kent three years ago, making him, at best, a sophomore when the squirrels were killed. I'll admit that theoretically there might be a few sophomores capable of sprinkling poison on an ear of corn without poisoning themselves, but that still means there's a three year-gap between crimes. Wouldn't a wacko like that have moved up to a human victim right away?"

"Maybe there was someone in between," I said.

"You're the one with the steel trap mind, Maddy. Was anyone within a hundred miles of Kent State mysteriously poisoned in the last three years?"

"Doesn't ring a bell."

"And what college student carrying a full load, and working part-time, and getting loaded, and trying to get laid, would have the time to frame Sissy James? Find out she was a former member of the Heaven Bound Cathedral who's having an affair with Buddy Wing's old protégé? Who has a secret child in Mingo Junction? Who she visits every Thanksgiving? This is Kent State we're talking about, not Yale."

"If it's that far-fetched why are we even wasting our time going to Kent?"

"You got me."

We were going to Kent State, of course, because the regular presence of strangers backstage at the cathedral would be an important part of Aubrey's stories on the murder. She'd explore the two possibilities: one, that the real killer was someone everybody knew; two, that the real killer was someone nobody knew. She'd play it straight, not trying to identify possible suspects, not even hinting at possible suspects. But everyone reading her series would know who all the possible suspects were. And everyone would come to the same conclusion: The Hannawa police were too hasty in accepting Sissy James's confession.

We drove through downtown Kent to the campus. Except for a few black squirrels and a few summer students, the campus was empty. We parked in a visitor's lot and walked past the slope where on that horrible spring day in 1970 the Ohio National Guard had turned and fired. We followed a sidewalk trimmed with beds of red geraniums to Taylor Hall.

Inside we waited for twelve minutes for Dr. Cooksey to come out of his office. He was a tall, overweight man of fifty. He was wearing faded tan Dockers and a white polo shirt. He was not happy to see us.

The walls of his office were covered with glossy publicity photos of network news reporters and anchors. All were upside-down. Perhaps to show his students what a daring iconoclast he was. Perhaps so they wouldn't feel in awe of the on-air stars they'd encounter once they graduated and went to work at some dippy little station like the one in Hannawa.

Anyway, Dr. Cooksey was not happy to see us and told us so: "I shouldn't even talk to you. It can't possibly do my students a lick of good."

I quickly turned to Aubrey, to see how she was reacting. Her eyebrows were raised. She was tapping her chin with her pen. Behind her on the wall was a grinning upside-down Dan Rather. "A story goes where a story goes," she said.

Dr. Cooksey leaned back in his chair and neatly inserted his fingers under his armpits. "But do you have a story, Miss McGinty?"

She ignored his question and asked the first of hers. "How many years have you been sending students to the Heaven Bound Cathedral?"

"I told you on the phone, seven or eight."

"I was hoping you'd looked it up."

"Eight."

"And Elaine Albert came to you with the idea?"

"That's right. She's who you should be talking to, you know."

"I would if she'd talk. Maybe you can put in a good word?"

"Not going to happen."

The hostility between Aubrey and the professor was simply chilling, and embarrassing. I know there's a natural animosity between print and broadcast people, but this was so nasty and personal. It was like Jerry Falwell and Larry Flint discussing celibacy on one of those cable talking-head shows. No respect whatsoever. No hope in the world of finding common ground.

"Do you know how many of your students were working there the semester Buddy Wing was killed?" Aubrey asked.

"Three, four, maybe five."

"Any chance you could find out for sure? Maybe give me their names?"

"Look, Miss McGinty. This thing isn't an official intern program where I get personally involved. All I do is post a flier that part-time jobs are available at the cathedral. The kids make the contact themselves."

"Doesn't the cathedral ever call you for references?"

Dr. Cooksey was losing and he knew it. "Sometimes."

"That semester?"

"Can't remember."

Aubrey wrote that down and underlined it several times. "You can see how these quotes are going to come out, don't you?" she said. 'Cooksey refused to say.' 'Cooksey said he couldn't remember.'"

"Quote whatever you want," the professor said. "But I do not keep a written record of those kind of calls. If Elaine, Mrs. Albert, calls about a student who's applied for a job, I check my grade book and attendance sheet and offer an opinion. I don't keep a record."

Aubrey, to her credit, wrote down his explanation. "So, what did you think when Buddy Wing was poisoned? You had three, four, maybe five students working there, after all."

He smirked. "You mean did I warn my students not to kiss any Bibles while they were over there? Naturally we talked about it in class the next week."

"Did any of them happen to tell you where they were backstage when he toppled over?"

"Gee whiz—I just don't remember any of those conversations."

Aubrey closed her notebook and put the cap on her pen. "Do you ever personally go to the broadcasts, to see how your students are doing?"

"I went a couple of times. Years ago when they first started hiring my kids. But I haven't been there for ages. I sure wasn't there the night Wing was poisoned, if that's what you're getting at."

When Aubrey stood up her hair swept across the Dan Rather photo, almost knocking it off the wall. "I wasn't getting at that. But thanks for the lead."

We left Taylor Hall and retreated through the red geraniums. Aubrey couldn't stop laughing. "Did you ever meet a bigger dickbrain in your life?"

"I've been around a long time—I'm sure I have. But he's right up there." I saw a tuft of wiry grass growing up through the mulch and stopped to yank it out. "You'd almost think he was covering up for one of his students, wouldn't you?"

"What he was covering was his own tookus."

"Oh, come on. You don't think he killed Buddy Wing?"

Now Aubrey laughed at me. "Remember when we first got there? And he said talking to us couldn't possibly do his students any good? What he meant was that talking to us couldn't do *him* any good. These professors are bunny rabbits, Maddy. Frightened little bunny rabbits. Their courses are their cabbage patches. And protecting the cabbage is what it's all about."

I found a second tuft of grass in the geraniums. Before I could find a third, Aubrey locked her arm in mine and steered me toward the parking lot. "Any idea how you're going to get the names of his students?" I asked.

She looked at me like I'd just told her I believed in Santa Claus. She pulled her notebook from her purse and flipped it open to a page marked with a paper clip. "Marcie Peacock, Amy Kamm, Zack Zimmerman and Kiralee Presello."

"Good gravy, why'd you drag me up here if you already had their names?"

She gave me several reasons: "To get some background. To get some color. To get some good quotes. To see the dickbrain squirm."

"That last one seems a bit personal."

"You bet it does," she said. "Newspaper people have a moral responsibility to strike a blow against television whenever we can."

"You're not serious—"

We'd reached the car. She fumbled in her purse for her keys. "Only half serious. This is the biggest story I've ever covered, Maddy. I have to be thorough. And careful."

We drove a few blocks to a Wendy's. I got a salad. Aubrey got a baked potato and chili. "So, where did you get the names from?" I asked.

Again she gave me the Santa Claus look. "From the church bulletin. They always list as many people as they can."

She was right about that. Have you ever seen a church bulletin that didn't have long lists of names, from the pastor down to the assistant baby-sitter in the nursery? "But how'd you get a bulletin from back in November?" I wondered. "I wouldn't think their shelf life is too long."

"Obviously I have an off-the-record source or two."

"Obviously."

"I wish I could tell you."

"The eyebrow woman?"

The corner of her mouth twisted cryptically. I tried again. "The students all checked out, I gather?"

"Four little kittens," she said.

# 15

**Tuesday, June 13**

As soon as Eric left for his morning Mountain Dew break Aubrey hurried to my desk—to show me her bruises and scratches.

"Good gravy, what happened to you?"

"Taurus Man attacked me last night," she said.

"Not—"

"No, I wasn't raped. Just slapped and scratched and threatened a little."

"A little?" There was one set of finger-shaped bruises on her right arm, just above the wrist. The other bruises were on her face, one above her left eye and one below her cheekbone. The scratches, just two of them, ran parallel from her left ear down across her chest. She had to open her blouse two buttons to show me where they ended just above her bra on the right side.

"You're sure it was the man in the station wagon? The guy Eric chased?"

"He was wearing a ballcap and bandanna, but it was him," she said.

"And this happened where, Aubrey?"

"Outside my building. He jumped out of the shrubs by the door. Batted me around for a couple of seconds and took off."

"And he threatened you?"

"He kept growling 'You better back off, devil girl.' I'm cutting down those fucking shrubs myself. You wouldn't have a chainsaw I can borrow?"

I'd hoped our problems with the man in the red station wagon were over. It had been two weeks since Eric chased him in Meri. We hadn't spotted him on our drive to Kent or anywhere else. Either he'd changed cars or changed his mind about the wisdom of following us. Now he was back in the picture. In a very scary way. "You have got to tell Tinker about this," I insisted.

"I already have."

That surprised me. Until now she'd hadn't said anything to Tinker or any of the editors about being followed or having her windows smashed. "Well, I'm glad you did," I said.

While we talked she kept checking the hallway to the cafeteria, to see if Eric was returning to his desk. Not only had Eric stopped sleeping with her since that unfortunate incident in Meri, he'd stopped associating with her altogether. "I'll see if I can get him to wear a bell around his neck," I teased.

She pretended not to hear me. "Telling Tinker was a close call," she said. "You know I don't want any of that sexist, poor-little-girl-reporter crap."

"I know."

"But getting roughed up and threatened—how good is that? I have to put that in the story."

She was amazing, wasn't she? A man grabbed her outside her apartment at night, slapped her around, clawed her chest, threatened her, and she could only think about what great copy it would make. "So you're convinced it's related to the Buddy Wing story and not your stories on the police or the prostitutes?" I asked.

"Hello? Back off devil girl?"

I motioned with my chin. Eric was coming. Aubrey swiveled just in time to see him duck into the men's room. "Why's he going in there?" she hissed.

I stayed on the subject. "You need more proof than 'Back off devil girl,' don't you?"

"I'm not going to back off and apparently neither is he. So by the time my series is ready to run, I'm sure there'll be plenty of proof. He'll slip up."

"Or slit your throat," I said.

She rolled her eyes at my melodrama. "The only remaining question is whether he's from Tim Bandicoot's happy little temple or Guthrie Gates' big bad cathedral."

"Does Tinker want you to make a police report?"

"Yeah."

"Why the frown? That's good for your story, isn't it?"

"He also wants me in my apartment before dark every night. He wouldn't tell a male reporter that."

I motioned with my chin again as Eric slid out of the men's room and pranced back to the cafeteria, as if a hive of wasps was following him. "Probably not. But it's good advice. I know I'll sleep better."

She smiled bravely. It just about broke my heart. She looked so vulnerable, yet so determined, like an overgrown first-grader mustering the courage to go back to school the day after getting pushed off the teeter-totter by a third-grade bully. "You're absolutely sure it was the guy in the station wagon?"

Aubrey went back to her desk and Eric returned to his. He tossed a Mounds bar at me and smiled sheepishly.

I felt so sorry for the poor lamb. Eric had not only stopped associating with Aubrey, he'd stopped associating with me. Which was a bit awkward given that I was his boss and our desks were only a few feet apart. He'd come face-to-face with some terrible truth that night in Meri. He'd experienced some dark epiphany about the world and his place in it. He held me responsible—partially at least—for unleashing the goblins eating away at his self-confidence. So I was delighted when he brought me a Mounds bar as a peace offering. I peeled back the wrapper and took a nibble.

"Don't forget I still need that computer check on Edward Tolchak," I said.

Aubrey had enough to wrap up her series on the Buddy Wing murder at any time. She'd dug deep into Buddy Wing's life and the rift with Tim Bandicoot that had torn his congregation in two. She'd compiled a long list of colorful characters that could be dangled out there as possible suspects, without ever actually saying they were suspects. Most importantly, she could prove that Sissy James was in Mingo Junction the night Buddy Wing was poisoned. She had all the examples of police ineptitude she needed.

But Aubrey wanted more. She wanted Sissy to confess on the record that she didn't poison Buddy Wing. And there was only one way to do that. Prove that Tim Bandicoot was a schmuck not worth protecting.

Luckily, Tinker was not only a patient managing editor, he was a managing editor under instructions from the newspaper's corporate overlords in St. Paul to boost the *Herald-Union's* sagging circulation. This Buddy Wing thing was going to be a great story. A national story. He would give his young, ambitious police reporter all the time she needed. And although he'd dutifully cautioned her not to look for the real killer—all that poppycock about that being the police department's job—I knew in my bones he wanted the real killer found. That's how a managing editor moves up to editor. He digs out stories that not only entertain readers and rile the powers that be, but also result in some action that serves the civic good: clean up a toxic waste dump, send a corrupt politician to jail, bring a cold-blooded murderer to justice. Win a Pulitzer.

◇◇◇

## Thursday, June 15

Thursday I took my Dodge Shadow to get E-checked. That's the state of Ohio's required emissions test to make sure the exhaust from your old car isn't single-handedly destroying the earth's atmosphere. They charge you $19.50 and if your car doesn't pass the test they make you fix it. My Shadow barely passed the last time and I was very nervous about this time. So I went to Ike's Coffee Shop first.

"Morgue Mama!" he sang out, as he always did. "What you doing goofing off in the middle of the day?"

"E-check."

"Don't be frightened. They only want to check your car—not you." He brought me a mug of tea and one of those tiny Ghirardelli chocolates wrapped in foil. "To bolster your courage," he said. "On the house."

"Better bring me the whole box," I said.

Ike is the dearest man. And a handsome man. And a widower in my general age range. He has a master's degree in mathematics and taught in the Hannawa City Schools. Back in the Eighties when the financially strapped school board offered early retirement to veteran teachers at the top of the pay scale, Ike snapped it up and opened the coffee shop. That's when I met him, a good fifteen years ago now. I sometimes wonder if it's our respective races that keeps us coffee-shop-owner and customer instead of something more.

Anyway, I spent an hour at Ike's, sharing snippets of conversation with him about the weather, my raspberries, and who was likely to win the fall congressional elections.

Fortified, I drove to the E-check station, and my Shadow passed the test again. It was only two o'clock. I should have gone back to work. But I felt like this afternoon belonged to me—a gift from the state of Ohio for being a good citizen. So I decided to shop for a new living room sofa. First I drove to Flexner's in Brinkley, where nothing is ever on sale. Then I drove to Albert's Furniture in Greenlawn, where everything is always on sale.

There are lots of Alberts in Hannawa. What were the odds that the Don Albert who owns the furniture store in Greenlawn was the husband of the Elaine Albert who directed the televised church services at the Heaven Bound Cathedral? What were the odds she'd be working the floor when I walked in?

I wanted to walk right out. But there wasn't another customer in the place, and Elaine had already spotted me, and was descending with a smile and a clipboard. She was a short, big-boned woman in a no-nonsense black skirt and eggshell white blouse. "I wanted to look at your sofas," I said.

"We have some wonderful sales today," she said.

I steered away from the leather sofas and concentrated on the models covered with stain-resistant fabric. Elaine stayed with me, pointing out all the little details about their construction and long wear. I didn't hear a word she said. She was Elaine Albert, director of the Heaven Bound Cathedral's televised services, one of two women Aubrey was dying to interview, the one who clearly was there the night Buddy Wing tumbled into the fake palms, who clearly knew more about the goings-on backstage that night than anyone alive. Whatever she was saying about grape juice stains was going in one ear and out the other.

"Could we sit down?" I asked.

"Sure, please," Elaine said.

I lowered myself into the corner of a fat moss-green loveseat. "The both of us," I said.

She studied me quizzically and lowered her full hips next to me. I think she was afraid I was going to faint or be sick or something.

I pulled down one of the yellow pillows from the top of the loveseat and cradled it in my lap. I started telling her the biggest string of lies I'd ever told in my life. "I do need a sofa," I began, "but I'd also like to talk to you. You see, I'm Marcie Peacock's grandmother—she was one of the Kent State students working for you at the cathedral the night the Reverend Wing died."

Elaine started hugging her clipboard the way I was hugging the pillow. "And?"

"Well, she's scared to death. The newspaper is digging into the whole thing again, it seems, and they think maybe one of the students is the real killer. Apparently the paper has some proof that the woman who confessed really didn't do it. That reporter has my Marcie simply frantic."

A sympathetic smile stretched across Elaine's wide German face. "You know, your Marcie is the first African-American student we've ever hired."

I could have just died. Elaine Albert had recognized me the moment I walked in. I apologized and tried to explain myself. Why she didn't toss me out I don't know. Maybe it was my obvious agony. Maybe she wanted to see what kind of information she could wheedle out of me. "I am genuinely concerned about those students," I said. "Once the paper starts running its series, they are going to come under suspicion."

"Along with a lot of people," she said.

As we sat on that sofa and talked, I was not the least bit afraid that she might be the real murderer. And it wasn't because she'd passed the lie detector test the police gave her. There was just something about her. A strange mix of icy confidence and serenity. If she'd wanted Buddy Wing dead for some reason, in my estimation she was the kind of woman who'd just pull out a pistol and shoot him.

Anyway, Elaine told me all about the college students who worked there—not about them individually so much—but about the kinds of jobs they did and where they would be at any given time before, during and after the broadcasts. She didn't believe for the world one of them poisoned Buddy Wing.

"What about someone disguised to look like a college student?" I asked.

"It gets pretty crazy back there," she said. "Sure."

I actually bought the sofa we were sitting on, $885, yellow pillows included. "Does it surprise you that Sissy James may not be the killer?" I asked as we walked to the door.

"After your visit here today," she said, "nothing surprises me anymore."

I went home and said good-bye to that scruffy beige monstrosity in my living room. Then I called the newsroom. "Aubrey," I said. "You'll never guess who sold me a new sofa."

"I can't talk. They just found Ronny Doddridge, deader than a doornail."

◇◇◇

# Friday, June 16

Ronny Doddridge was the big-eared security guard at the Heaven Bound Cathedral. Aubrey and I had encountered him on our first visit there. He had showed us the way to Guthrie Gates' office. On our second visit he'd showed us the door. Because it was a suspected suicide, Aubrey's story was only nine short paragraphs:

## Cathedral security guard found dead after 9-1-1 call

HANNAWA—Police responding to a 9-1-1 call early yesterday morning found the body of 47-year-old Ronald "Ronny" Doddridge in his home on the city's near east side.

Police said it appears Doddridge made the emergency call himself before taking his own life. The West Virginia native had worked as a security guard for the Heaven Bound Cathedral since 1992.

Neighbors said Doddridge was not married and lived alone in the small, frame house he rented on Pulver Court.

Police said Doddridge died of a massive head wound. A 9 mm Smith & Wesson semi-automatic pistol was found next to his body, they said.

Police spokesman Lt. Benjamin Wiley said dispatchers received the 9-1-1 call at 3:22 a.m. Thursday. The caller, believed to be a middle-aged male, repeated three times that "A man's been shot," then hung up.

Dispatchers traced the call to Doddridge's home and officers arrived on the scene at 3:55 a.m. Wiley said Doddridge's body was found on the kitchen floor.

Wiley would not confirm that a suicide note was found, although a neighbor told the *Herald-Union* that officers responding to the 9-1-1 call told him they had found a note pinned to Doddridge's bathrobe.

The Rev. Guthrie Gates, pastor of the Heaven Bound Cathedral, issued a statement calling Doddridge "a good and decent man who took great honor in serving the Lord."

Aubrey was too busy to go to Speckley's for lunch. So we walked up to the Mr. Hero in the Geisselman Building. The temperature was in the eighties and that meant the downtown sidewalks were as hot as a waffle iron. We shared a foot-long ham and Swiss with brown mustard and tomato. We both bought pink lemonades. We sat in a window booth with closed Venetian blinds.

My stomach was so queasy I was just nibbling my half of the sandwich. "I have to tell you, Aubrey," I said, "this Doddridge thing really scares me."

She was chomping like a horse. "You don't think it was suicide? Come on—just by looking at him you could tell there was a lot of bad stuff going on inside his head."

"That's exactly my point, Aubrey. Maybe he knew something about Buddy Wing's death. Or had some strong suspicions he was sharing with others at the church. And maybe that worried the real killer. Somebody clever enough to poison Wing the way he did, and pin it on Sissy with all that evidence, easily could've made Doddridge's death look like a suicide."

"And you think maybe the murderer will keep killing. Ronny Doddridge. Aubrey McGinty. Dolly Madison Sprowls, maybe?"

"It's crossed my mind."

She dismissed my fears by taking another enormous bite from her half of the sandwich.

"I'd think it would cross yours, too. You're being followed. Your car windows have been—"

"And I've been slapped around and threatened. But this really looks like an honest-to-God suicide."

"You're awfully nonchalant about all this."

"What I am is awfully hungry," she said.

I let the subject drop and watched her chew. She was not only hungry. She was exhausted. She'd spent all morning trying to follow up on the Doddridge story, with little success. The police were still freezing her out over the ruckus her stories on the chief's reorganization plan caused. I'm sure whatever information she was getting was coming from disgruntled officers far down the food chain, information that had to be checked and double-checked. "Any idea what the suicide note said?" I asked.

"I can't confirm it yet," she said, "but Doddridge apparently apologized to the congregation for not protecting Buddy Wing better."

I wrapped my half of the sandwich and wedged it into my purse. I'd try to eat it later. "This is all getting so complicated."

Aubrey took a long, noisy drag on her lemonade. "So, Maddy, tell me about that new sofa."

# 16

**Thursday, June 22**

On Tuesday, the county coroner ruled Ronny Doddridge's death a suicide. On Wednesday, Aubrey came back from police headquarters with a copy of the suicide note. It was written directly to the Reverend Buddy Wing:

> *Dear pastor,*
>
> *I am so sorry I let you down. Surely I am going down to hell where I deserve to be. When the devils came back to get you I was hiding like a school boy to smoke a cigarette, as I am sure both you and Jesus already know. I was born no good and remain so.*
>
> *Ronald James Doddridge*

A powerful note. Unfortunately we could not run it word for word, not while the case was still open. And even though the coroner had rendered his expert judgment, the police would take their good time—six months or more—before officially proclaiming that Doddridge took his life without undue or illegal interference of another person or party. So for her Thursday story Aubrey had to paraphrase:

## Doddridge out for smoke night Rev. Wing poisoned

HANNAWA—Before putting a pistol to his head last Thursday, Heaven Bound Cathedral security guard Ronald "Ronny" Doddridge wrote a note apologizing for taking an unauthorized cigarette break the night the Rev. Buddy Wing was fatally poisoned.

According to sources close to the police investigation, the note was addressed directly to Wing and began with the salutation, "Dear pastor."

SEE NOTE PAGE A9

It was another good story. Having encountered Ronny Doddridge herself, on those two occasions, she was able to describe his appearance and mannerisms to a tee. She talked to his neighbors again about his daily habits, getting a measure of his friendliness. "He was something of a loner," said the woman who lived across the street, "but when you waved at him he'd always wave back."

Aubrey also talked to the eyebrow woman, who confirmed, off the record of course, that Doddridge, like herself, was indeed a secret smoker.

Aubrey also talked to Guthrie Gates.

Well, Gates had to talk to her, didn't he? The security guard at his church had not only killed himself, he'd also pried open two old cans of worms: Buddy Wing's murder and the rift between Buddy and Tim Bandicoot.

Aubrey interviewed Gates on the phone, long after I'd gone home for the day, so I have no way of knowing exactly what she asked him. But given his answers, she had clearly asked him what he thought Ronny Doddridge meant by "when the devils came back to get you."

"We preach belief in a literal devil," she quoted Gates as saying, "though I can't say by the note whether Ronny was speaking literally or metaphorically. But there's no doubt Pastor Wing's murderer was possessed by the devil in some way. I only wish I'd known brother Ronny was hurting so."

Before work on Thursday morning, I met Aubrey at Ike's. We got our coffee and tea to go and walked up to the reading garden at the main library. We sat across from the pink metal monstrosity by the famed Cincinnati sculptor Donald Raintree Tubb, a blindfolded pig gleefully riding a bicycle made entirely of sausage links. "So, are we still buying the suicide note?" I asked.

"I think we are," she said. "The handwriting comparisons and the motive all seem to add up."

I sucked a tiny of taste of tea through the slit in the plastic lid on my paper cup. "Then assuming the note is legit—what exactly does it tell us?"

Aubrey had been staring at the pig on the bicycle. Now she turned her face toward me, the breeze off empty Central Avenue plastering her loose red hair across her eyes. "You read my story, right? When I asked Gates what he thought *when the devils came back to get you* meant, he immediately reduced it to one devil. But Ronny had said devils."

"You think Ronny meant real devils?"

"Real human devils. Devils that came back—meaning they'd been there before."

"Let me guess—the devils who'd been there before are Tim Bandicoot and his followers, the ones who pooh-poohed Buddy's talking in tongues."

"That would be my guess."

"And you think Doddridge knew that for sure?"

"No way of knowing. But Ronny Doddridge wasn't as dumb as he looked."

No he wasn't. Aubrey's story on him had surprised me totally. Ronny Doddridge wasn't just some poor sap in the church who needed a job. For fourteen years, he'd been a deputy sheriff in Mineral County, West Virginia. Six months after he was forced to resign for repeatedly drinking beer in his patrol car, Buddy Wing brought him to Hannawa as the Heaven Bound Cathedral's first security guard. Ronny was the nephew of Buddy's dead wife. But there was apparently more to it than family obligation. Buddy hired him just five months before the very public flap that sent Tim Bandicoot and two hundred members of his flock off to that abandoned Woolworth's store on Lutheran Hill. Buddy Wing knew there was going to be trouble and wanted someone loyal, and maybe experienced with a gun, to watch his back.

Aubrey showed me her watch. It was almost ten. We left the bicycling pig and headed up the hill toward the *Herald-Union*. "It just doesn't make any sense," I said. "Why would Doddridge kill himself if he was onto something? Wouldn't he take what he knew to the police? Or Guthrie Gates? Or you? Why would he just scribble that cryptic little hint about devils coming back and then shoot himself in the head?"

"Overwrought with guilt?" she ventured.

"Not so overwrought to leave a big hint," I said.

Aubrey put her arm around me, like I was a silly child. "You really don't think he killed himself, do you?"

"I don't know what I think," I said. Then I promptly told her exactly what I thought: "The real killer has already framed Sissy James. But now you're about to prove her innocent. That will mean an all-out investigation by a police department with egg on its face. So the killer kills again, preemptively pointing the police in the wrong direction, toward someone in Tim Bandicoot's church. The killer has already scattered some new evidence around probably, just like he did with Sissy—probably."

Aubrey laughed. "My oh my. Aren't you the super sleuth."

"You don't think it's possible?"

"I think it's possible."

We stopped at Central and North Smiley and waited for the WALK sign. I used the opportunity to slide out from under Aubrey's arm. We were only a block from the paper and the last thing I wanted was for one of my many enemies in the newsroom to catch me being palsy-walsy with a reporter. To protect one's image, one must be always vigilant.

We reached the paper and used the street entrance, something employees rarely do. We greeted Al Tosi, the day security man at the desk, and rode the elevator to the newsroom. "So what's on your agenda?" I asked Aubrey before we went our separate ways.

Alec Tinker's voice ambushed us. "Ladies!"

"Ladies?" Aubrey shriekcd playfully. "Someone's not reading their sexual harassment handbook."

He pressed his palms together prayerfully and bowed apologetically.

"Or the religious practices handbook," I added.

He told us that Tim Bandicoot and Guthrie Gates were coming in at one, together, to discuss Aubrey's investigation. "And you're invited, too, Maddy."

"Good gravy," I said, "why am I invited?"

The meeting was held in Bob Averill's office on the fifth floor. It's a long, sterile office, huge round window at one end, display case filled with old Underwood typewriters at the other. The gray walls in between are lined with a century's worth of important front pages: the Japanese surrender, men walking on the moon, the Kennedy assassination, the violent UAW strike of 1958 (which my Lawrence covered), the 1908 school fire that killed forty-two children, a couple dozen pages in all. Bob doesn't have a desk, just a glass-top coffee table circled by comfortable leather chairs. The coffee table that afternoon held what it always holds: the most recent edition of the paper, neatly folded, and an aloe plant in a green ceramic bowl.

Tim Bandicoot and Guthrie Gates were already sitting when Aubrey and I arrived. So was Tinker. So was Bob. We sat down quickly and nodded pleasantly to everyone.

I never felt so out of place in my life. Bob was wearing an expensive suit about the same shade as his walls. Tinker had worn one of his better suits for the occasion, dark blue with red pinstripes, meaning he knew that Gates and Bandicoot were coming in at least a day in advance, while only giving us three hours' warning. The two evangelists, usually resplendent in white double-breasted suits with wide zig-zaggy neckties, were both dressed in charcoal. Aubrey, for her part, was wearing a snug pair of faded jeans and a sleeveless red blouse. I was wearing my absolutely worst-fitting pair of khakis and a T-shirt with a Canada goose on the front that I'd bought years ago on a vacation to Mackinac Island. Aubrey's jeans won out over my goose as the focal point for the four important men in suits.

"I understand you have some concerns?" Bob said to Tim and Guthrie when our nodding was completed.

They grinned bravely at each other, and Guthrie said, "Yes, we do."

Their concern, of course, was Aubrey's upcoming series on the Buddy Wing murder. They were fearful—that's the word Tim used, *fearful*—that Aubrey had mistakenly gotten the impression that the two congregations were unfriendly toward each other.

"The fact of the matter," Tim said, "is that Guthrie and I have been brothers in the Lamb for many years. While some feathers were ruffled, years and years ago, that is all behind us now. Relations between our congregations could not be better."

"Quite copacetic," Guthrie added.

I quickly swallowed the giggle that was suddenly dancing on my tongue. Instead I made this horrible noise, as if I was blowing my nose without a handkerchief. It was that word *copacetic*. Imagine that old be-bop jazz word coming out of the mouth of Guthrie Gates. Back in my college days it was big word among the Meriwether Square crowd. Everything then was either "copacetic" or "most copacetic."

"You okay?" Bob asked me.

"I'm fine," I said, wishing I'd had the nerve to say everything was copacetic.

Tinker looked at Bob for permission, and then, apparently getting it through some telepathic process taught to the newspaper chain's muckety mucks, reassured the two visitors that the *Herald-Union's* intentions were not to stir up trouble between the two churches. "We can't be too specific, as I'm sure you can appreciate," he said, "but we have some evidence that Sissy James did not murder Buddy Wing. When we publish what we've found—if we publish—there's been no final decision in that regard—our stories will pertain only to the murder."

It was a cautiously worded bit of corporate boilerplate that Aubrey simply couldn't let stand. "Of course, when a newspaper publishes any story, it's our duty to put things in context," she added.

Tim Bandicoot frowned sourly. "Context can mean a lot of things," he said.

"We'd like whatever assurances you can give us that Miss McGinty won't dredge up any more than's necessary," Guthrie added.

Bob shifted from his left buttock to his right. "We don't dredge, gentlemen, we report."

It was the appropriate thing for an editor-in-chief to say, of course, but dredge is what newspapers do, and should do.

Guthrie was repentant. "I shouldn't have said dredge."

Tim was not. "Your paper, Mr. Averill, has a history of treating religion like it belongs on the sports pages. Hallelujah City. All that stuff."

Bob set himself square on both buttocks. "We did not coin that phrase, Mr. Bandicoot. That was that radio guy—Charlie Chimera."

"You've certainly repeated it enough times," Tim Bandicoot said.

Bob pawed the air. "Everybody's repeated it—but the point is, the *Herald-Union* is not anti-religion." He then explained our earlier coverage of the split between Tim and Buddy Wing. "Buddy was a very public figure, not only locally but nationally. And when a very public figure does very public things, like casting an assistant pastor out of his congregation during a live television broadcast, that is going to be reported."

Bob had hit a nerve with Guthrie Gates. "Pastor Wing did not cast Tim out. He merely said that the gift of tongues was about to come over him and that all who might be offended should listen elsewhere."

Tim Bandicoot leaned forward and clasped his hands together. He closed his eyes. But he did not pray. He growled slowly like a Doberman strapped into a muzzle. "Guthrie, I was never offended when Buddy spoke in tongues. We simply had a difference of opinion."

Guthrie held up his hands and spread his fingers in surrender. "Sorry. I've gotten us off track."

I can't say if Tim was prepared to let the matter rest. But Aubrey sure wasn't. She leaned back and crossed her legs like a man, wrapping her hands around her pointing knee. "It's more than a difference of opinion, isn't it? It's a fundamental difference in belief. Buddy believed that speaking in tongues was proof of being baptized in the Holy Spirit. And those who didn't, weren't. That's what you believe, too, isn't it, Guthrie?"

He nodded nervously. "But it has nothing to do with Buddy's death."

"Whether it does or it doesn't," said Aubrey, "it's part of the big picture that we have to report."

Guthrie pushed back his bangs. They were beginning to turn dark with perspiration. "I don't see why."

Tinker was about ready to say something diplomatic to keep the conversation dull and businesslike. Bob, however, did his Richard Nixon impersonation, dropping his eyebrows and shaking his jowls, a signal to let Aubrey keep going. Which she did.

"Well," she said, "the woman now in prison for Buddy's murder was one of those two hundred people who followed Tim out of the cathedral. And the one Tim was sleeping with, to boot."

"There's no reason to go there," Guthrie pleaded. He seemed oddly more uncomfortable with Tim's carnal sins than Tim himself.

Aubrey ignored him. "So, if Sissy James is innocent, then somebody set her up. Somebody who knew about the affair. Somebody who knew his or her way around the cathedral. Somebody with a most wicked sense of humor—big glob of poison right on Buddy Wing's wagging old tongue. How can we not print all that?"

Guthrie came out of his leather chair like a jack-in-the-box. "You are not a police officer, Miss McGinty. You are not judge and jury. You're just some damn little—"

Aubrey's lips thinned and tightened. "Reporter?" she asked. "Or were you going to say girl?"

I was sure Bob or Tinker would say something now. But neither did. They let Aubrey say whatever she wanted.

"We are not going to point fingers, and we are not going to pass judgment on anyone," she said. "We are just going to report."

"And embarrass a lot of good people," Tim said softly.

"If people in your congregations are embarrassed," Aubrey answered just as softly, "it will be from the embarrassing things other people in your congregations did."

Guthrie, still standing, issued a mean-spirited "A-men." Tim knew it was aimed at him. He sprang out of his leather chair and pushed Guthrie back into his.

Tim Bandicoot and Guthrie Gates had come into Bob Averill's office as brothers and were now acting like it. They crashed into each other like two bull walruses competing for a dewy-eyed cow on a rocky beach in the North Atlantic. There wasn't any punching or swearing, just pushing and an occasional growl from deep inside their straining guts.

Bob Averill, the veteran of so many heated discussions in his office, went to his phone and called security. Tinker, a managing editor who someday hoped to be an editor-in-chief just like Bob Averill, pulled the coffee table out of the way, saving the aloe plant and the neatly folded copy of that morning's paper. Aubrey and I stayed put in our leather chairs and tried not to pee our pants laughing.

The hatred between Tim Bandicoot and Guthrie Gates was understandable. They were both bright and ambitious young men. They'd found themselves under the same roof, climbing the same ladder. Two heirs, one throne. What good was going to come of that? So if that speaking in tongues business hadn't erupted, something else would have come along to drive one of them out. But the tongues business did erupt. And it turned a nasty sibling rivalry into an even nastier battle between an aging father and an errant son.

That rift between Buddy and Tim was hardly small potatoes. It was a big, big deal. When Aubrey first started looking into the murder, I went to Nanette Beane, the paper's religion editor, and asked her what she knew about speaking in tongues. Well, naturally, she didn't know diddly. Before becoming religion editor she'd been the food editor and before that she'd covered suburban school board meetings. But she did have a number of reference books strung across the back of her desk and she found one called *The Fundamentals of Fundamentalism* and it contained a chapter on the subject.

Buddy Wing was a Pentecostal.

Pentecost—I have to admit I didn't know this—was the seventh Sunday after Jesus's resurrection, when he appeared before his disciples. They were so filled with the Holy Spirit they began to speak in tongues, the Bible says. So that's what Pentecostals still do today: They fill themselves with the spirit and say things no one but God understands.

Some Pentecostals believe different people are given different gifts—so if you don't speak in tongues, that's okay, you can still get into heaven. Others are not so forgiving: If you don't have the gift of tongues you aren't really saved. Buddy Wing apparently fell into that second group. So when Tim Bandicoot came back from Bible college, his head brimming with theological flexibility, and started suggesting that the Heaven Bound Cathedral might do better in the here-and-now, television viewer-wise, if Buddy toned down a few of his more controversial practices, like healing people through the television screen, like handling rattlesnakes every year on his birthday, or like speaking in tongues, well, you can only imagine what Buddy thought.

Tim had grown up in the church. His parents were original members of the Clean Collar Club. He was the son Buddy never had. I'm sure Buddy tried everything he could to correct Tim's errant thinking. At some point he must have realized it wasn't going to happen and he brought in Guthrie Gates and began grooming him.

Why didn't Buddy just send Tim on his merry way, to start his own church, to spread the good word in his own way? Maybe he had tried to do that. Maybe Tim wouldn't leave gracefully. Maybe Tim had the power of his convictions and was determined to stay and fight. Maybe Tim, religiously speaking, knew a cash cow when he saw one and wasn't about to walk away. Maybe Guthrie's sudden appearance as a rival only stiffened Tim's resolve. Who knows what kind of psychological stuff was going on inside, and among, Tim Bandicoot, Guthrie Gates and the Rev. Buddy Wing?

All we know is that things slowly came to a head, and one night, with the television cameras grinding away, Buddy Wing cast Tim Bandicoot from his flock.

The fancy Greek word for speaking in tongues, by the way, is glossolalia: *glossai* means tongue, *lalein* means to babble. But what believers speak is not Greek. It is a heavenly language, perhaps the language spoken by the angels, or God himself. When humans speak it, they have no idea what they are saying. When humans hear it, they have no idea what they're hearing. They are simply in the spirit.

"*Shalbala-she-shalbala,*" Buddy cried out from his pulpit the night he cast out Tim Bandicoot. "The gift of tongues has come over me. All who might be offended better listen elsewhere. *She-shalbala-shebendula-shebendula.* Out of this holy place you who reject the gift, you who pretend to be saved." His finger surveyed the congregation, the choir and the dancers and the orchestra, and like the jittery needle on a compass found Tim Bandicoot seated alongside Guthrie Gates in the row of huge gold chairs behind his pulpit.

Can you imagine the humiliation felt by the two hundred who retreated toward the exit signs that night? Can you imagine the self-righteousness felt by the thousand who applauded them out?

◇◇◇

Tim Bandicoot and Guthrie Gates left as they'd come—together. Except this time the *Herald-Union's* own version of Ronny Doddridge, day shift security guard Al Tosi, who stood five-six and weighed four pounds for every one of his sixty-two years, was waddling behind them. Both Tim and Guthrie were crying.

Tim had apologized profusely after the shoving match. Guthrie had only sniffled indignantly, "I suppose you're going to print this, too?"

Which was a good question. Was their meeting in Bob Averill's office off the record? Or was it fair fodder for Aubrey's series—to help give context to the rift between the tongue-speaking followers of the Rev. Guthrie Gates and the non-glossolalianites in the Rev. Tim Bandicoot's New Epiphany Temple?

# 17

As soon as I got to my desk Aubrey motioned for me to come to hers. I hurried across the newsroom, tea bag still soaking in my mug. "Can't you wait until a woman's awake?" I complained.

She wanted me to hear the message on her phone. She handed me the receiver and punched the replay button. The voice was precise and sweet in the phoniest way:

> *Aubrey...this is Annie Bandicoot. Something really important is going to happen Sunday at Tim's church. And I thought you might want to be there. Services start at ten...bye-bye.*

Aubrey put her hands behind her head and swiveled back and forth in her chair. With her elbows sticking out like that she looked like an angel ornament swinging from a Christmas tree. Her smile was absolutely Satanic. "What do you make of that?" she asked me.

"Assuming it was really Annie Bandicoot?"

"Yeah. Assuming that."

"Then I'd say something important is going to happen. Something they want reported."

"They? Or just Annie? Remember what she said: 'I thought you might want to be there.' *I* thought, not *we* thought."

Dangling tea bag or no, I took a sip from my mug. "It's probably innocent enough. But it does make you wonder why Annie made the call and not Tim, doesn't it?"

"So many possibilities, Maddy: Tim is so distraught after his little shoving match with Guthrie Gates that wifey-poo has to do his dirty work. Or wifey-poo, tired of seeing her man muck things up, takes matters in her own hands. Or maybe the Bandicoots are in cahoots, going on the offensive together to cover their guilt."

"Bandicoots in cahoots," I said. "I like that."

She ignored me. "Maybe that wasn't Annie Bandicoot on the phone at all. Maybe that was someone from Guthrie's church, wanting me to show up at Tim's church, so Tim would see me and go off on me and look like a complete jerk, which I would dutifully include in my series."

I had a possibility of my own: "Maybe somebody's going to spike Tim's water pitcher."

Aubrey turned her wings back into arms and silently applauded my deductive powers. "Whatever's going to happen, you and I, Dolly Madison Sprowls, are going to church Sunday."

## Friday, June 30

Eric finally came out of his funk and completed the computer search on Edward Tolchak, the neighbor who kept shooting out the Heaven Bound Cathedral's parking lot lights. Unfortunately, as Aubrey already had surmised, the search came up with nothing useful. After getting out of jail for the third time, Tolchak had filed a civil suit against the Heaven Bound Cathedral. The cathedral settled out of court, removing two of the light poles, installing Venetian blinds on Tolchak's windows, planting a row of blue spruce along his property line and paying him $25,000 for the mental anguish he'd suffered. I gave the findings to Aubrey.

◇◇◇

# Sunday, July 2

Sunday morning Aubrey and I drove to Lutheran Hill. So did the man in the red Taurus station wagon. We spotted him behind us shortly after Aubrey picked me up. "Do you think Annie Bandicoot left a message on his phone, too?" Aubrey asked. She was neither angry nor afraid. Not even anxious. She was enjoying all this.

When we reached the New Epiphany Temple and pulled into the gravel parking lot, the man in the station wagon made a quick turn onto a side street and parked. He was protecting his license plate number like it was the secret formula for Coca-Cola.

The old Woolworth's store was filled to the gills. We found a pair of empty chairs near the back. Aubrey nudged me and pointed at the huge cross behind the pulpit. It was twinkling.

A quintet of musicians took their positions in the corner and started playing—two guitars, trumpet, drums and an electric piano. People started clapping in time. Many were rocking their shoulders and bobbing their heads. I noticed I was tapping my toes. Then Aubrey took a camera out of her purse and put it in her lap. "Good gravy," I whispered, "you're not going to take pictures, are you?"

"I was asked to come and cover an important event. Of course I'm going to take pictures."

"You start snapping that thing during the service and they'll descend on us like a plague of locusts."

No sooner said, the back door swung wide and a muscle-bound man with a backwards baseball cap and a television camera on his shoulder slid inside. Behind him was Tish Kiddle. Aubrey hissed "television whore" loud enough for half the congregation to hear.

The thrones on the stage suddenly filled up with elders. A couple dozen people from the congregation filtered to the stage and sang this absolutely wild hymn that sounded an awful lot like the Isley's Brothers' *Do You Love Me?*

Then Tim and Annie Bandicoot appeared at the pulpit together. The congregation seemed to shrivel. Clearly this is not what usually happened at the temple's Sunday morning service. Annie lovingly rubbed her husband's shoulder and then stepped to the microphone. She said this: "Tim is going to talk to you, and I want you to know that what he is going to say, he has already said to me, and to our children. I want you to know that we love him and trust him and believe in him. And we believe in you."

Then she said this: "Jesus said to the Pharisees, 'He that is without sin among you, let him first cast a stone.' So should you decide to cast stones at my husband when this is finished, I will be standing at his side."

Aubrey looked at me and mouthed that line from the Tammy Wynette song, *Stand By Your Man*.

It was clear where this whole thing was going. Jesus had said that cast-the-first-stone stuff to the Pharisees after they brought a woman to him charged with adultery, and reminded him that the punishment under the old laws of Moses was death by stoning.

Tim Bandicoot hugged his wife and stepped to the microphone. "I am guilty of the sin of adultery. And it was with a woman you all know. A woman who today sits in prison, for the murder of our beloved Buddy Wing."

Aubrey finished scribbling the quote and then snapped a series of photographs.

Tim's confession was filled with tears and whimpering and loud prayers peppered with scripture. There was plenty of crying in the audience, too. Every now and then someone would pop from their folding chair and implore him to "Go and sin no more"—the same thing Jesus said to the woman after he'd saved her from the Pharisees' stones.

I must say that Tim Bandicoot's agony looked genuine to me. And I have some experience with the agony of unfaithful men: Dale Marabout's, when I found him on the floor with the kindergarten teacher; my husband Lawrence's, when I found him in the garage with the secretary from the labor union. I could tell from Aubrey's frozen smirk that she did not believe Tim Bandicoot's contrition was for real.

But then he said this: "There are those who believe Sissy did not kill Pastor Wing. There are those who believe Sissy confessed to that terrible sin to protect me. Though I surely broke Buddy's heart, I did not stop it from beating. I did not kill Buddy Wing."

He started to cry again, and shake. Annie took him in her arms and they swayed like wind chimes. To get a better angle, Aubrey slid into the aisle and sank to her knees, clicking off more shots.

Tim gently pushed his wife away and, with arms stiffly anchored on his pulpit, directly addressed the long-legged reporter kneeling in the aisle. "I do not know if Sissy is innocent or guilty, Miss McGinty. But I will go to her prison cell, and I will beg that if she has not spoken the truth, she speaks it now."

Tim and Annie left the stage. Aubrey tried to follow them into the hallway behind the stage, but a large black man in a brown suit stopped her. The musicians started playing and the choir started singing. The congregation clapped and danced and the tears poured.

Aubrey and I trotted out the door like the hyenas we were. Tish Kiddle and her cameraman were right behind us.

"That sneaky bitch," Aubrey fumed as we hurried to her Escort.

I was not sure who she meant. "Tish Kiddle or Annie Bandicoot?"

She fumbled through her purse for her car keys. "Try to keep the objects of my disdain straight, Maddy. Tish is the whore. Annie is the sneaky bitch."

"Does it really surprise you they invited Channel 21, too?"

"This is my story, Maddy."

"I think the Bandicoots consider it their story," I said.

Aubrey glowered at me—as if I was guilty of something. "It's because of my digging that they're in this spot. You'd think they'd respect that."

"I don't think protecting your scoop is very high on their list of worries."

Aubrey mellowed. She giggled at her own arrogance. "It should be."

We sped past the church. The red Taurus station wagon pulled from the side street and followed us.

I understood why Aubrey was livid. It *was* her story. She'd spent weeks researching the murder, wheedling information out of one reluctant source after another. For weeks she'd seen that fat, black Page One headline in her head:

```
Did Sissy really
kill Buddy Wing?
```

Now Tish Kiddle would be breaking her story on tonight's TV news.

I did all I could to comfort her. "They'll lead with it tonight—unless there was some terrible accident on the interstate—but they won't have any details, or any background. After tonight they'll just be reporting what you've already reported."

Aubrey fished through her purse for her cellphone and thumbed in a number. "How do those TV people live with themselves . . . Tinker? Sorry to call you at home on Sunday."

There was no time to drive me home. We went straight to the paper and Aubrey spent the next five hours writing her story. And while she wrote, Tinker, who'd rushed to the news-room in musty jogging shorts and a Cleveland Indians T-shirt, lorded over the weekend skeleton crew on the metro desk. The story would run across the top of Page One. Tim Bandicoot's confession to adultery would be the main thrust of the story, but it would state very clearly in the second paragraph that the public admission came in the wake of an ongoing *Herald-Union* investigation into the murder of Buddy Wing. We were going to be scooped by the local TV news, but we would push, and push hard, whatever advantage we had. We would let our readers know, and not in a shy way, that while TV 21 simply stumbled into the story, we uncovered the story, that Tim Bandicoot was confessing for one reason and one reason only, because of the *Herald-Union*'s dogged journalistic excellence.

Aubrey's photos came out pretty good. Tinker chose one of Tim and Annie hugging. He told the make-up editor to blow it up big. And run it in color. And crop it tight, so every wrinkle of agony on Tim's face showed, so the wedding ring on Annie's hand showed. The headline on the story was plain and powerful:

```
Preacher confesses to affair
  with convicted murderess
```

While Aubrey was writing, and frantically trying to get her sources on the phone, including Guthrie Gates, Tinker dragged me off to the cafeteria. We shared a piece of stale carrot cake from the vending machine. He asked me for my impression of Tim Bandicoot's confession, not once but five times. He was pumped up about the story but also worried. Originally Aubrey was supposed to continue her investigation for another month, and then take another two or three weeks to write her stories. The stories would be run by the paper's lawyers and discussed ad nauseam in editorial meetings. The graphics people were going to design a special logo to go with the stories, a Bible with a dripping cross.

But now, thanks to Annie Bandicoot, Aubrey would not only have to start writing her stories right away, we'd have to start running them right away. It was going to be a crazy couple of weeks.

Just as Tinker and I were playfully fighting over the little sugar carrot on the cake, Bob Averill poked his head in the cafeteria. He pointed at Tinker and motioned for him to follow. To me he said, "Enjoy your snack."

At six everybody gathered around the television in the conference room to watch the news, 21 at Six. Tish Kiddle, reporting live from the dark and empty church, had almost nothing:

"Members of the New Epiphany Temple remain in utter shock tonight following the unexpected confession by the Rev. Tim Bandicoot that he'd had a long sexual relationship with Sissy James, the confessed murderer of Bandicoot's old mentor, nationally known evangelist Buddy Wing."

After weekend anchorwoman Jamie Stokes said, "Oh my," and weekend anchorman Bill Callucci said, "What more can you tell us, Tish?" Tish said, "TV 21 has learned—and TV 21 is the first to report this—that new evidence may have surfaced suggesting that Sissy James may not be the real killer."

Jamie Stokes asked Tish to, "Keep us posted." To which Tish promised, "I'll be working through the evening on this exclusive breaking story and I'll have the very latest on 21 at Eleven."

"We'll look forward to it," Bill Callucci said. Swiveling in his chair to take advantage of a new camera angle, he said, "Speaking of confessions, I must confess my weakness for blueberry pie." It was his segue into TV 21's coverage of the Bowenville Blueberry Festival.

When Aubrey finished writing her story, Tinker and Bob took her upstairs for another two hours of planning. It was eight o'clock before she came down, sticky with exhaustion. She apologized profusely for stranding me at the paper all day. We drove to Lipini's for pizza and then at nine started for my house.

When I drive home at night I always take West Tuckman. It's wide and well-lighted and the neighborhoods for the most part are safe. Aubrey that night took West Apple, which, although a much straighter shot across town, slices through some very iffy neighborhoods. It even intersects with infamous Morrow Street, where the hookers Aubrey wrote about do their business.

While her old Escort looked a lot worse than it drove, I was still nervous and checked the door locks I don't know how many times. That got on Aubrey's nerves. "Will you just relax?"

That's about when the flashing blue lights appeared in the rear-view mirror and Aubrey hissed the f-word. She slowed down until the lights were right behind us, then pulled into an abandoned gas station. We were just two short, dark, rundown blocks from Morrow Street. "Be careful," I said. "Two years ago some nut pretending to be a cop raped six women before he was caught."

Aubrey adjusted her mirror and studied the car pulling in behind us. "Looks like the real deal," she said.

"So did the rapist's car," I said.

"Will you just stop it, Maddy? I've been going through red lights since we left the paper."

Aubrey was reacting calmly, though I did notice that she still had the car in gear, to speed off, I suppose, if it wasn't a real police officer—not that a Ford Escort is actually capable of speeding off.

The officer was suddenly at Aubrey's door, rapping on her window with his knuckles. She opened her window about three inches. The jibber-jabber of the police radio on his belt calmed me a little, but I still kept my hand on the door latch in case I had to go running into the night and hide in a dumpster or something. "Sorry to say you went through a couple of red lights, ma'am," the officer said. He was young and chubby and friendly looking. "May I see your license and registration?"

Aubrey dug them out of her purse. The officer thanked her and took them back to his cruiser.

"I've been through this routine a billion times," Aubrey said, finally turning off her engine. "He'll come back in three minutes and say, 'Ma'am, this isn't the best of streets at night, and I know you were probably nervous. So I'm going to let it go. Take West Tuckman next time.'"

"Which you should have," I said.

Fifteen minutes later we were still waiting and Aubrey was hissing the f-word again.

Another police car pulled in. Its lights were not blinking. The two officers conferred for a minute or two, then strolled side by side to Aubrey's car. "Would you please step out, Miss McGinty?" the newly arrived officer said. "You too, ma'am."

We got out. The friendly chubby officer gave Aubrey her license and registration and retreated to his car. We were alone with the new officer.

We recognized him immediately. It was 3rd District Commander Lionel Percy. He was not a tall man but he was muscular. He was wearing his hat but you could see around his temples that his head was shaved. His uniform was impeccable, as if he'd just taken it out of the dry-cleaning bag.

"How lucky can a man get," he said, "the famous Aubrey McGinty running red lights in my district."

"Let me guess," Aubrey answered. "You're going to put the fear of God in me."

"It is good to fear God," he said.

Aubrey smiled and tucked her fingers under her arms defiantly. "Especially when he's in uniform?"

"Cute," he said.

"And so are you," she said, trumping him again.

I could see the frustration in Percy's eyes. He'd undoubtedly been waiting for this chance to intimidate Aubrey for weeks. Her stories on the police reorganization plan, and then on his district's prostitution problem, had caused him a lot of grief with the mayor and City Council. And now he had her trapped in an abandoned gas station, on a dark empty night, and lo-and-behold, she was giving back better than he was giving. He must have been going nuts inside.

Percy tried again. "You know Miss McGinty, I've been a police officer in this city longer than you've been alive—"

"Which ought to bring you pretty close to retirement age," Aubrey said.

"—and I've suffered through my share of newspaper reporters. Squeaky clean white kids from the suburbs. For you, the inner city is just a place to play make-believe. Write about all the shitty things the degenerate city people do to each other. Prove your moral superiority. Make mama and daddy proud. Win a bunch of *journalism* awards you can roll up and diddle yourself with."

"That's pretty much why I do it," Aubrey said.

"Write what you want, Miss McGinty. The mayor's going to howl and the council's going to squeal, and the chief's going to salute and click his heels. But nothing's going to happen. Lionel Percy is, and will remain, commander of the 3rd District. And you'll be left dangling out there all alone, lots and lots of people mad at you."

Aubrey slowly opened her car door and leaned on it. Even leaning she was taller than Lionel Percy. "And you won't come riding to my rescue? How disappointing."

I hurried around to my side of the car. Our doors slammed at the same time. Aubrey put the key in the ignition and closed her eyes. "Please start," she said.

The Escort did start and we chugged away. "Now wasn't that something," Aubrey said coolly. Her long legs were shaking.

# 18

**Monday, July 3**

Aubrey started calling Marysville at a quarter to eight Monday morning. She was hoping that some efficient soul in the warden's office would pick up the phone before starting time. She did not want Tish Kiddle talking to Sissy before she did.

At three that afternoon she was still trying to get past the voice mail. At five she finally spoke to a real live person and made her request for a visitation.

TV 21 did a follow-up story on its six o'clock, news. Tish had nothing new, just old footage of Buddy Wing staggering backward into the fake palms. "What are the police saying?" anchorman Bill Callucci asked Tish as she stood in the empty parking lot at the Heaven Bound Cathedral. "Well Bill, in an exclusive interview with TV 21, Hannawa Police Chief Donald Polceznec told us exclusively that his department has no plans to reopen their investigation—at this time."

"So they might reopen it in the future?" asked anchorwoman Jamie Stokes.

"That's clearly a possibility," Tish answered.

"And you'll keep us posted?" Bill Callucci asked.

"Will do," answered Tish.

Tish's lazy reporting delighted Aubrey. Tinker, too.

Aubrey's story for Tuesday reported that while police stated publicly they had no immediate plans for reopening the case, the *Herald-Union* had learned that Chief Polceznec had asked the department's top homicide detective Scotty Grant to review Tim Bandicoot's statements to see if a further investigation was warranted.

◇◇◇

## Tuesday, July 4

Having to wait out the holiday drove Aubrey crazy. But actually it was something of a blessing. It gave her a long, uninterrupted day to start writing her series. I spent the day at home, weeding and napping, and after the sun went down, listening to the dogs in the neighborhood bark every time some damn kid lit a cherry bomb.

◇◇◇

## Wednesday, July 5

After a long day of furious writing and frustrating phone calls, Aubrey finally heard from the prison. "Sorry," the woman in the warden's office said. "Sissy James does not wish to see you at this time."

Aubrey went immediately to Tinker, who immediately took her upstairs to see Bob Averill. An enormous decision had to be made. Should the paper go ahead with a full-blown series as planned? Without Sissy's admission that she didn't kill Buddy Wing? Or would it be wise to scale things down? Run a story here and there? Over the months pile fact upon fact like a many layered Dobosh torte, until the police were forced to reopen the case?

During their meeting, Bob excused himself on the pretense of having to use the restroom and called me in the morgue. "This is very important, Maddy. When you went with Aubrey to Mingo Junction—you personally heard Sissy's cousin say that she was there all weekend?"

"I was standing right next to Aubrey," I said.

"You're absolutely sure? We could look awfully foolish if our journalistic ducks—"

"They're in a row, Bob."

"So, you're sure?"

"Good gravy, Bob."

So the decision was made. We'd still go with the full-blown series, starting on the following Wednesday. That would give Aubrey one week. If she got through to Sissy James, good. If she couldn't, then we'd go with what we had.

## Thursday, July 6

I put in an extra hour at my desk doing nothing then drove home. I covered a frozen chicken patty with bottled spaghetti sauce and Parmesan cheese and baked it in the oven for fifteen minutes. I poured a warm can of Squirt over a tumbler of ice cubes. I had my dinner on the back porch, watching what I hoped were rain clouds rolling in from the west. My lawn and flower beds desperately needed a soaking.

I felt so alone sitting there. And angry at myself because I did.

I'd lived by myself since 1963, when Lawrence and I divorced. The first few years were terrible but I got so used to being alone that little by little I convinced myself I liked it that way. Now Aubrey McGinty had sucked me into her life. She'd filled my evenings and my weekends. She'd filled my head, and I suppose even my heart, with a sense of adventure, a feeling of family.

I took my tray into the kitchen and checked the cupboard to see how many tea bags I had left. I had enough for six months. I drove to Ike's for more.

"Morgue Mama," he sang out.

"One for here, Ike, and a couple boxes for the road."

I was still there at nine when the rain hit. When Aubrey's little white Escort pulled to the curb.

Aubrey bought a bottle of cranberry juice and a bag of barbecue potato chips. She joined me at my table by the window, pushing aside my boxes of tea bags. "Anything fit to print today?" I asked.

"That's why I stopped when I saw your car. You'll never guess whose windows were smashed out."

"Oh my—not again."

"Not mine—Tish Kiddle's." She dug a printout of her story from her purse. She kept up a running commentary while I read. "Can you believe she drives a Lexus? You see where she lives? Saffron Hills? Do you know how pricey those condos are? Good God, how much money does that fluff-cake make?"

Tish Kiddle's paycheck did not interest me. Her smashed car windows did. "You think this means she's onto something?"

Aubrey slid down in her chair and glumly folded her arms. "At the very least somebody's afraid she is." She flipped back her hair and stared me. "You think I'm pretty enough for TV news?"

I'd come to Ike's to talk to Ike. To relax in his slow, easy voice. Now Aubrey was buzzing all over me, like a bee at a picnic. I was simply not in the mood for her ego, or her jealousy, or her youth. When Aubrey headed for the restroom, I headed for my car.

It was still raining—not as hard as before but enough to keep my windshield wipers clacking. The lights along the downtown's empty streets were dim, mutated blurs. I turned onto West Tuckman. It wasn't that late but the rain had chased everybody home to the suburbs.

Just west of the monstrous old YMCA building, a pair of headlights filled my rear-view mirror, bright, then dim, then bright again. I pushed on the gas pedal. I made sure my doors were locked. The headlights got closer. Flashed again. I sped up more.

I scolded myself for panicking. I lifted my chin and squinted at the mirror. To see what kind of car it was. To see what kind of danger I was in. But it was too dark, and it was raining too hard, and the headlights were too close and too bright.

I was driving through the 3rd District now, Lionel Percy's domain. But if that was a police car following me, wouldn't its blue roof lights be blasting? Wouldn't its siren be squealing? I decided not necessarily. I reached Potter's Hill, where the city's old ceramic industry once flourished. Now it was a lifeless strip of used car lots and empty storefronts with tattered For Sale or Lease signs in the windows.

I ran the red light at Halprin Street. So did the car behind me. You can imagine what was going on inside my head. Car windows being smashed. Men jumping out from bushes slapping and scratching. Lionel Percy popping up like a jack-in-the-box clown. Preachers tumbling backward into pots of fake palms. The street was slick with standing water. I drove faster anyway. In a few minutes I would be in Meri. There would be people there, brighter street lights and glowing neon.

I started chastising myself, in that special shrill whisper we save for our own ears: "It's your own damn fault. You didn't have to get involved with that crazy girl. You could have stayed right in your safe little Morgue Mama world making people miserable. But you had to tag along like the sidekick on some old Saturday morning western. And now here you are about to be beaten, killed or worse. You old fool. You're as full of yourself as she is."

I also started thinking about ways to defend myself—kicking, biting, screaming, calmly talking myself out of trouble, running like a rabbit—but I quickly realized that my age was my only defense. "Who would hurt a sixty-seven-year-old woman?" I whispered. "Then again, who would murder a seventy-five-year-old preacher?"

The traffic light at Teeple was yellow when I slipped under it. It was a dark neighborhood crowded with tall frame houses, drooping trees and uneven slate sidewalks. There were a few more cars on the street. Unfortunately not enough to stop the demon behind me from riding my bumper.

Two blocks from Meri the car behind me started beeping. It was a weak, oinking beep, no more threatening than the timer on my microwave. "Good gravy," I growled. I pulled over and watched Aubrey trot toward me through the rain. I rolled down my window and claimed my two boxes of Darjeeling tea.

◇◇◇

# Friday, July 7

On Friday I went into work at seven. In case I was needed. In case something surprising happened I didn't want to miss.

Aubrey was already at her desk, a Walkman snapped over her ears filling her ears with God knows what kind of noise while she typed like a maniac.

Just after eleven, I heard her howl. She danced toward me like a flamenco dancer, chopping her feet and clicking her fingers. She leaned across my desk until our noses were almost touching. "Guess who just called me? Tim Bandicoot. Tomorrow morning he's going to Marysville, and you and I are going along."

## Saturday, July 8

At two in the morning my phone rang. It was Aubrey and she was worried—about her own behavior.

"You've got to promise me I won't screw this up," she said.

I swung my feet over the edge of the bed, hoping what she'd just said would make more sense if I was sitting up. "You want *me* to promise that *you* won't screw up?"

"You know I will, Maddy. All those hours in the car with that idiot. I'm bound to say something that sets him off."

I knew what she was talking about now. In just a few hours we would be driving to Marysville with Tim Bandicoot, to get Sissy James to admit her innocence. I slid to the floor and shuffled toward the wicker chair by the window. Sometimes I curl up there when it's too hot to sleep, but mostly I use it as a staging area for my laundry. That night it was piled with bathroom towels that still needed folding. I pushed them onto the floor and sat. "You'll just have to concentrate," I said. I could hear the soft clink of computer keys. "Are you still at work?"

She yawned. "Where else would I be?"

I was going to say something motherly about the need for a good night's rest. But then I remembered the all-nighters Dale Marabout used to pull when he was a young police reporter. Sometimes the stories demand it. "There's some gum in my desk if you need it," I said.

"That's what I'll do tomorrow," she said. "I'll cram my mouth full of gum so I can't talk. When Timmy boy says something tempting I'll just, 'Yom-yom-yom-yom-yom.'"

"Good plan," I said. "Can I go back to bed now?"

There were a few seconds of very serious silence. "What do you make of all this?" she asked. "Tim Bandicoot inviting us along, I mean."

"Maybe it's Sissy's idea."

"Not in a trillion years. I don't think it's Tim's idea either. He's got to hate my guts."

"His wife's idea then?"

"Has to be."

"For good or ill, you think?"

"I'd say for ill."

"Really?"

"Annie Bandicoot's motives might be pure as snow—loving supportive wife just trying to make nice—but I think we're talking Bride of Machiavelli here."

I'd tried to fight it but I was wide awake now. I got on my knees and started folding towels. "You think we're walking into some kind of a trap? You thought that about the church thing on Sunday."

"Maddy, you're not following the bouncing ball. Not us walking into a trap. Annie Bandicoot trying to avoid one."

"Get the gum, Aubrey. You're getting punchy."

"Think about it. Sweet little Annie gloms onto Tim Bandicoot when she's still in Sunday school. He's handsome and ambitious and heir to the throne. She marries him when she's only nineteen. For a while the future looks peachy. But then Tim starts questioning Buddy's ways—all that speaking in tongues business. Buddy starts having second thoughts. He brings in Guthrie Gates and starts grooming him as his heir. Then Buddy suddenly gives Tim the boot. Tim tries to build a new church. But after six years he's still preaching to that scraggly rabble on Lutheran Hill. Worst of all, he's schtoomping some loser bimbo. This isn't *Stand By Your Man*. This is *Save Your Man's Sorry Ass*.

So Annie puts on a wig and some funny glasses or something and waltzes into the cathedral and poisons the man who did her man wrong. And she frames the bimbo. Maybe Tim's new church will take off now. Maybe Tim will behave himself now."

I was down to the wash cloths. "You're saying he knows his wife killed Buddy?"

"Maybe he knows. Maybe he suspects. Maybe he's too afraid to find out."

"And then you come along and start digging into the murder?"

"That's right—and then I come along. Tim handles it pretty well at first. He really doesn't know anything for sure—so he doesn't have to lie. But the nosy bitch reporter keeps prying. Proves Sissy couldn't have done it. Things start to unravel. Tim and Guthrie try to bury the hatchet. They come to the paper hand in hand. They end up shoving each other like a couple of feuding five-year-olds. Annie has to take the bull by the horns now. She tells her man, 'You're ruining everything we've worked all these years for. Sunday morning you're going to come clean and confess your sins to the world. And then you're going to Marysville and rescue Sissy, and you're taking the nosy bitch reporter with you.'"

I crawled back in bed. In the moonlight the stacks of towels on the floor looked like the skyline of a tiny city. "A good offense is a good defense," I said.

"Bingo," she said.

I arrived at the *Herald-Union* at eight. Aubrey met me downstairs in the lobby. She had a travel mug of coffee in one hand and a granola bar in the other. Her bag hung from her shoulder. She looked horrible. I imagine I did, too.

When Tim Bandicoot pulled up in his minivan, Aubrey made me sit up front. She got in the back and curled up against the door, sipping and chewing with her eyes closed. Her strategy, apparently, was to sleep all the way to Marysville. "She's been writing all night," I explained.

For the longest time Tim and I talked about safe, dumb things—the newest effort to revitalize the downtown, how far the suburbs were spreading into the countryside, whether the Cleveland Indians were going to catch the Chicago White Sox in the standings. Then just as we were getting on I-491, Aubrey came to and leaned between the banana-shaped front seats. "I thought maybe your wife would come along," she said to Tim.

I saw his eyes peek over the bottom of the rear-view mirror. I expected him to make some benign excuse. But he didn't. "You and my wife in the same car? There's already been one murder."

We took I-491 to I-76 to I-71. Fifteen minutes north of Columbus we exited onto U.S. 36 and sped west to Marysville. At the prison we were taken to the same room where we'd talked to Sissy before. We sat on the same blue sofa.

All morning I'd been dying to see the expressions on Sissy's and Tim's faces when they first saw each other, to get some visceral sense of how they really felt about each other. Would they have the same look or different looks?

When Sissy came in she was already crying, clutching a wad of tissue the size of a major league baseball. She smiled the second she saw Tim.

Tim didn't smile. But he did start crying. He stood up and she wrapped her arms around his neck and they hugged and took turns refilling their depleted lungs. There was some kind of love going on there. What kind I didn't know.

Sissy shook Aubrey's hand and then mine. She settled into the hard wooden chair across from the sofa. There was some perfunctory chit-chat about the weather and the prison food and how things were going at the church—all fine—and then Tim got the ball rolling by offering a prayer. We all bowed our heads and closed our eyes. We all peeked.

"Sissy," Tim said, "both Aubrey and Mrs. Sprowls know about our past relationship. So do a lot of other people."

Sissy nodded and pressed the back of her hand against her lips, bracing for the sorrow to come.

"I have confessed it to the congregation," he said, "and it has been reported in the media. Our relationship was wrong."

Sissy closed her watery eyes and nodded.

"And I take full responsibility for all that has happened," he said.

His confession and her nodding went on for several minutes. Aubrey took notes. I dabbed my eyes with the tip of my pinkie.

Finally Tim got to the reason for our visit. "Sissy, if you are being held wrongfully in this prison, I have to know—so I, and we, and everybody who cares about you, can help you."

Well, his sentence structure was as awkward as a toad in a basket of apples, but it was a start.

"I killed him," Sissy said.

She might as well have said, "I am a Greyhound bus." That's how believable it was.

"I do not need protecting," Tim answered.

Aubrey closed her notebook and fed her ballpoint through the top spiral. She laid it next to her on the sofa cushion. She leaned forward. "I bet you were really confused when the police showed up at your house. It was only six o'clock. You were getting ready for work. Like everybody else in Hannawa, you knew Buddy Wing was dead. You'd read the newspaper stories and knew exactly how and when he died. While Detective Grant was questioning you in the kitchen, other cops were searching your property. You told the detective you didn't know anything. Then they found all that stuff in your garbage. You knew instantly somebody wanted you to take the blame. But who? Tim Bandicoot? Your spiritual leader? Your lover? You knew Friday night was Family Night at the temple. You knew Tim always did something with his family. You knew that particular Friday night he was supposed to take his sons to the basketball game in Cleveland. But did he? Detective Grant started pressing you to confess."

Sissy continued her Greyhound bus defense. "I was not covering up for Tim or anybody else—I don't see why everybody has such a hard time understanding that."

"Because," said Aubrey, "you were still in Mingo Junction that Friday night. You were there the entire weekend. With your cousin Jeanie and her daughters—and your daughter Rosy."

Sissy was stunned. A secret more important than her life had been told. Her eyes blamed Tim.

"We learned it on our own," I heard myself say.

Sissy's fingers dug into the varnish on the chair arms. She began to pant, as if giving birth to Rosy all over again. "It was not Tim's baby."

Aubrey left the sofa and kneeled in front of Sissy. "We are not interested in the father of your child, or who you thought you were covering up for. We just want to hear from you that you didn't do it."

The growl of an unexorcised demon escaped from Sissy's quivering lips. "Just so you can get a good story."

"Yes, so I can get a good story," Aubrey admitted. "A story that will get you out of here. The real world's a mean place, Sissy, as you discovered a long time ago. It's mean with selfish people covering up their mistakes and saving their asses. Prosecutors don't reopen cases without public pressure. Judges get re-elected by putting people in prison, by not letting them out. Everybody's eyes are fixed on their own precious futures. Nobody looks back until they're forced to look back. And that's what we're going to make them do now. We're going to force them to look back. Force them to free you and find who really killed Buddy Wing."

Sissy dried her eyes with her ball of tissue. She sat up straight and put her knees together and rested her folded hands on top of them. Aubrey stretched out her arm and motioned impatiently for her pen and notebook. I gave them to her.

"Tell the truth," Tim said softly.

Said Sissy James: "I did not put poison on Pastor Wing's Bible, or in his water pitcher. I was in Mingo Junction, Ohio, on that Friday night, visiting my cousin and my daughter."

It was the confession Aubrey wanted. But Aubrey wanted more. "Did you confess thinking that Tim might have been the killer?"

Sissy checked Tim's face for permission. "All I knew was that somebody wanted me to take responsibility for what happened."

Aubrey still wanted more. "You're saying you still don't know who that somebody is?"

I popped up like a piece of burnt toast. "That's not our job, Aubrey."

Aubrey twisted toward me. The unexorcised demon was now residing in her.

"We've got all we need for now," I said.

Aubrey smiled, grimly. She un-clicked her pen and flipped her notebook closed. She stood up. "Mrs. Sprowls is right. We have all we need for now."

Tim Bandicoot stepped across the coffee table and pulled Sissy to her feet. He kissed her forehead. "I'll get you a good lawyer. We will make this thing all right."

Our meeting with Sissy James did not last much longer than that. Tim led us in prayer again and Sissy meekly begged Aubrey not to report that Rosy was her daughter. Aubrey promised that she would not report it, unless others reported it first. We drove back to Hannawa.

◇◇◇

Was I surprised that Aubrey made that promise? No, I was not.

Aubrey and Sissy shared a common past, sexual abuse. They were two young women seeking safety and acceptance, and if possible, some kind of love. Of course Aubrey would make that promise.

That evening at Ike's when we discussed it, Aubrey explained her promise differently: "Sissy having a daughter by some john is terrific stuff. But it's worth sacrificing, for now. This little series isn't going to be the end of it. There'll be lots of follow-up stories. I'm going to need Sissy's gratitude."

# 19

I did not want to have lunch with Dale and Sharon Marabout. And I'm sure Dale wasn't crazy about the idea either. But Sharon would not let it go. She wanted to thank me in person for helping *her hubby* get that freelance job.

"It'll be fun," she kept assuring Dale.

"It won't be as bad as you think," Dale kept assuring me.

I'd successfully put them off for weeks. But now with the whole Buddy Wing thing only a few days from exploding all over the front page, I knew it would be best to put the lunch behind me.

Right after Meet the Press, I did a little grocery shopping and then drove to Speckley's. Dale and Sharon were waiting outside by the door. They smiled simultaneously and gave me a his-and-hers finger wiggle. I wiggled my fingers back. I was dreading this.

Sharon was short and on the cusp of plumpness. Plumpness is not a good thing when you're in your twenties trying to fit into the latest snare-a-man styles. But when you're in your forties, as Sharon Marabout was now, it serves you well. It smoothes out your wrinkles and gives you a sensuousness that skinny women your age would die for. "Sharon, so good to see you again," I said.

"Maddy," she said, "we should do this more often."

In the twenty-two years since I walked in on them naked on the apartment floor, I don't think I've seen Sharon a half-dozen times. Yet she always treats me like a close friend of the family, sending me Christmas cards and inviting me to important family gatherings. I never send them a card and I never go to their gatherings. Sharon is a wonderful woman and a good match for Dale. They have great kids. I just wish she'd stop treating me like Dale's favorite aunt. I was his lover, for Pete's sake! For five years! Surely she realized that everything he taught her about sex I'd taught him.

"Yes, we should do this more often," I said, pretending to be as nice as she really was. "We really, really should."

Speckley's was packed. The best we could do was a table in the adjoining banquet room. As soon as we were in our chairs Sharon giddily announced she was getting the meat loaf sandwich and au gratin potatoes. Apparently Dale didn't bring her to Speckley's very often. It was, after all, our place. When the waitress came we all ordered the meat loaf and potatoes.

After our iced teas came, Sharon apparently gave Dale one of those imperceptible wife-signals, because he immediately launched into a gooey expression of gratitude no man would give on his own: "We just wanted to show our appreciation for helping me in my time of need," he said. "It was really lovely."

Time of need? Really lovely? I knew who'd come up with those lines.

All I'd done was find a freelance assignment for Dale after he'd blown a fuse and quit the paper. That assignment was coming to an end and what Dale would do for money now was anybody's guess. Still, that assignment, as temporary as it was, clearly had renewed his self-confidence. He was going to be okay.

Sharon pronounced the meat loaf the best she'd ever had, the au gratin potatoes incredible. All three of us ordered the key lime pie. We chatted through I don't know how many refills of iced tea. I checked my wristwatch I don't know how many times.

During our lunch, the conversation had repeatedly drifted to Aubrey's series on the Buddy Wing murder. Dale had written a crime series or two during his years on the police beat and understandably wanted to know exactly how she was organizing it. I told him what I knew:

The first story, scheduled to run on Wednesday, would lead with Sissy James's confession that she did not poison the Rev. Buddy Wing. It would rehash Ronny Doddridge's suicide and Tim Bandicoot's own recent confession of his affair with Sissy. It would also rehash Buddy's death and his nasty split with Tim Bandicoot over speaking in tongues. But this story wouldn't contain too many details. This was the teaser story.

Thursday's story would go back to the very beginning, Buddy Wing's childhood in West Virginia and his migration to Hannawa to begin his ministry. It would discuss Buddy's theological beliefs and the nuts and bolts of building his evangelical empire, from the salad days of the Clean Collar Club, to the erection of the Heaven Bound Cathedral. It would end with the coming of Guthrie Gates. A sidebar would explore Hannawa's emergence as the "The Hallelujah City."

Friday's story would re-examine Tim Bandicoot's falling out with Buddy over speaking in tongues, the snake handling and the like. Ronny Doddridge's sudden appearance as security guard would be recounted, and so would the lingering anger and suspicion—and the spying—between the two congregations. One sidebar would tell Tim Bandicoot's life story: his childhood in Buddy Wing's church, his Bible college years, his marriage to Annie, their fall from grace and their struggles at the New Epiphany Temple. Another sidebar would recount some of Buddy's troubles: his wife's death from lung cancer, his run-ins with Wayne F. Dillow and Edward Tolchak, his church's many near-bankruptcies, how over the years he survived the Tonight Show jokes about his having Jesus's phone number for example, the snide comments about how he dressed and talked and wore his hair.

On Saturday Aubrey would tell the world about Sissy's pitiful childhood, the stripping and prostitution, her rescue by Jesus Christ, her affair with Tim Bandicoot, her confession to the murder. As Aubrey promised, the story would not say a word about little Rosy.

Sunday's story would be the big finale. It would state emphatically that Sissy was telling the truth, that she was in Mingo Junction that Thanksgiving weekend, visiting her cousin, as she did every year. The story would examine the length somebody went to frame her, the evidence sprinkled in her garbage and the spare bedroom where she worked on her crafts. The story would ask: If Sissy James didn't do it, then who did? There would be several sidebars. One would examine the police department's hurried investigation. One would ask why Tim Bandicoot and Guthrie Gates, and others who knew Sissy, so readily accepted her confession; that story also would tell readers where those good Christians were the night Buddy was poisoned. Another sidebar would show just how easy it was for the real murderer to enter the inner bowels of the cathedral and paint that poison cross on the Bible, fill that pitcher with poisoned water. The final sidebar would tell Aubrey's story—the broken car windows, the threats and the bruises, the red Taurus station wagon that pursued her while she sought the truth, and, yes, how Tim Bandicoot and Guthrie Gates got into a shoving match in Bob Averill's office.

Accompanying Aubrey's stories on Sunday would be an editorial imploring the Hannawa police to reopen the case.

## Monday, July 10

I came in at eight and went straight to Aubrey's desk. A felt-tip pen was sticking out of her mouth like a cigar. Her fingers were draped across her keyboard like ten sleeping salamanders. Every few seconds a few fingers would twitch awake and a string of words would race across her computer screen. Several diet Coke cans were in her wastebasket. Several Milky Way wrappers, too. "I hope you didn't work all night," I said.

She tilted her head back until she was looking straight up into my face. She yawned noisily, like the Cowardly Lion in *The Wizard of Oz*. "I should have," she said.

So I let her work and went to my desk to collect my mug. Had it only been four months since Aubrey McGinty first called me Morgue Mama to my face? Asked to see the files on Buddy Wing? It seemed more like four years—one of those officially packaged four years, like college or a presidential term, with a distinct beginning, an endlessly horrifying but exhilarating middle, and an abrupt end.

And it was going to end abruptly, in less than forty-eight hours. Once those big presses downstairs started rolling with that big story splashed across the top of Page One, the journey that put Aubrey and me in the same wobbling canoe would be over. Her life would go in one direction and mine in another. We'd talk, when there was something to say. We might even reminisce if the opportunity arose. But things would not be the same.

At ten-thirty I heard Aubrey yell, "Who has time for this crap?"

She yelled that after getting a call from the police department's PR guy, informing her that Chief Polceznec was going to hold a news conference at eleven. Tinker sent Doreen Poole to cover it. She came back at noon with the lead story for Tuesday's paper:

## Beleaguered police chief says he'll retire early

Sylvia Berdache hurried to a one o'clock press conference at City Hall, providing a sidebar to the story:

## Sad to see his "old amigo" step down, mayor appoints Ted Duffy interim chief

I just knew Lionel Percy sent one of his flunkies out for cake and ice cream. Ted Duffy was a well-known paper-pusher in the safety director's office, in Sylvia's words, "a real marshmallow who wouldn't even rock the boat in his bathtub."

A little after two, Eric Chen appeared at my desk with a grin on his face. He handed me a printout, the way a boy hands a doctored report card to his mother. Eric wanted nothing to do with Aubrey these days, not after that night in Meri, but I was still his boss. I'd told him to keep checking the computer files for information on the various people connected to the Buddy Wing story, especially Annie Bandicoot.

When I read the printout I clutched my throat, in case my heart had any idea of escaping. "Good job," I said.

I took a long, steadying drink of my room-temperature tea and trotted to Aubrey's desk. "Eric just brought me this," I said, sliding the printout into her hands. It was a short story, written months earlier by religion editor Nanette Beane:

> HANNAWA—Right after serving their own families Thanksgiving dinner, the wives of six local ministers left for eastern Kentucky Thursday night, their cavalcade of minivans and station wagons loaded with food, clothing and toys to make this Christmas a little brighter for families in that economically ravaged region.
>
> "It's a little thing for us to do," said Joy Brown, wife of the Rev. Donald Brown, pastor of Culver Ridge Methodist Church, "but it'll be a big thing for the families down there."
>
> Brown, coordinator of the trip, said the women would spend Friday and Saturday visiting homes in Lee and Owsley counties and then attend Sunday morning worship services at the Baptist church in Korbin Knob, a small mountain

town approximately 80 miles southeast of Lexington.

Other women making the trip were Ellen Hopsen, wife of the Rev. Ernest Hopsen, Tamarack Episcopal Church, Hannawa Falls; Jennifer Moeller, wife of the Rev. Richard Moeller, Greenlawn Reformed Church, Greenlawn; Sophia Wildenhein, wife of the Rev. Ralph Wildenhein, St. Marks Lutheran Church, Brinkley; Annie Bandicoot, wife of the Rev. Tim Bandicoot, New Epiphany Temple, Hannawa; and Cynthia Short, wife of the Rev. John Short, Spire Hill United Church of Christ, North Hannawa.

Items for the mission were donated by members of the six participating congregations.

I pointed to the date the story ran, which is included in the computer file of every story that we publish, along with what page it appeared on, which editions it ran, and who wrote it.

Aubrey stared at the story. "Wonder boy couldn't have found this a week ago?"

"At least he found it," I said.

She let the story float to her desktop. "Thanks, Maddy."

"It's not going to mean a lot of rewriting, I hope."

"Couple of paragraphs."

I went back to my desk. The news that Annie Bandicoot was on a mission trip to Kentucky the night Buddy Wing was murdered would only take a little rewriting, just as Aubrey said. She was not, after all, identifying possible suspects and their whereabouts that night. She could just mention it in passing:

*For Annie Bandicoot, who was in eastern Kentucky the night of the murder, distributing food, clothing and toys to the poor, the arrest of Sissy James must have been especially distressing . . .* Aubrey would just have to write something like that.

Yes, the rewriting would be easy for Aubrey. A quick cut and paste. Rewiring her brain would be harder. She'd been certain, I'm sure, that when the police reopened the case, their investigation would uncover all the evidence they needed to put Annie Bandicoot in that cell now occupied by Sissy James.

Aubrey left the newsroom a few minutes after four. I left at five. I didn't feel like cooking so I had a quick bowl of miniature shredded wheats. Then I opened a package of Fig Newtons and turned on the TV 21 news. They led with a fatal truck-car accident on the interstate and then covered Chief Polceznec's surprise retirement. Then they went live to Disney World, where Tish Kiddle had apparently fled after the windows of her Lexus were smashed out. It was the first part of her week-long series on Vacation Fun in the Florida Sun. "Tish, my sweet little lamb," I said to the TV screen, my teeth gooey with fig, "you are no Aubrey McGinty."

# 20

**Tuesday, July 11**

I went to bed Monday absolutely certain I'd call in sick the next day. Aubrey's series on the Buddy Wing murder was starting on Wednesday and that meant Tuesday would be frantic, like the day before a space shuttle launch or a military invasion. There would be a million last-minute changes. There would be unavoidable arguments and ugly fits of egomania. All day long the twin demons of anticipation and dread would be going at each other like a couple of barnyard roosters. Yet the second my eyes popped open, I knew I'd not only be going in, I'd be going in early and staying late. I didn't want to miss a thing.

When I got to the paper Aubrey was already at her desk. Tinker was already in his office. I collected my mug and headed for the cafeteria. Eric was already there, drinking Mountain Dews with a couple of the boys from sports. I took my tea back to the morgue and started marking up the paper. I couldn't keep my eyes off Aubrey. Her hair, not washed for a day or two, was pulled back into a ponytail. Her knees were propped against her desk and her keyboard was on her lap. She'd type a bit, then think a bit, and then yawn and take a sip of coffee, and then check her watch.

At noon I went to the cafeteria and stared at the vending machines for a while, coming pretty close to buying one of those dreadful ham and cheese sandwiches wedged in the slot like a warped piece of drywall. I went to Ike's instead. "Morgue Mama, what's wrong with you today?" he asked when I walked in. "You look like you're going to corkscrew yourself right out of your pantaloons."

"Aubrey's series on Buddy Wing starts tomorrow," I said. He'd already poured water for my tea and I pointed to a huge peanut butter cookie in the dessert case.

"From everything you've told me, it'll all go fine," he said.

"It's what I haven't told you that worries me," I said.

Ike handed me the cookie and waved off my money. "Why you always keeping secrets from me, Maddy?"

In the afternoon I stayed as busy as I could. Occasionally Aubrey would look at me and pretend she was pulling out her hair. I'd just nod and we'd exchange a tired smile.

Shortly after five, I saw her hang her purse on her shoulder and head for the elevator. I grabbed my purse and followed. I slipped in just as the door was closing. "Sorry about lunch," she said.

I watched her punch the parking deck button. "Going home?" I asked.

"Shopping," she said.

"For anything in particular?"

"Tranquillity. But I'll end up buying shoes."

And so Aubrey and I drove to the mall in Brinkley, in my Dodge Shadow. The shops were already filled with clothes for fall and winter. I didn't buy a thing. Aubrey found a sexy pair of pink mules on the clearance table at Payless. I dropped her off at the paper at seven-thirty. "Go home and relax," I said.

She squeezed my arm and slid out. Before slamming the door she bent down and wiggled her fingers. I wiggled back. I watched her go inside. We'd been gone all that time and not once did either of us mention her Buddy Wing stories. What a relief that was.

◇◇◇

At home I tried to eat a tuna fish sandwich and tried to watch TV. I washed my face and brushed my teeth and got into a baggy pair of pajamas. By now Wednesday's front page was ready to go on the press. Unless something big broke, the press would start rolling precisely at midnight.

At eleven the phone rang. It was Tinker. "It's really necessary that I be there?" I asked.

He just said, "Maddy," the slow, stern way my father used to say "Maddy" when I tried to buck my chores or listened to my radio too late at night.

I drove back to the paper.

Except for a sprinkling of copy editors in metro and sports, the newsroom was empty. I went to Tinker's office but he wasn't there. So I got my mug and headed for the cafeteria. The last thing I needed at a quarter to midnight was a hot mug of Darjeeling tea. But I made some.

I slowly sipped my way back to the newsroom, my pinkies sticking out from my mug like tiny airplane wings. I was standing in the no-man's-land between the morgue and sports when the elevator doors parted and Aubrey stepped out. As bad as she looked all day, she looked even worse now. Her hair was hanging like broomstraw from a Cleveland Indians ballcap. She was wearing a baggy tee shirt and even baggier sweatpants. She also was wearing the new pink mules. She walked straight for me. "Tinker called you in, too?"

I sipped and nodded.

"Christ—I wasn't asleep five minutes."

"That's five minutes more than I had. Any idea what he wants?"

Her hands were tucked under her armpits. She was twisting nervously. "Some question about my story—I can't believe he called you in, too."

"I wish he hadn't."

We stood there, Aubrey twisting, me sipping. Finally Tinker popped out of the elevator. Another man, middle-aged and bald, was with him. They walked straight to Aubrey's desk on the fringe of the metro department. It was a minute before midnight but both were wearing business suits. Tinker motioned for us to join them.

Tinker introduced the other man. "Aubrey, Maddy, this is Stan Craddock, his firm does legal work for the paper."

Aubrey pulled back her hand after one short nibble of a shake. "So there's a legal problem with my story?"

"Unfortunately," Tinker said. "That's why I wanted Maddy here. She was with you most of the time." He asked Aubrey to call up her story for Wednesday.

She sat at her desk and clicked on her monitor. "It's still running tomorrow, isn't it?"

Said Tinker, "That's why we're here at midnight."

Aubrey typed in her security code. The monitor's sky blue screen filled with boxes. She called up her story. Aubrey's back immediately flattened against her chair, as if she'd been struck in the chest by an invisible fist. She had seen the story's byline:

```
By Dale Marabout
```

Her eyes went quickly to the story's first paragraph. So did ours. It was a straightforward, hard news lead, the kind veteran police reporters like Dale Marabout can write in their sleep. It was still in the computer format reporters write in—ragged right, an unflattering sans serif type font:

HANNAWA—Police early this morning arrested *Herald-Union* reporter Aubrey McGinty for the November murder of the Rev. Buddy Wing.

She was expected to be charged and arraigned later today in Common Pleas Court.

Detective Scotty Grant called the 24-year-old newspaper reporter's alleged involvement in the poisoning death of the nationally known television evangelist "both bizarre and frightening."

"I've been investigating murders in this city for 22 years, and I've never seen a case twist around like this," he said.

Grant said that McGinty fatally poisoned Wing after being assured of a job with the *Herald-Union*. "She killed Wing so she could later prove the wrong person was in prison, and make a name for herself," he said. "She almost got away with it."

Aubrey stopped reading. She pressed her hands together, as if to pray, and then rubbed her nose. Her eyes slowly lifted toward me.

"It was your lies," I said. I was cowering behind my mug like it was one of those long shields the Crusaders carried. "The first lie made me curious. The second lie made me suspicious. The third convinced me."

Aubrey slumped in her chair and wrapped her arms around her waist. "What kind of nonsense have you been telling people?"

I ignored her silly effort to throw the suspicion onto me. "Lie number one was that gift certificate you used to buy that jacket at Old Navy, after we made our first visit to the Heaven Bound Cathedral."

Aubrey rolled her eyes, and made sure Tinker and Stan Craddock could see them roll. "Maddy, I explained all that."

"Yes you did. After I confronted you about it."

She bristled, just a tiny bit. "After you snooped into my private life."

"I told you then, Aubrey. I don't snoop. I get intrigued."

"I told you the truth."

"Yes you did. The old files I looked at bore that out. Your sister had been sexually molested for years by your stepfather—I'm betting you were, too—and after she took him to court, and after he was acquitted, she took her own life. I can only imagine what kind of guilt you felt. You told the social workers and the police nothing had ever happened to you, that you'd never seen nor heard your stepfather do anything to your sister. Were you afraid? Had he threatened you? Of course you've tried to keep your sister alive."

Aubrey was furious. "Psycho-babble bullshit, Maddy. You've got me in a lot of trouble over your stupid psycho-babble bullshit."

Another man joined us. It was Scotty Grant, chief detective in the Hannawa Police Department's homicide unit. There was no need for an introduction. Aubrey knew who he was.

"At the time," I continued, "I figured you were looking into the Buddy Wing murder because of your mistrust of the legal system. Your sympathy for its victims. I was very impressed."

Aubrey's eyes drifted back to her computer screen. She scrolled down. We all read:

> *Herald-Union* Managing Editor Alec Tinker confirmed that McGinty had been investigating the Buddy Wing murder since March. She had presented him with compelling evidence that Sissy James, the 27-year-old Hannawa hospital worker who confessed to the murder, was in fact innocent.
>
> James is now serving a life sentence at the Marysville Reformatory for Women.
>
> Detective Grant said police now believe James confessed to protect Wing's former protégé, the Rev. Tim Bandicoot, who was expelled from the Heaven Bound Cathedral after a much publicized rift over the practice of speaking in tongues.

"Lie number two came on Easter Sunday," I said. "Right here at the paper. You and Eric were in the cafeteria going over your files. Remember when I asked why you had two copies of the church directory? You told me you went back for an older one—because former members of the church were more likely to be suspects than present ones. Quick thinking. But I'd already seen that the two directories had the same date on the cover."

Aubrey artfully put a look of mild shock on her face. "That can't be right."

I plowed ahead. "One possibility is that someone at the cathedral mistakenly gave you a current directory when you asked for an older one. Nobody at the cathedral remembers such a visit, by the way."

"I did go back—"

"The other possibility, of course, is that you already had a church directory when you asked Guthrie Gates for the first one, during that visit with me."

Aubrey changed her expression to one of confusion, as if I was some demented old duck. "So what point are you trying to make here, Maddy?"

"That you lied about having two identical directories when you didn't need to lie," I said. "You could have said, 'I figured since you and Eric were helping we'd need two,' or 'I found another one in the morgue files you gave me,' or 'Don't you remember? Guthrie gave us two.' I would have believed any of that. But you intentionally lied. Because you'd had that other directory for months. You panicked."

Aubrey's eyes were drifting. I turned to see what she was looking at. Two uniformed police officers were leaning against the wall in sports. "You're completely wrong about this," she insisted hollowly.

I felt my own eyes tearing up. "I spent the next two weeks trying not to think the worst—I really did—but unfortunately for you I'm one of those miserable old buttinskys who just can't say no to her curiosities. Take that day we were watching the police tapes at my house. Matter-of-factly you said procaine was used only in hospitals. But that's not true. Paramedics carry all sorts of emergency medicines, including procaine. I don't think it's a coincidence that three weeks before Buddy Wing was poisoned you decided to write a story on Rush City's EMS unit. You rode with them for four days and wrote a wonderful story about how they rushed around the county saving kids who drank Drano and old men having heart attacks. Could it be that once you'd decided on Buddy Wing as your victim, and then chose poor Sissy James as your suspect, you researched how she might do it? You learned she worked at a hospital, and knowing as much about poisons as you do, you decided on procaine as your poison of choice. But as the big day got closer, you began to worry. Would the procaine be enough to kill him? Especially in the cruel, clever way you planned to administer it? So you added the lily of the valley."

Aubrey smirked, thinking she'd found something to discredit my analysis, I suppose. "Knowing as much about posions as I do? Where in that feeble mind of yours did you come up with that?"

I smirked right back at her. "This is no time for false modesty, dear. You know plenty about poisons. But before we get to that, let me tell you about lie number three. It was the most serendipitous thing. You remember that day in May when Dale Marabout popped his cork and quit? I felt just awful about it. And after stewing about it all week I went to Bob Averill, to explain all the stress Dale had been under. Your name came up and before I knew it I was telling him about my suspicions. He thought I was crazy. But after I told him about the church directories and your EMS story in *The Gazette*, and the way you found the real killer in the football coach case, and how you covered the squirrel poisoning at Kent—well."

Before Aubrey arrived at the paper that night, Bob Averill and Dale Marabout had stationed themselves in a storage room by the elevator. Now they were standing behind us, like a couple of Houdinis materializing out of thin air.

"I'd like to say it was my idea," Bob said, "but it was actually Maddy's. She thought we should secretly hire Dale to investigate your investigation—on a freelance basis."

Aubrey swiveled in her chair. "And you believe the crap he's written, Bob? He's been trying to fuck me since the day I got here."

Bob Averill was shocked into silence. I was not. "If you mean in a sexual way," I said, "God only knows what goes on inside a man's head. But if you mean getting even with you for stealing his beat, that's simply not true. Dale was pissed at Tinker, never you."

Dale couldn't resist. "For the record, I'm still pissed at Tinker."

Tinker's lips began to bubble. Before he could say anything, Bob held up his hands, like a pope calling for quiet from his balcony above St. Peter's Square. "Now-now. We don't need another shoving match here."

He was referring, of course, to the episode in his office between Tim Bandicoot and Guthrie Gates.

"We figured it would be wise to have Dale follow you around town," Tinker now said to Aubrey, "not only to see if you'd give yourself away, but also in case you tried to hurt someone else. And because we were afraid you might recognize Dale's car, Dale drove his wife's, a red Taurus station wagon."

The "*ssshit*" that leaked from Aubrey's lips was better than any confession.

I continued: "We were just beginning to think it was a waste of time, when you made up that business about the man in the station wagon attacking you. Tinker thinks you did it to make your story sexier—reporter risks life and limb to get the truth—but I think you did it to get Eric back."

Aubrey was suddenly like a girl in junior high, denying to her friends that she liked some goofy boy with braces. "I beat myself up to get Eric back? Puh-leeze."

I knew everyone wanted me to get on with my story. But I also knew that Aubrey—murderer or not—had fallen in love with Eric. And I knew that Eric—world-class doofus or not—had fallen in love with her. Keeping Eric in the dark had been the toughest part of this whole affair for me and I felt the need to confess, so she could go to prison knowing that at least one person, once upon a time, had truly loved her.

"Eric didn't know anything about Dale following you," I said. "He didn't know anything about anything. That night in Meri when he chased Dale down the alley, he was truly trying to protect you. When I saw him staggering back across the street, I figured it was all over. But discovering that the mysterious man in the station wagon was none other than Dale Marabout, and that Dale was following you because you very likely were the real killer, and that I was behind the whole blessed thing—well. Eric was so confused he couldn't even talk."

Whatever Aubrey felt inside she was keeping inside. "That's all so sweet. But if that was Dale in the red Taurus then it was Dale who attacked me. Because, regardless of what any of you say, I was attacked that night."

Dale grinned at her victoriously. "That night—Monday, June 12—the Taurus and I were staying at the Motel 6 in Rush City, after spending the day talking to your old co-workers at *The Gazette*."

Aubrey threw up her hands, as if being caught in a series of lies meant nothing at all. "So I was foolishly blinded by love, desperately trying to get my *boyfriend* back. So what?"

Dale leaned over Aubrey's keyboard and scrolled his story down a bit. "You might want to read this."

Aubrey swiveled back and read:

> Detective Grant refused to discuss publicly the evidence that lead to McGinty's arrest. Nevertheless, from a variety of sources the *Herald-Union* has been able to piece together the chilling story of a murder painstakingly planned and meticulously carried out.
>
> That story actually may have begun three autumns ago on the campus of Kent State University, where McGinty was just beginning her senior year.
>
> McGinty, like many students in the journalism department, worked on The Stater, the daily campus newspaper. Like other students, she planned to use those stories to get her first job after graduation.

> "The better your stories the better
> your chance of landing on a big paper,"
> Dr. Edward Firestone, faculty advisor
> for The Stater, told his student reporters
> again and again.
>
> Three weeks into the fall semester, the
> university's famous black squirrels began
> dying. Their carcasses were found in
> flower beds and at the base of the huge
> oaks that dot the sprawling campus.
>
> The carcasses of 22 squirrels were
> found before campus police announced
> that the squirrels died after eating ears
> of corn laced with chlordane, a power-
> ful chemical used to control crickets
> and other insects.

I don't know how fast Aubrey was reading, but I was well into Dale's background on how the squirrels were first brought to Kent when she started laughing. "This is some real crap reporting, Marabout," she said.

Dale smiled and motioned for her to read on:

> "I remember that Aubrey handed
> in a completed story on the squirrel
> deaths before the editors could assign
> somebody to cover it," Firestone told
> the *Herald-Union*. "We were impressed
> with her initiative and gave her the
> green light to cover the story the rest of
> the way."
>
> In all, McGinty wrote 16 stories
> about the squirrels, including one detail-
> ing the campus police department's
> inept handling of the investigation.
>
> No suspect was ever identified and
> the poisonings stopped before the
> semester ended.

> According to college transcripts,
> McGinty took an elective course in
> criminal toxicology during the spring
> semester of her junior year.
>
> Patrick Byner, dean of Kent's Crimi-
> nal Justice Studies program, told the
> *Herald-Union* that it is rare for students
> not majoring in law enforcement to take
> what he called "such an arcane, gradu-
> ate-level course."
>
> Byner said the course deals with
> techniques for investigating deaths by
> poisoning.

Aubrey smirked at what she'd read. "You can't print innuen-
does like these."

"We were pretty close to printing yours," Tinker answered.
"Anyway, we hope that by the time this goes to press you'll have
confirmed them."

Aubrey turned back to her computer screen, as anxious as
the rest to read what came next, I think:

> During the spring semester McGinty
> applied at a number of larger news-
> papers, including the *Herald-Union*. She
> did not receive an offer from any of
> those papers, however. Three months
> after graduation she accepted a job
> with the small daily in her hometown,
> the Rush City Gazette.
>
> According to Gazette Managing
> Editor Marilyn Morely, McGinty made
> no secret of her desire to move on to
> a larger newspaper as rapidly as pos-
> sible. "She tried to make even the most
> routine stories seem important," Morely
> said.
>
> One story that wasn't routine was
> the murder of Rush City High School

football coach Charles "Chuck" Reddincoat. A month after police charged the
father of a boy dropped from the team
for harassing younger players, McGinty
presented evidence pointing to what
police admitted was "a more likely
suspect."

Dale's story went on to recap Aubrey's investigation into the
coach's murder. How, based on her information, police found
bloody overalls and a gun at a hunting cabin in Coshocton
County. How that evidence led to the arrest and conviction of
the cheerleading advisor's jealous husband. How Aubrey had
spent the night following the murder at a motel just three miles
from the hunting cabin.

Aubrey sighed sarcastically. "You have descended into the
ooey-gooey depths of innuendo again, Marabout."

Dale was enjoying himself. "You'll be happy to know that the
police in Rush City are already taking another look at the case."

Aubrey answered coldly. "Are they?" She resumed reading:

McGinty's coverage of the killing,
and the police department's arrest of
the wrong man, were among the clippings she sent to the *Herald-Union*'s
newly appointed managing editor, Alec
Tinker.
"I was very impressed," Tinker said.
"She was just the kind of reporter I was
looking for. I promised her a job as soon
as there was an appropriate opening."

Can you imagine how hard it was for Dale to write that part
of the story? Calmly taking notes while Tinker all but admitted he forced him off his beat? So he could replace him with a
younger and more energetic reporter? I was so proud of Dale at
that moment. We all kept reading:

Tinker and McGinty kept in touch
for more than a year, exchanging e-mail
messages and periodically having lunch.
Last August he told her a police reporter's job would be available shortly after
the first of the year.

"I had decided to reassign a number
of reporters and considered Aubrey as
my number one candidate for the police
reporter position," Tinker acknowledged.

Aubrey started nodding, the way any reader thoughtfully
nods when he sees where a story is headed. "So after killing the
squirrels and the football coach, I killed Buddy Wing, for the
good clips?"

"Are you sure you don't want to stop here and talk to Detective Grant in private?" I asked.

"And miss the rest of Dale's brilliant reportage?"

She pronounced that last word, *reportage*, as if she was a
snooty French cabaret singer.

She continued reading.

We all continued reading.

# 21

I left my house as soon as it was light outside and crept through rush hour traffic toward the interstate. The roads were clear but there was snow in the brown clouds rolling out of the southwest, the direction I was heading. Thank God I had a Thermos of hot Darjeeling tea.

I-491 wound through the hills south of Hannawa for several miles before connecting with I-71, the wide asphalt spine that runs down the center of Ohio from Cleveland to Cincinnati. Just north of Jeromesville it started to rain, humongous drops that overpowered my wipers and made me feel like I was driving under water. I slipped in behind a semi pulling a trailer stacked with new Jeep Cherokees. I was content to stay behind him all the way to Columbus if that's how far he was going. I remembered how Aubrey McGinty had talked about getting an SUV someday, a bright yellow one, after she got her Visa card under control.

It was hard to believe that a full year had gone by since Aubrey first dragged me to the Heaven Bound Cathedral to start her investigation into the Buddy Wing murder. Who would have guessed it was Aubrey herself who painted that poisonous cross on his Bible, and filled his water pitcher with water laced with lily of the valley?

I might never have acted on my suspicions about Aubrey if Dale Marabout hadn't quit the way he did. It had stirred me up something terrible. I went to Bob Averill's office thinking my only motive was to get his job back. But I wasn't in there two minutes before I was spilling the beans.

After I'd convinced Bob that Aubrey might be the real killer, he called Tinker up to his office, so I could convince him. At first Tinker resisted the possibility. He'd recruited her after all. But as I went through the bits of evidence I'd collected, he began to see journalistic gold. "If you're right, we've got a huge story about how we brought one of our own to justice," he said. "We'll be up to our necks in awards."

Tinker wanted to create a secret team of reporters to investigate Aubrey's investigation. Bob nixed the idea immediately. "Reporters are genetic blabberers," he said. "Aubrey would find out in five minutes."

Dale Marabout's name just popped out of my mouth.

So we all met with Dale at my house. After an hour of pleading over coffee and an Entenmann's low-fat cherry cheesecake, he agreed to do the story, for an outrageous freelance fee that included the continuation of his health-care coverage.

Dale's first task was to double-check my own suspicions about Aubrey. He went to Rush City and gathered whatever records he could about her stepfather's molestation trial and her sister's suicide. He talked to her old high school teachers. Despite the horrors of her home life she was a very good student. She was editor of the high school newspaper, first-chair French horn player in the band. One teacher confided that Aubrey also was rumored to be a tad bit promiscuous. That same teacher confirmed that Coach Reddincoat had quite a well-known zipper problem himself, not only with the young teachers but also with senior girls about to graduate.

Dale found no evidence that anything sexual ever happened between Aubrey and the coach, coerced or consensual. Yet she certainly was aware of his lechery, just as she was aware of her stepfather's. So when she came back to Rush City as a reporter, and needed a worthless human being to kill, to get those good clips she needed to get a better job, well, there he was, a well-known abuser of impressionable young women, currently having sex with the cheerleading advisor. Best of all, he'd been threatened in public by the irate father of a boy thrown off the football team for urinating in the gymbags of underclassmen.

After choosing the coach as her victim, Aubrey went to work framing Darren Yoder, the hapless husband of the cheerleading advisor. She learned he owned a hunting cabin in Coshocton County. Motel records showed she made two trips to that rural county, one prior to the murder, one immediately after.

As Aubrey expected, the Rush City police arrested the football player's father. She waited patiently for a month until Yoder went to his hunting cabin. That's when she called the police. When they searched the cabin they found a .45 in the attic and a half-burned pair of bloody overalls in the woodburner.

Why did Aubrey use her real name at the motel in Coshocton County? The same reason she used her real name at motels in Hannawa before poisoning Buddy Wing. She was a newspaper reporter. She didn't have any money. She had to use her credit cards. Considering her self-confidence I'm sure she saw very little danger in it.

◇◇◇

The days Dale Marabout spent in Rush City were fruitful. He not only figured out how and why Aubrey killed Coach Reddincoat, he developed a hypothesis—a hypothesis-in-progress at least—of how and why she killed Buddy Wing. He explained it to me over lunch at Speckley's, on a napkin:

"STEP ONE," said Dale as he scribbled, "Aubrey chooses a victim—somebody well-known whose death will rile people up. Coach Reddincoat in Rush City, Buddy Wing here in Hannawa."

He scribbled STEP TWO. "Then she looks for the two schmucks she's going to frame. The obvious one who gets arrested right off the bat and then the less obvious one she'll uncover later."

I was nodding like one of those bobble-head dogs some people feel compelled to put in the back window of their cars. "It's anybody's guess what goes on inside the noodle of a killer," I said, "but you can see her progression. She poisoned the squirrels and got some pretty good clips. But nobody got arrested and the story fizzled out. The only job offer those dead squirrels got her was from the Rush City *Gazette*. She'd fix that with the football coach. And when that worked to a tee she figured, what the hell, do it again in Hannawa."

Dale started twirling his felt-tip through his fingers like a majorette's baton. He was perplexed. "Didn't she think solving two almost identical cases would make somebody suspicious?"

I watched his felt-tip fly across the aisle and land under a table of old women who'd already gotten their food. He looked at the tangle of support-hosed legs and winced. I gave him a ballpoint from my purse. "That's why she killed Buddy Wing before she got to Hannawa," I said. "How could she be a suspect if the victim was dead several months before she arrived in town?"

Dale clicked my pen and sheepishly wrote STEP THREE. "After she's got her schmucks in a row, she starts on the fun part, figuring out how to kill her victim and how to plant the evidence."

By the time I reached Mansfield snowflakes as big as nickels were freezing on the pavement. I slowed to thirty-five. I wanted a mug of tea to calm my nerves but there was no way I was going to drive with one hand while I poured it. I wrapped my hands around the top of the steering wheel and plowed on. My Thermos was right there on the seat beside me. It might as well have been a thousand miles away.

His hypothesis-in-progress finished and folded, and tucked in his shirt pocket, Dale Marabout set out to prove Aubrey killed Buddy Wing.

His first stop was Tinker's office. He learned that on the last Saturday in August, Tinker had driven to Rush City, and over a quick lunch at Wendy's promised Aubrey a job after the first of year.

Two weeks later Aubrey checked into a Quality Inn just two miles up the road from the Heaven Bound Cathedral. She stayed Friday and Saturday night. Over the next three months she would spend five more weekends at that motel, putting nearly $1,500 on her Visa and Discover cards.

At the time of Dale's investigation there was no way to prove Aubrey had spent those weekends planning Buddy Wing's murder. Yes, we could surmise that she was learning her away around the Heaven Bound Cathedral, selecting Sissy as her patsy, and all the rest, but there wasn't one whit of proof she was doing anything more evil those weekends than shopping for shoes at the Brinkley mall.

Later, of course, we'd learn everything about those weekends from her written confession, which, by the way, she typed out herself on a borrowed laptop in the city jail.

From that confession, we learned she'd already chosen Buddy Wing as her victim by the time Tinker promised her a job: "I also was considering WFLO's Charlie Chimera. He was both hated and loved. His show was a lightening rod for nutballs. He had three angry ex-wives. But Buddy Wing ultimately had the most going for him. He was famous nationally as well as locally. He was on TV all the time—so the whole world could watch him die. He had enemies that could be exploited. And in the final analysis, he was infinitely more evil than that idiot on the radio."

As soon as Tinker promised her a job, she started to investigate Buddy Wing in earnest. She wrote: "I taped his broadcasts and watched them over and over. He always kissed his Bible approximately halfway through his sermons. Dropping dead at his pulpit would be very dramatic and make the police think his murder was for religious purposes."

During her first weekend in Hannawa, Aubrey attended services at the Heaven Bound Cathedral. She walked the back hallways and saw the list of Kent State television students in the bulletin. On one of her visits she appropriated a copy of the church directory. "I knew from my first visit to the cathedral poisoning Buddy Wing was going to be easy," Aubrey wrote in her confession. "Security was almost non-existent. There were faceless college students running around. I'd only been out of school for two years. All I needed was a Kent State sweatshirt and an eager look in my eyes."

She also spent several hours that weekend at the city library's main downtown branch, reading microfiche copies of the *Herald-Union*'s many stories on Buddy Wing and his controversial church.

So Aubrey learned early on about the nasty split between Buddy and Tim Bandicoot over speaking in tongues, and the rivalry it spawned between Tim and Guthrie Gates. "My first inclination was to make Gates look like the killer," she wrote. "I could easily plant some kind of evidence to get him arrested. Then during his trial, or maybe after he was already in prison, I could prove he didn't do it."

But that all changed, Aubrey confessed, during her second weekend in Hannawa. Early Saturday morning she drove to Tim Bandicoot's house in Hannawa Falls. She parked at end of the cul-de-sac, just as she did that Friday night in May when we followed him to Borders with his family. When Tim left his house, Aubrey followed him first to his church on Lutheran Hill and then to the rundown house in the city where Sissy James lived. She saw Tim and Sissy kiss at the door. She hid in the overgrown shrubbery and watched through the bedroom window as they pulled each other's clothes off. "I could see immediately that Sissy James would make a much better killer than Guthrie Gates," she wrote. "Sex always makes for a better story."

Aubrey spent the next two weeks researching Sissy's life. She learned Sissy was born in Mingo Junction and still had relatives in that God-forsaken river town. She learned Sissy had been arrested several times for prostitution in her teens and twenties. She learned Sissy was one of the two hundred members of the Heaven Bound Cathedral who followed Tim to Lutheran Hill.

She learned Sissy worked as a food-service aide at Hannawa General Hospital. She learned Sissy was one of those unfortunate women addicted to crafts.

"Sissy's hobby was perfect," Aubrey wrote. "She had a spare bedroom filled with jars of paint and little brushes. I couldn't believe my luck."

Aubrey then went to work picking the poisons she'd use. She'd taken that course in criminal toxicology and still had the textbook. She looked for a poison that Sissy theoretically could steal from the hospital. She took a liking to the heart drug procaine. She leafed through an EMS training manual at the library and confirmed that paramedics carried it in their drug boxes. She called the EMS director in Rush City. "They were thrilled to death I wanted to ride with them and do a story," she wrote.

Everything was falling into place for Aubrey regarding Sissy James. Sissy had a motive: she was Tim Bandicoot's lover and one of those driven from Buddy Wing's flock; as a hospital worker she had access to drugs; as a maker of worthless cutsie-wootsie crafts, she had the manual skills necessary to paint that poisonous cross on Buddy Wing's old family Bible. Sissy had the opportunity: as the other woman, she would be home alone on Family Night.

Wrote Aubrey: "I was convinced the police would immediately suspect Tim Bandicoot of the murder. They'd quickly discover he had an alibi for Friday night. But they'd discover just as quickly that he had a lover on the side, an emotionally unstable proselyte with a questionable past. They'd go to her house and find all the evidence they needed."

During our lunch at Speckley's, Dale and I had assumed Aubrey chose the "real killer" in advance. But that's not what she did at all.

Wrote Aubrey: "I realized it would be too chancy picking my second suspect right away. Tim Bandicoot was the perfect choice—sleazeball evangelist sets up his crazy girlfriend and all that—but if I wanted to have Buddy Wing drop over dead on live TV, which I really did want, then it couldn't be Tim. He would have that Family Night alibi. So would Annie, a perfect choice otherwise. Through my research I'd found several other potential suspects. But how could I be sure the one I chose wouldn't produce an iron-clad alibi? So I decided to put off my decision on the second suspect until I was working at the *Herald-Union*, when I could investigate them all thoroughly."

I got off the interstate at Mt. Gilead and pulled into The Leaf. It's a wonderful little restaurant right off the exit ramp that serves breakfast 24 hours a day. I had a quick half-mug of tea in the car then went inside for a three-cheese omelet. Every waitress in the place reminded me of Sissy James—bone-tired working-class women dedicated to survival no matter how much crap the world throws at them.

Sissy has survived more than most, hasn't she? With Buddy Wing's help she crawled out of the sewer of prostitution, only to be enslaved in an illicit love affair with a weak-willed married man—Tim Bandicoot—an equally odorous predicament. Then Aubrey McGinty chose her as Schmuck Number One. Given her excellent training in victimhood, Sissy immediately confessed to a murder she did not commit, which I'm sure delighted Aubrey to no end.

Now with my help, and Dale Marabout's help, and ironically Aubrey's help, Sissy James is free of the sewer again. After Aubrey's confession, the city prosecutor hurried back into court. The judge dismissed the charges against her and she was freed. What happened to Sissy was tragic. But all in all, things have worked out well for her: Nine months in Marysville for stupidity is a lot better than life without parole for murder.

After returning to Hannawa last fall, Sissy returned to the Heaven Bound Cathedral. "Our sister has come home," Guthrie Gates announced from the pulpit during his televised Friday night service. She was applauded and cheered.

Guthrie, by the way, has put Sissy in charge of the cathedral's new outreach ministry to the city's prostitutes. Guthrie told me he got the idea from Aubrey's series on the women who work along Morrow Street.

Keesha, the prostitute Aubrey used in her lead, is not one of the women Sissy is trying to save. Keesha is dead.

I left my waitress a $5 tip and coaxed my Dodge Shadow back onto the interstate.

During the first week of November, Aubrey rode with the Rush City paramedics and stole two bottles of procaine and a syringe from their drug box. She went to a crafts supply store and bought several little bottles of gold paint, and some tiny brushes. She practiced painting crosses on an old Bible she bought for a dollar at a yard sale. She timed how long it would take the paint to dry. "I knew procaine was a lethal drug," she wrote in her confession, "but I began to worry whether Buddy would ingest enough to kill him. So I looked in my textbook for another drug, as a backup. In the appendix, right below the procaine entry, I found lily of the valley. I discovered that even the water in a vase can be fatal if swallowed. I knew from my visits to the Heaven Bound Cathedral that Elaine Albert always put a pitcher of water on the pulpit. It was perfect. I found a greenhouse in Akron that grew lily of valley and I bought five live plants. I soaked the stems and leaves until I had a very lethal quart of water."

Thanksgiving night Aubrey drove to Hannawa and checked into the Quality Inn. She spent all day Friday in her motel room watching television. At six, she put on one of her old Kent State sweatshirts and drove to the Heaven Bound Cathedral with her duffel bag of tricks. She walked right in. She went to the kitchenette in the nursery and filled a water pitcher with the tainted lily of valley water. When Buddy Wing left his office for the make-up room, she scooted in. She closed the door and painted the cross on his Bible. She took the Bible and the water and Buddy's notes to the pulpit. She drove back to the motel and watched Buddy Wing die. At midnight she drove into Hannawa and planted her evidence in Sissy's garbage cans.

In March, Aubrey came to work at the *Herald-Union*. She immediately sucked me into her madness. For weeks I followed her all over Hannawa. I thought I was helping her prove that Sissy James didn't kill Buddy Wing.

What I was doing, of course, was helping Aubrey find the perfect person to set up—that poor soul whom Dale Marabout aptly labeled on his napkin hypothesis as her second *schmuck*.

By the end of June it was clear to me just who that schmuck was going to be. It was going to be Annie Bandicoot.

Annie Bandicoot not only had a basketful of motives for poisoning Buddy Wing—revenge for his kicking Tim out of his church, getting Sissy James out the picture, clearing the way for the Bandicoots to become the king and queen of Hallelujah City—she also had the opportunity. Friday night was Family Night at the New Epiphany Temple. But that particular Friday night was Father and Son Night. While Tim and his sons were in Cleveland watching the Cavaliers beat the Knicks, Annie was waiting at home.

Aubrey, of course, owed that particular piece of information to Sandra Leigh Swain, the make-up woman we'd jokingly called the eyebrow woman. What a fruitful source she turned out to be: she not only told Aubrey that Annie didn't have an alibi, she told her that Sissy did! "Prior to my conversations with Sandra Swain, I did not know about Sissy's Thanksgiving weekend trip to Mingo Junction," Aubrey wrote in her confession. "I was thrilled. I knew I could prove Sissy's innocence."

Another thing Aubrey didn't know beforehand was that Sissy had a daughter. Maybe I'm letting my own heart get the best of me, but I think that revelation played heavily on Aubrey's conscience. So, at the same time she was coldly looking for a second person to frame, she was frantically trying to free Sissy for all the right reasons.

◇◇◇

I'd been back on the interstate a good fifteen minutes when flashing blue lights suddenly filled my rear-view mirror. It was daylight. I had hundreds of cars and trucks for company. But those lights sent a shiver from the back of my eye sockets to the tip of my tailbone. It's something how fear stays with you, isn't it? I've been away from LaFargeville for fifty years but every time I see a pasture of cows I feel the hoof of that old Guernsey breaking my toes again, the way it did that afternoon long ago when my father was teaching me to milk. And now those flashing lights were filling me with the same panic I felt that rainy night in July when Aubrey followed me home from Ike's.

Of course I knew it wasn't the Taurus Man following me that night. The Taurus Man was Dale Marabout. And I knew it wasn't any of the other suspects Aubrey had concocted. But I did fear it might be Lionel Percy again. It had only been four nights since he'd scared the bejesus out of us on West Apple, and he did not seem like the kind of man who could be satisfied scaring someone just once. You don't know how relieved I was to hear the pathetic beep of Aubrey's little Escort.

Which is funny. During all those months I suspected Aubrey of killing Buddy Wing, I never once feared for my own life. Maybe I was just too full of my own cleverness. My own deceitfulness. Maybe I was so fond of the *good* Aubrey that I couldn't believe the *bad* Aubrey would hurt me.

Which was ridiculous. Looking back now with a clear head, I doubt Aubrey would have hesitated two seconds if she'd discovered I was onto her. She'd already sacrificed two decent men and a lot of squirrels for her brilliant career, hadn't she? Why wouldn't she sacrifice a squirrelly old librarian?

Anyway, the terror sparked by those blinking blue lights quickly fizzled. I pulled over. A baby-faced State Highway Patrol officer walked up to my open window. "Your turn signal's been blinking for many many miles, ma'am," he said.

Dale Marabout's secret investigation did not always go as smoothly as I'd hoped. My first scare, of course, came that Tuesday in late May when Aubrey started drilling me in the morgue about Dale's new freelance job. When she'd surprised him at the library the night before—where he was busy researching the poisons she'd used to kill Buddy Wing, by the way—he'd told her he was working on a project for a local company. Aubrey assumed he'd "descended into the dark, slimy world of corporate PR," as she put it. I let her go right on thinking that. The next scare came a week later in Meri when Eric Chen's chivalry got the best of him. Luckily Eric was humiliated into silence. Then just two weeks after that, when police found Ronny Doddridge's body, I was sure Aubrey had killed him. I can't tell you how relieved I was when the coroner ruled it a suicide. That poor, big-eared lamb was dead but at least I wasn't responsible for it.

My fears returned right after the Fourth of July when the windows on Tish Kiddle's Lexus were smashed. No mystery who did the smashing. "What's Aubrey going to do if Tish stays on the story?" I worried to Dale.

"There's not a chance in hell Tish Kiddle will stay on the story," he said. He was right. Forty-eight hours later Tish Kiddle was broadcasting from sunny Orlando.

TV 21's report on Tim Bandicoot's public confession about his affair with Sissy James did bring matters to a head, however. Tinker told Aubrey to start writing her series and Bob Averill put in a call to Detective Scotty Grant. Bob Averill made me go to police headquarters with him. "Sorry we didn't tell you about this earlier," Bob told Scotty Grant. "We weren't sure of our facts yet and we didn't want to get you folks involved in a crazy goose-chase."

Grant was surprisingly grateful. "Nobody likes chasing gooses," he said.

So it came down to that final Sunday, Monday and Tuesday. While Aubrey was imprisoned in the newsroom racing to meet her deadline, Dale Marabout was at home racing to meet his, turning a dozen reporter's notebooks full of scribbled notes into a story.

By now Scotty Grant had advised Tim and Annie Bandicoot of the situation. They were prayerful and cooperative. Officers searched their property. Under the driver's seat of Annie's Saturn they found a Bible covered with hand-painted gold crosses.

Under the passenger's seat they found a curly auburn wig and pair of red-framed lollipop glasses big enough to disguise even the most familiar face. It still wasn't enough to arrest Aubrey, however. Dale's evidence was largely circumstantial and the items found in Annie's car bore neither a suspicious fingerprint nor fiber.

Sunday, after I had lunch with Dale and Sharon at Speckley's, I drove to Bob Averill's pricey condominium in White Lake. Tinker and Scotty Grant were there. "Okay, Maddy," Bob said, bringing a tray of snapping highballs from the kitchen, "tell us what you've got in mind."

I told them about Aubrey's surprise birthday dinner for Eric. "She wanted me to help her make a cake and a lasagna. Cakes are nothing. But a lasagna, that's a pretty time-consuming dish, even when you've got all the ingredients handy. Lots of layers. Lots of steps. If you forget to put one of the ingredients on your shopping list—say the ricotta cheese—and somebody has to go back to the supermarket, well that just stops you in your tracks, doesn't it?"

Bob sloshed his mouthful of highball, like it was mouthwash. "Just how does this lasagna of yours help arrest Aubrey, Maddy?"

I toasted the three impatient men and after a miniature sip, bedazzled them with my shrewdness: "Dale needed everything he could get on Aubrey's past. I'd been to Aubrey's apartment before, and seen her cardboard boxes marked SHIT FROM COLLEGE and SHIT FROM HOME. The evidence that might be in those boxes was simply gnawing a hole in me. So when Aubrey asked me over to help her make a lasagna, I was tickled pink. I gave her a list of ingredients to buy and intentionally left off the ricotta cheese. So right when I was up to my elbows in boiling noodles, she had to run out to the supermarket. I figured that would give me time to snoop. I found her college transcripts—which listed that odd elective course she took in criminal toxicology—and I found the textbook from that course, with a number of poisons marked with a yellow highlighter, including procaine and lily of the valley."

Scotty Grant was as excited as a thirteen-year-old finding his father's *Playboys*. "And that stuff is still in her apartment?"

I nodded proudly. "It is. And that's my idea. Aubrey plans to frame Annie Bandicoot. But what if she suddenly discovers, at the very last minute, that Annie wasn't really at home that Friday night? That she had a solid alibi?"

Tinker at least was keeping up. "She'd have to frame somebody else."

"Absolutely. And she'd have to plant some convincing evidence. And what does she have that she could grab in a hurry?"

"I'm guessing it's not a slice of your leftover lasagna?" Bob joked.

"Her toxicology textbook," I said.

"It would have her fingerprints all over it," Tinker said.

"Xeroxes wouldn't," Scotty Grant said.

I toasted him. Everybody dutifully sipped. I told them my idea and they went for it.

So, Monday afternoon, while Aubrey was working feverishly to complete her stories, I brought Aubrey the story from the morgue files that Eric had found—the one about Annie Bandicoot being in Kentucky over the Thanksgiving weekend with a gaggle of other preachers' wives.

It was a real story. Annie really was in Kentucky over Thanksgiving. It just wasn't that particular Thanksgiving. It was five Thanksgivings ago. I simply had Eric alter the date on the computer file. Aubrey didn't question that doctored story for a minute. What reporter would? If something's in the morgue it's the gospel truth.

Aubrey tossed the story on her desk and went back to work, as if it was no big deal. But I knew it was a big deal; at least I had my fingers crossed that it was.

Scotty Grant followed Aubrey home Monday evening. At ten-thirty she drove to an open-all-night Kinko's. Scotty watched from his car as she copied several pages from a book. She was wearing gloves. Then she drove to a Walgreen's drug store and bought a can of lighter fluid, a box of stick matches and a plastic bottle of Evian water.

I had a hunch Aubrey would try to frame Wayne F. Dillow. He had motive and opportunity and a wonderful old brick barbecue in his backyard where evidence could be planted without a fuss. My hunch proved correct. Aubrey arrived at Dillow's a little after midnight. She parked far up the street and slipped through several dark backyards. Scotty Grant watched from a neighbor's evergreens while she dribbled the copies with lighter fluid and then set them on fire. She let them burn for only a few seconds before dousing them with the Evian. She had done the same thing with the blood-stained overalls she planted in Darren Yoder's hunting cabin. She was making it look like Wayne Dillow was trying to destroy evidence that would prove he poisoned the faith-healer who betrayed his beloved wife.

That Tuesday night at the paper Aubrey had pooh-poohed the circumstantial evidence in Dale's story. But when she read the part of his story that reported all of this—what could she do but confess?

◇◇◇

I left I-71 and took US36 into Marysville. The prison officials checked me in. It was the fourth time I'd visited Aubrey since she was sentenced in September. She is serving two life sentences for aggravated homicide. She will serve them without hope of parole. She will serve them consecutively. She is lucky. The prosecutor wanted death.

I was ushered into the same little room where Aubrey and I met with Sissy James. I sat on the blue sofa. When Aubrey came in she sat next to me. "How's the flag-making business?" I asked.

Her answer was sharp and sarcastic, pure Aubrey McGinty. "I'm getting more patriotic by the day."

I handed her the copy of the *Herald-Union* I promised. She unfolded it and scanned Dale Marabout's latest story on Lionel

Percy. Alec Tinker had not only rehired Dale after Aubrey's arrest, he'd put him back on the police beat. For the last few months Dale had been joyfully covering Percy's metamorphosis from much-feared police commander to hapless inmate shoveling out cow barns at the state prison farm in Grafton.

Percy's troubles, by the way, began the same week Mayor Kyle Finn appointed Ted Duffy interim police chief. Duffy had spent a lifetime nurturing a reputation as a timid, go-along-to-get-along bureaucrat. But inside lived an ambitious man with a long memory. During his first week as interim chief, he met secretly with State Attorney General Eileen Bachelor. Her probe brought down Lionel Percy and two scooping handfuls of corrupt underlings. It also changed Mayor Kyle Finn's re-election plans.

Aubrey refolded the paper and slipped it under her arm. "So, Maddy—what brings you to Disney World?"

I felt light-headed and clammy, like I had the flu. I wrapped my long arms around my waist and told her. "Well, there's been a murder at Hemphill College—"

"I didn't do it."

Her sarcasm put me at ease. "It was an old classmate of mine, Gordon Sweet. We all called him Sweet Gordon because that's the way his name appeared on class rosters. Sweet comma Gordon. Anyway, he went on to become a professor there. In archeology. He specialized in some kooky field called *garbology*—digging into landfills to see how average people really lived. He was an eccentric old Beatnik but as harmless as a marshmallow. The police are clueless."

Aubrey's eyebrows elevated ever so slightly. "And you want me to help you find the murderer? You've got some big balls for a tiny old woman."

# 22

Ike put my Darjeeling tea and a Ghirardelli chocolate on the table. It was almost closing time. The street was empty and so was his coffee shop. "How'd your visit with that crazy girl go?" he asked.

I patted the chair next to mine and he dutifully sat. I was tired from the long drive but I needed company. "It went fine," I said.

He unwrapped the chocolate for me. "I'll tell you one thing—if you'd bamboozled me the way you bamboozled her, I don't think I'd be inviting you to my prison cell."

"I wouldn't accept your invitations if you did," I said.

We both laughed. It's hard to say whose laugh was sadder.

He slid the flat square of chocolate across the table on its foil wrapper, like a bribe. "You played that Aubrey McGinty like a fiddle, just like you play everybody else, me included."

I broke the chocolate in two and slid the big half back to him. "You're giving me way too much credit."

Ike nibbled like a gerbil. "You and me are so much alike it's scary," he said.

"Alike? How are you and I alike?"

"Underrated and overlooked," he said. "These young business-types that prance in and out of here every morning—to them I'm nothing but the old black guy who pours their coffee.

Not a damn one of them knows I taught high school math all those years, that I probably taught their own mamas and daddies, that in a roundabout way I'm responsible for their own big-shot success. Old black guy pouring the coffee, that's all I am."

"And me, Ike?"

"You're Morgue Mama. Keeper of the musty-dusty old files. What everybody forgets, is that behind that sour, tea-sipping frown you wear like a TRESPASSERS WILL BE SHOT sign, resides the shrewdest damn woman in Hannawa, Ohio."

"What a lovely compliment."

"I meant it to be. Aubrey McGinty was so impressed with her own sick genius, she couldn't see you had a hundred times the brains she did. Hundred times the curiosity and a hundred times the guile."

Ike got up and locked the door. He grabbed a whole handful of Ghirardelli chocolates from the counter and sat back down, resting his legs on an empty chair. "You ever ask her why she killed those men?" he asked. "The real, deep-down-in-the-soul reason?"

"I don't have to ask her. I know why. At a very early age she learned that bad people take what they want from good people. So why shouldn't good people take what they want from bad people?"

Ike nodded in slow motion. "You think she sees herself as a good person?"

"Aubrey is a good person," I said, "except for that bitter little knot in her brain that kills people."

Ike unwrapped another chocolate for us.

**RF**

To receive a free catalog of other Poisoned Pen Press titles, please contact us in one of the following ways:

Phone: 1-800-421-3976
Facsimile: 1-480-949-1707
Email: info@poisonedpenpress.com
Website: www.poisonedpenpress.com

Poisoned Pen Press
6962 E. First Ave. Ste 103
Scottsdale, AZ 85251